PINEAPPLE

CIRCUS

A Pineapple Port Mystery: Book Thirteen

Amy Vansant

Vansant Creations, LLC / Amy Vansant
Annapolis, MD
http://www.AmyVansant.com
http://www.PineapplePort.com

Editing/Proofreading by Effrosyni Moschoudi, Connie Leap & Meg Barnhart
Cover by Steven Novak

DEDICATION

To Archer, our new puppy—and the whole fifteen pounds
heavier than we thought he'd be. I love every pound of you!

CHAPTER ONE

Baroness von Chilling took her heart medication and tugged at the nightdress pinching her middle. The cat she'd adopted during her tenure working in the Boudreaux & Bo's Family Circus' fortune-teller's tent lay curled on her bed.

Kitty purred as she approached her.

Breathless, Baroness sat resting, preparing for the effort it would take to swing her dry-skinned, dimpled legs beneath the sheets. A sharp *clacking* noise, something like tiny plastic boulders bouncing down a metal mountain, clattered in the adjacent room.

Baroness groaned.

I thought I turned off the ice maker...

She enjoyed the open feel of her small modular home in The Big Top fifty-five-plus community for retired circus performers, but every noise could be heard every*where*. In her opinion, whoever dreamed up *open plan* deserved to be burned at the stake.

Whenever she complained, neighbors suggested she close her bedroom door.

As if she hadn't thought of that.

Idiots.

If she closed her bedroom door, Kitty scratched and howled to get out. If she opened it, the cat went right back to bed. They'd been playing this game since they first met.

Stupid cat.

Baroness pushed away from the bed, steadied herself on her arthritic feet and shuffled toward the kitchen, hips aching. A lot of good the clairvoyance gift she'd inherited from her mother had done her. If she could have predicted the pains in her eighty-six-year-old joints, she would have put stones in her pockets and walked into the sea at seventy-two.

"Baroness."

A voice spoke in the darkness.

Von Chilling gasped and wobbled on her feet, reaching out to steady herself on the back of the sofa.

It wasn't the ice.

A shadowy figure stood inside her front door, large and triangle-shaped. It took her milky eyes a minute to adjust before she realized the intruder wore robes.

Her robes.

She recognized the stars and moons she'd Bedazzled on the dark fabric decades ago.

"Who are you?" she asked, pointing with a crooked finger. "Be gone before I curse you for *eternity*." She used her scariest voice, one heavy with portent and husky with seventy years of smoking. A Romanian accent dripped from every word, though she'd grown up in Newark, New Jersey.

The figure took a few steps forward into the light cast by the moon through her skylight.

"You know me?"

She squinted. "No. Who—"

More of the face slipped into the glow cast by the streetlights outside her kitchen window.

I do know that face.

"What are you doing?" she demanded to know, convinced no answer could make her feel more at ease.

The figure spoke again.

"How's it feel to be judged?"

Baroness turned to run. Hands fell on her shoulders before she'd taken two shuffling steps. Fingers tightened around her throat. She collapsed beneath the weight of her attacker, who rolled her onto her back, pinning her to the ground.

With a knee on her chest, Baroness couldn't breathe. She squirmed to free herself. She clawed at the thumbs pressing at her windpipe.

The irony of her sudden urge to live wasn't lost on her.

It was almost funny.

As the darkness closed in around her, she shifted her attention to the bedroom.

Kitty was nowhere to be seen.

Probably hiding.

The creature she'd saved couldn't be bothered to do the same for her.

Stupid cat.

The fingers around Baroness' throat released, and she took a gasping breath. From beneath the robes, her attacker produced a crystal ball—*her* crystal ball—and held it above her skull.

The intruder spoke as the crystal ball raised higher.

"Not so powerful now, are you, Baroness?"

CHAPTER TWO

Abby, Charlotte's soft-coated Wheaten terrier, was the first to see the truck pull up to Charlotte's house. She barked once, and Charlotte jogged from the kitchen to the window, stopping only to set a small platter of crackers, cheese, and pepperoni on the living room table.

She peered through her curtains, trying hard not to look like a lunatic.

At the curb, a woman and a man sat in a truck, talking.

Her mysterious Aunt Siofra "Shee" McQueen had arrived.

Shee had called a day before to arrange a visit, but Charlotte didn't mind the impromptu nature of the self-invite. She couldn't be any more excited. Shee was her only link to her parents and a life she barely remembered. She'd been young when her father died in an accident. She'd lost her mother later to cancer. After that, she'd been shipped to her grandmother Estelle's modular home in the fifty-five-plus community of Pineapple Port, only to have her grandmother die soon after that.

Even with all that tragedy she'd been lucky. The community raised her, mothering spearheaded by the neighbor across the street, Mariska.

She couldn't have asked for a better substitute mother to raise her. Thanks to Pineapple Port, she had a family larger than most.

Still...to find out she had *blood* relatives left...

She was excited.

In addition to meeting Siofra, she'd discovered her grandfather Mick was still alive, though he lay in a coma on the opposite side of Florida.

Shee was the only *speaking* link to her past.

From what she could divine from the brief time she'd spent working a kidnapping case with Siofra in Jupiter Beach, her aunt was a *certified badass.* She didn't know the whole story but hoped to learn from her. Anything Shee shared could only enhance her own burgeoning private investigation skills.

Charlotte watched her visitors through the window, giggly with anticipation.

Get out of the truck...

The couple sat.

Is that her?

The woman in the passenger seat looked like Shee, but who was driving? She hadn't said someone else was coming. Was it Mick, her grandfather? Was he better?

The woman glanced at the house.

Okay. That's definitely Shee.

She could see enough to tell the driver was a man, a *big* one, but little else.

Charlotte looked at her watch.

They'd been sitting in the truck for five minutes.

She heard a click and watched, enthralled, as the couple climbed out of the truck and started toward the house.

Finally.

Squelching a squeal of excitement, Charlotte placed herself behind the door.

Waiting.

They'd reached the stoop. She heard them talking outside.

Minutes went by.

Come on.

Charlotte opened the front to find her aunt standing there,

her fist raised to knock.

"Hi," she said.

She bent to grip Abby's collar, pulling the curious dog back to make room as she unlatched the screen door.

Shee smiled and glanced at her big friend.

"After you," said the man.

The couple walked inside, navigating the excited terrier. Charlotte scrambled for something to say. She motioned to the dog.

"This is Abby."

She swallowed.

I sound like an idiot.

She eyeballed the man. Handsome, probably Shee's age—he was built like someone who'd spent a long time doing things that required *strength*. She nearly asked him if he were an actor, but she suspected even an action-star wouldn't radiate with such genuine *toughness*. He smelled good and looked well-groomed, but his visible scars belied a life *not* spent in the lap of luxury.

She thrust an open palm toward him. "I'm Charlotte."

He stared at her hand as if he wasn't sure what it was.

"I'm sorry, this is Mason," said Shee, bumping him with her elbow.

He seemed to awake from a trance. "Hi," he said, smiling and shaking her hand.

Charlotte motioned to the sofa. "Have a seat. Can I get you something to drink? Iced tea? Water?" The dog's attention shifted to the pepperoni on the platter and Charlotte pushed her away with her leg.

Shee mumbled something she didn't hear.

"Iced tea would be great," said Mason.

Charlotte flashed a smile and slipped into the kitchen. Sliding the iced tea from the fridge, she took a deep breath.

Why am I so nervous?

She realized she *really* wanted her aunt to like her. No—*more than that*—she wanted her to *respect* her as a fellow crime solver. She wasn't sure what Shee was—she could be CIA for all she knew—but she had *skills*.

She took another second to let her heartbeat slow and then toted the teas to the living room. Abby sat beside Mason, getting pets beneath his own giant paw.

"We're kind of in brunch territory, so I put out this stuff," Charlotte said, nodding at the plate of crackers. "If you'd prefer something more breakfasty—"

"No, this is fine," said Shee.

Charlotte placed the glasses on the living room table her boyfriend, Declan, had given her from his pawn shop. She looked around the room. All her furniture was from the pawn shop.

Can they tell?

Charlotte realized Mason was staring at her, his jaw cracked open. Unsettled, she looked to Shee and noticed for the first time the bruises on her aunt's face. One eye was blackened, and she had a smattering of small cuts on her face and arms.

How did I miss that?

"What happened?" she asked, gesturing to her aunt's face.

Shee's hand fluttered to her bruises. "Oh. Little car accident."

"Oh no, are you okay?"

She nodded. "Air bag did more damage than anything else."

Silence again.

"So, to what do I owe the visit?" Charlotte asked. "How are things at the Loggerhead?"

"Good..." Shee jumped in her seat. "Oh, Mick—your grandfather—he's awake. Out of the coma."

Charlotte gasped. "He is? Oh, that's *great*."

"Yeah, I'm sorry. I should have told you sooner..."

"Is that why you came?"

"Hm?"

"To let me know?" Charlotte glanced at Mason.

He was still staring.

She couldn't put her finger on his expression. It wasn't

wolfish. He seemed...*stunned.*

Shee put her hand on his knee. "Um, yes and no. We have something else we have to tell you..."

Mason cleared his throat and nodded. "We do."

"We do," echoed Shee. "There's no easy way to say this, so I'm just going to do it."

OMG. It hit Charlotte where this was going. *Her grandfather had awoken, but something else was wrong.*

"Is he okay?" she asked.

Shee seemed confused. "Who? Mason? Sure. He's just—"

Charlotte shook her head. "No, *Mick.*"

"Oh. He's *fine.* Sorry, I can see how you thought that's where I was going. It's not him—"

"I'm your father," blurted Mason.

Charlotte looked at the giant, certain she'd misheard him.

"What?" she asked.

He hooked a thumb at Shee. "She's your mother."

"What?" Charlotte followed his gesture to watch Shee close her eyes.

A laugh spat from Charlotte's lips. She felt her shoulders un-bunch a notch.

I get it. They're kidding me.

She was about to speak when she noticed the look on Shee's face. It seemed *awfully* serious for a person in the middle of a joke.

"This isn't exactly how I had this planned..." Shee glared in Mason's direction. "But it's true. We're your parents."

Charlotte blinked at them.

What?

Shee continued. "I found out I was pregnant with you right before he was deployed—"

"I didn't know," said Mason. "I'm in the Navy. *Was. Was* in the Navy."

Shee squeezed his leg. "Anyway, my sister Grace couldn't have a baby and I wasn't ready, so I gave you to her—"

Charlotte swallowed.

Her mother's name was Grace.

She's not kidding.

"I didn't know," said Mason again.

Charlotte looked at him.

Shee plowed on. "When Grace died, I was in hiding, so I couldn't take you back. Someone was after me, and it would have been too dangerous. Long story. Anyway, Mick gave you to Estelle—"

"I didn't know," said Mason.

"*She's got it,*" snapped Shee.

Charlotte heard her grandmother's name, and everything became even more real to her. All the facts were right. The story checked out.

This can't be happening.

Mason cleared his throat.

Shee took a deep breath. "You grew up here. You know that part. I stayed in hiding. We *just* stopped the guy who was after me and now I'm here—"

"*We're* here," said Mason. "I just found out about you. Like a week ago."

Charlotte looked at him. Somehow, his repetition had broken through her shock.

"You didn't even know I *existed*?" she asked.

He shook his head.

She looked back at Shee. "Why didn't you tell him?"

Shee stared at her, much the way Mason had earlier—jaw slack.

Shee closed her mouth. "Um, at first, I was afraid the news would distract *him*. Get him killed. Then, after a while, I guess it just felt like it was too late."

Charlotte found herself speechless.

"It's not like he could have taken you instead of Estelle," Shee added.

Mason sniffed. "I don't know, maybe if someone had offered me the chance—"

"*This* was a better option." Shee growled the words.

Mason shrugged.

Shee took a deep breath and turned her attention back to Charlotte. "I know this is a lot to digest."

Charlotte nodded and said the sentence repeating in her head.

"You're my parents."

Shee and Mason both nodded.

Charlotte stood. She wanted to run. She needed to process. She wanted them to leave, but she wanted them to stay—

"I actually have to be somewhere," she said. She didn't, but the words came out of her mouth anyway. "But maybe we could have dinner or something?"

Shee and Mason both jumped to their feet.

"Absolutely. Our treat. You pick the place," said Shee.

Shee.

Her *mother.*

Charlotte bit her lip. It felt as if she had locusts buzzing in her brain, under her skin—

Dinner. Arrange the dinner. I eat dinner. I eat dinner with—

That was it. She needed her people around her to help buffer *everything.*

"Could I bring a few people?" she asked. "There are people I'd like you to meet. People who raised me, and my boyfriend...."

"*Absolutely,*" said Shee. "Anyone. Everyone."

"Absolutely," echoed Mason. "Anyone."

Charlotte nodded. "Okay. Maybe around five?" She offered them a sheepish smile. "We eat kind of early around here."

"Sounds good." Shee pushed Mason out from behind the table.

Charlotte walked behind them as they moved to the door.

They're leaving. What if they run? What if I never see them again?

"Wait," she said.

The couple turned.

Charlotte opened her arms and moved in for a hug. Shee did the same, gripping her.

"Charlotte..." she said.

Charlotte panicked.

Okay. Too much. Move on.

Charlotte released her mother to hug Mason. When she stepped back from him, Mason put the side of his fist against his lips and looked away.

Shee jumped ahead to open the door and then spun on her heel to turn back, her shoulder bouncing off Mason's chest as he shadowed her too closely.

"We'll see you tonight," said Shee, glowering at Mason, who flashed a quick, awkward smile.

Charlotte nodded. "Okay. See you tonight."

"Bye," they said in unison as they exited.

Charlotte waved and then shut the door, unsure if her heart was beating *so* fast she could no longer feel the individual thumps, or if it had stopped altogether.

What just happened?

She leaned her back against the wall, sliding until her butt hit the floor.

Abby licked her face. She put her arms around the dog and squeezed, staring at the opposite wall, her whole body vibrating with nerves.

After a minute, she released the terrier, clambered to her feet and glanced at her watch.

Dinner with my parents at five.

She had seven hours to find some way to distance herself intact from the train that had just hit her.

Pineapple Port's orphan had *parents*.

CHAPTER THREE

Before Charlotte could consider how her world had changed, someone knocked on the front door. She scanned her living room, thinking Shee and Mason had left something behind.

Nothing.

Her stomach did a little flip.

Is this the part where they come back to scream 'April Fool!'?

She took a deep breath and opened the door.

Her neighbor across the street and resident mother figure, Mariska, stood on her stoop.

"Who were *they*?" she asked, moving into the house, though her gaze remained locked on the curb where the truck had been parked. Charlotte had to step out of her way to avoid being trampled.

"Who?" asked Charlotte, though she knew *who*. No doubt Mariska had been watching the visitors from her window. Charlotte wouldn't have been shocked to discover she'd been outside the whole time with her ear pressed against the side of the house.

Mariska turned to point out the front window. "That handsome couple in the black truck. The people who were just here. Do they need a detective?"

Charlotte lifted the cheese and cracker plate and held it out.

"Cheese? Pepperoni?"

Mariska's expression lit and then darkened. "Wait. You put out cheese and crackers? You knew they were coming?"

"Of course I knew they were coming. *Polite* people don't just show up *unannounced*."

She stared to see if her comment registered, but Mariska's attention had shifted to the food. She knew her comments would lose in a battle against cheese, deli meats, and crackers every time.

She moved to take the plate to the kitchen. Mariska touched her arm to stop her and snatch some cheese.

"Don't waste the cheese and meats. It's sweating a little, but that's okay. It isn't bad." She nibbled a chunk and then pushed the rest of the block into her mouth. "Ooh. That's good. What is it?"

"Aged Gouda."

"It's kind of..."

"Nutty."

"Mm. Yes. Nutty. That's it. Delicious. Was it on sale?"

Charlotte chuckled knowing she might never have to answer any questions about her parents. She could keep distracting Mariska with cheese and cured meats until the woman forgot why she came and wandered back home again.

She placed the tray on the counter and stared past Mariska at the two ice teas dripping condensation onto her tropical-themed coasters.

Everything sweats in Florida.

The people, the teas, the cheese...

Sadly, they'd have to sweat a little longer. Mariska had set up camp, picking at the snack tray, blocking passage between the kitchen and the front room.

"So who were they?" she repeated, nibbling a slice of pepperoni.

Shoot. She remembered.

Charlotte took a breath. Part of her didn't want to tell, as if saying things out loud made everything too real. She also wanted to look into the couple, maybe do a few background checks...

Should I get a DNA test?

Mariska stared at her from above a loaded cracker. Charlotte realized she had to say *something*. She'd told Shee and Mason she wanted Mariska and the others to come to dinner.

She stared at Mariska who peered back at her, munching one cracker, another on deck in her opposite hand. Her snacking was escalating.

She's going to freak out.

There was no avoiding it.

Here we go...

"They were my parents," she said.

The words sounded strange to her own ears.

Mariska stopped chewing. "Hm?"

"They were my *parents*."

Mariska seemed frozen. Charlotte wondered if something had burst loose in her brain.

"Are you okay?" she asked.

Mariska sniffed. "I thought you said they were your *parents*."

"I *did* say that."

"Why would you say that?"

"Because that's what they told me."

Mariska looked down and brushed the crumbs off her bosom before wandering toward the sofa. "I think I need to sit down."

"Me, too."

Mariska took a seat on the sofa and then picked up Shee's iced tea to take a sip.

"We need to report them," she said.

"Report them?"

"They're scammers. They're obviously up to no good."

"I don't think—"

Mariska pressed her lips tight. "I got an email today saying my subscription for some computer thingy was renewing, but I *know* I never signed up for anything like that. It said to call if it was in error—"

Charlotte put her palm against her chest. "You didn't call or click on anything, did you?"

Mariska looked at her as if she were the dumbest girl on the planet. "*No.* You told me to delete things like that."

"Whew. Good."

"But my point is, there are scammers *everywhere.*"

"There are." Charlotte sat in the chair across from the sofa. "So, you think these people are after my fortune?"

Mariska lifted her hands into the air. "Who knows what they're after? They could be after your social security number or, or—" she waved a hand in the dog's direction. "They could be after *Abby.*"

"You think they're pretending to be my parents so they can steal Abby?"

"Who knows? They could earn your trust, so you ask them to babysit. Who knows what these people want?"

Charlotte snorted a laugh. "How did they know I was an orphan?"

"Pssht. Everyone knows you're an orphan."

"Oh, I forgot. There's Little Annie and then *me.*"

"Did they offer any proof?"

"They didn't bring a DNA test, no."

"So, see? They're scammers."

Charlotte sighed. "I don't think so. It was my Aunt Shee from Jupiter."

"The woman you told me about?"

"Yes. Apparently, she's my real mother and my mother was her sister."

Mariska scowled. "How does that make sense?"

"She wasn't in a place where she could keep me, so she gave me to her sister."

Mariska frowned. "That's irresponsible."

"Her sister couldn't have a baby and wanted one."

Mariska's expression softened. "Oh. I guess that's a little different...but, *still.* What about the father?"

"He was overseas or something. Military."

"What branch?"

"Navy."

"Hm. That's too bad. Bob was in the Marines. I could have asked him if he knew him."

Charlotte tittered. "I doubt everyone in the Marines knows all the others."

"You'd be surprised."

"I *would*. Well, good news—you can ask them all the probing questions you like tonight."

Mariska perked. "They're coming back?"

"We're all having dinner. You, Bob, Darla, Frank, me, and them."

"We are? Where?"

"I didn't pick a place."

"I feel like pasta."

"Okay..."

"Frank can arrest them if they're lying."

"I don't think—" Charlotte's phone rang, and she stood to retrieve it from the kitchen counter. The name on screen said it was Frank.

"Speak of the devil. Hello?"

"I've got a robbery," said Frank's gruff voice. "You said you wanted to investigate a good robbery, and I've got one."

Saved.

"Oh, great, text me the address. I'll be there in a second."

She hung up and turned back to Mariska. "I have to go. Frank is letting me work a case with him."

"What should I wear to dinner?" Mariska stood. "Are we having pasta? Do you want me to see what coupons I have?"

"No. I—"

"We should go someplace public."

Charlotte cocked her head. "So they don't murder us?"

"Exactly."

"Isn't every restaurant public?"

Mariska shrugged. "Not a speakeasy."

"Do you know of any speakeasies?"

"No."

Charlotte grabbed her car keys. "How about you help me pick a place while I'm with Frank?"

Mariska offered her a sharp nod. "Yes. I'll do that. Can I get Darla to help?"

A thousand reasons why Mariska and Darla picking a restaurant could go horribly wrong flashed through Charlotte's mind, but she pushed them all away.

"Sure."

CHAPTER FOUR

Stephanie Moriarty burst into the Hock o' Bell pawn shop, her hands clenched into fists on either side of her head, her face red.

"Declan!"

A pair of ladies admiring the shop's Josef collectibles turned to gape at the sobbing blonde as she wove her way through used furniture in four-inch heels.

Declan stepped out of his office, cringing. Some of the worst days of his life had started with his ex-girlfriend, Stephanie, sobbing. The time she told him she'd cheated on him. The *other* time she told him she'd cheated on him. The *other other* time—

"*Declan.*"

Stephanie walked past the counter and threw her arms around him, collapsing as if she'd finished a marathon. He stood rigid as she pressed her face against his chest. From the opposite side of the room, the old ladies cocked synchronized eyebrows in his direction. He flashed them a tight smile.

"Would you like to come into the office?" he muttered to Stephanie.

He felt her head nod against him and put an arm around her to half-lead, half-drag her into the back. Her legs had apparently lost the ability to support her weight.

Inside his office, he peeled her from his body like a piece of lunchmeat and closed the door.

"What's wrong?"

He kept himself from adding *this time.*

"The FBI called me," said Stephanie, dabbing an eye with an invisible tissue.

He plucked a real tissue from the box on his desk and handed it to her. "Okay..."

Stephanie closed her eyes tight and tilted back her head. "My mother's *dead.*"

Declan stared as she peeked through her fingers back at him. "Did you hear me?"

He nodded. "Your mother—the murderer, the famous Puzzle Killer—is *dead*?"

Stephanie shrugged one shoulder. "We don't need to bring up her less attractive qualities right *now*..."

"No, we definitely do. Her whole thing is *tricks.* What are the chances she's actually dead?"

"No. It's official this time. I told you, the FBI called me."

"The FBI, or someone your mother hired to pretend they're the FBI? Do you have a body?"

"I don't have a body, but I assume they do. She didn't fall off a cruise ship—she was *shot.* There's no mistake." Stephanie glowered at him. "You know, you're being kind of a jerk about this."

"Oh, I'm *sorry.* Maybe it's because the woman tried to kill *me, Charlotte,* and *you,* like, six times."

"It wasn't *six.*" Stephanie traced a finger along the edge of his filing cabinet. "So, I'm not getting *any* sympathy out of you on this one?"

"'Friad not."

She pouted. "But I was just getting to know her."

"Which almost got you killed."

Declan couldn't say Jamie Moriarty's death had come as a terrible disappointment. The world and everyone in it, especially people *he* knew, were a lot safer without her around.

The news did pique his curiosity, though.

"So she was shot?" he asked. "By the cops?"

"By somebody in some roadside motel." Stephanie's lip curled. "Like some kind of *hobo*."

"I'm pretty sure the very definition of *hobo* precludes them spending time in motels," muttered Declan.

Stephanie rolled her eyes. "Whatever. Who'd you learn that from? Your genius girlfriend?"

"Right. Charlotte's an expert in hobo trivia. *Who* shot your mother?"

She looked away. "I don't know. They wouldn't tell me." She spun on her heel to evil-eye at him. "I'll find out, though. Don't worry about that."

Declan held up his palms. "Easy there, killer. You're the new kinder, gentler Stephanie now. Remember?"

She grunted.

"So, was Jamie trying to kill this person at the hotel?"

"I don't *know*."

Her lip curled again, and Declan chuckled.

"You're more annoyed by the *way* she went than by the *fact* she went. You wanted her to go out in a blaze of glory, Bonnie-and-Clyde-style."

"Maybe. She had *way* too much style to die in a grubby motel. A Four Seasons, *maybe*, but..." Stephanie looked up at the ceiling. "If she looked down from heaven and saw her body lying on a motel carpet—"

Declan's chuckle grew to a full laugh. "I don't think you have to worry about her looking *down*."

"Yeah, well," Stephanie gathered herself up and stretched her back. "Whatever. I had to tell someone. I'll get out of your hair." She opened the office door and headed out.

Though he had every right to rejoice over the passing of a serial killer, Declan found himself feeling a little guilty for not having acted more sympathetic. With a sigh, he followed her back into the shop.

"Hey," he called after her. "Seriously, though. Are you okay?"

"I'm fine," she said over her shoulder. Before opening the front door, her attention shifted to the ladies by the Josef figurines.

"They're all fakes," she said.

The women gasped and looked at Declan.

He shook his head. "She's kidding. They're real."

The women put down the statues they'd been inspecting.

"No, I *promise*. They're real."

No amount of cajoling could have slowed the women's retreat. They tucked their purses a little closer to their bodies and left the store.

CHAPTER FIVE

Mariska knocked on Darla's door and doubled over, breathing heavily. The door opened.

She didn't move.

"Are you okay?" asked Darla.

Mariska squinted with one eye and held up a peace sign. "Two seconds. I'm dying."

"What happened? You're panting like a dog. Are you having a stroke?"

Mariska nodded. "Maybe. I ran over here."

"Ran? I'd help you, but I can't open the screen door with you blocking it."

"Oh, sure. I'll move. Why don't I drive myself to the hospital, while I'm at it? If you were a surgeon, would you ask your patients to sew themselves up?"

Darla huffed. "For crying out loud, just take a step back."

Mariska moved to a lower step as if Michelangelo's solid marble statue of David were strapped to her back.

Darla opened the door. "Okay. Now come in and sit down. You're making *me* tired."

Mariska straightened. "Stop being so pushy." Digging deep, she found the energy to enter Darla's house. She ambled to the kitchen and flopped into a chair.

"I think I broke a hip."

Darla pulled a bottle of water from her refrigerator and placed it in front of her friend. "I doubt it. What's going on?"

Mariska held up her index finger, asking for a moment while she gulped half the water.

Darla sighed. "Whatever this is, I'd have already known it by now if you'd *walked* over here like a normal person."

"Agreed. Running was a bad idea." Mariska wiped her forehead with a kitchen towel. "Okay. I'm good now."

"I, on the other hand, need a new kitchen towel." Darla slid open a drawer and pulled out a fresh towel covered with baby ducks. "So what's so important?"

Mariska took a deep inhale. "Charlotte has parents."

Darla gaped at her and then frowned. "Shoot."

"Shoot?"

"You *are* having a stroke."

Mariska clucked her tongue. "*No.* It's true. They just left her house."

"Who did? Her *parents*?"

"*Yes.*" Mariska took another gulp of her water. "We're having dinner with them tonight."

"Who is?"

"You, me, and them. And Charlotte, of course." She thought for a moment. "Oh, and Declan, I imagine...and Frank and Bob."

"Wait, wait, wait." Darla waved her hands. "I thought her parents were dead? I mean, she's *the orphan*."

"Her parents who died were actually her aunt and uncle. Her real parents were..." Mariska couldn't think of the word. A few moments later, she added, "...*busy.*"

"*Busy*? Who's *busy* for almost thirty years? Where were they? In line at the DMV?"

Mariska fanned her face with the now sweaty towel. "I don't know. She told me who they were, and I think I sort of blacked out. I might have missed some details."

Darla chuckled. "You're usually such a stickler for details."

"Shush it. Anyway, we can ask them all the questions we

want tonight."

"Wow. What do they look like?"

"Very attractive couple. Tall."

"Wow..."

Mariska took a deep inhale and huffed a sigh.

Darla's brow knit. "Now what's wrong?"

Mariska felt something like panic burbling in her chest. "Do you think she'll still love *us*?"

"Charlotte?"

"Yes. Now that she has parents, we're just...*neighbors*..." Mariska felt her eyes tearing and wiped them with the towel.

"Oh honey, of course she'll still love us." Darla opened her arms. She moved in for a hug and then reconsidered. "You're a sweaty mess. Pretend I gave you a big hug."

Mariska nodded and blew her nose into the towel.

Darla shook her head. "You put one more bodily fluid into that towel, and this will be a crime scene."

"Sorry. I'll take this home and wash it," Mariska mumbled.

"Hey, so... dinner—where are we going?"

Mariska perked. "Oh, that's the other thing. She asked *us* to pick a place for her while she's off with Frank doing something."

"Doing what?"

"Robbery training or something."

Darla pouted. "*I* taught her how to pick locks."

"Not *how* to rob, how to catch a thief."

"Oh. That makes more sense. Who's paying for dinner?"

"I think they are."

"Charlotte and Frank?"

"The *parents*."

"Oh." Darla rubbed her hands together. "Ooh, sky's the limit then."

Mariska hooked her mouth to the side. "Maybe we should pick a fancy place but then one more middle-of-the-road, just in case."

"Good idea." Darla opened her refrigerator and scanned the shelves. "I need cheese."

"It's early. Do you have donuts?"

"I meant I need cheese in case her parents stop by. Not for *now*."

"Oh." Mariska toyed with her now empty water bottle. "But *do* you have donuts?"

Darla shook her head. "No. We should go get cheese and donuts."

"That's a good idea. We can talk about restaurant ideas on the way to the store."

Darla clapped her hands together. "Let's take my new golf cart. Wait 'til you see it."

She grabbed keys and pulled enough reusable shopping bags from her closet to shop for the population of Peru. Mariska followed her outside, where Darla motioned to a shiny golf cart parked beside her car as if she were Vanna White asking her to admire the vowels.

"Isn't she pretty?"

Mariska goggled at the gold-flecked dark blue paint. "She *is*."

"Looks like a night sky, doesn't it? I named her Midnight. Some guy was selling her cheap, and ours was falling apart."

"Lucky you."

They hopped into the cart, and Darla motored them out of the neighborhood. At the main road, she stopped to wait for the light to change. Pineapple Port's proximity to the food store across the street was one of the reasons Mariska had chosen the community when she moved from Maryland.

"What about Johnny's?" she asked, motioning to the food store's adjacent strip mall.

Darla shrugged. "Is that fancy enough?"

"Maybe not."

At the crossing, another golf cart pulled up beside them. Painted in black and yellow stripes, the cart had the word *Stinger* painted across the front. The top of the lower-case 'g' in the word had been recreated as an angry-faced bee.

Mariska smiled at the driver, but the thin, curly-haired

woman glared back at her.

"I like your cart," added Mariska.

The woman's expression jerked as if she'd been slapped across the face. She exchanged a look with her friend on the bench seating beside her. The friend turned to flash a haughty scowl, her short, masculine haircut never moving.

Mariska whispered to Darla. "What's wrong with those two?"

Darla looked past her to eyeball the other ladies, her expression souring.

"Is there a problem?" she asked.

The women ignored her, speaking in hushed tones to each other.

Darla looked at Mariska. "What crawled up their diaper and died?"

"I don't know."

"That's my cart," said the other driver.

"What?" asked Darla and Mariska in unison, heads swiveling.

"I said, *that's my cart*." The woman punctuated each word by poking a boney finger toward Midnight.

Darla laughed. "You're off your nut, lady. This is *my* cart."

"Where'd you get it?"

"It came in a cereal box. Where do you think I got it? I *bought* it."

"From whom?"

"That's none of your beeswax."

The woman grit her teeth. "That cart is stolen."

Darla rolled her eyes. "I doubt it. My husband is *Sheriff*. He doesn't buy stolen merchandise."

"She lost it in a pink slip race," said the short-haired woman in the passenger seat.

The driver glanced at her friend and Mariska heard her hiss.

"*Shut up, Tabby.*"

She turned back, looking even more angry. "I was *cheated*

out of it."

"She used some kind of rocket fuel," piped Tabby.

The driver shuddered, as if resisting the urge to turn and chastise her mouthy friend a second time.

Mariska watched as Darla's anger seemed to melt into dispassion. Her friend shrugged.

"That's your problem. *My* cart now."

The light changed and the bumblebee cart driver stomped on her gas. Her vehicle leapt forward like a jungle cat and tore across the street.

"We'll meet again!" the driver called over her shoulder as she buzzed across the street.

Darla stomped on her own pedal. Midnight putted forward. The other cart hit the opposite curb before Darla reached the mid-way point. She looked at Mariska.

"We'll meet again?" said Darla. "Who says that?"

She cupped her hand around her mouth. "Hey, Tabby, your husband called, he wants his haircut back!" she bellowed as the other cart shot into the parking lot.

"Why are you picking on Tabby? The other lady was meaner," said Mariska.

Darla glowered at the road ahead of her, gripping the wheel with both hands. "She's no *lady*. And I only knew the other one's name—I panicked." She rolled up onto the sidewalk. "Anyway, her hair was stupid."

"I thought it was sort of smart. Especially in the heat—"

Darla threw daggers at her. Mariska changed the topic.

"Did you see how fast she went? I didn't know golf carts could go that fast."

"I'm guessing she removed the governor," said Darla. "They keep carts from going too fast, so people don't tear around the courses."

"Oh. I guess Midnight has a governor?"

Darla patted the cart's dashboard. "Not for long."

CHAPTER SIX

Charlotte pulled up behind Sheriff Frank Marshall's cruiser and parked her 240 Volvo Station Wagon.

She'd been drawn to her old car the moment she spotted it on the dealer's lot. She discovered *why* later—without realizing it, she'd remembered it from her childhood.

It had been her mother's.

Except it wasn't now, was it? What did the magical coincidence of buying her mother's old car *mean* now that the woman she thought was her mother was her *aunt*?

Shee was her mother. Alive and well.

Charlotte parked the car and stared at the dashboard, wrestling with feelings she couldn't identify.

She already felt guilty she could barely remember the woman she'd known as her mother as a child. Now that she knew Grace wasn't her *real* mother, she felt even more guilty—as if she were cheating on her with Shee.

At the same time, she felt excited to get to know her real mother. Her real *parents*.

She turned off the engine and stared through her windshield at Frank. He stood on the sidewalk outside a small rancher located not far from Pineapple Port in one of Charity, Florida's less fancy neighborhoods. The front yard behind Frank was neat and well kept, but the home's peeling stucco ensured it blended with the neighbors and their less fastidious landscaping.

She took a deep breath.

Time to get to work.

Working a case would be the easiest way to push aside the confusing mishmash of thoughts and emotions swirling inside her.

Frank grinned as she exited the car to join him.

"You're going to love this," he said as she approached.

"Why? What is it?"

"You'll see."

They mounted three cracked cement stairs and opened the screen door without knocking.

Inside, Charlotte found the living room neat, but in need of updating. She could tell the worn carpet had been recently vacuumed with lavender-scented carpet powder, but no amount of attention would change its outdated golden hue. The ruffle-covered sofa looked as if it had been plucked from a seventies furniture catalog and dropped into the home, untouched. The avocado-colored reclining chair showed signs of wear.

A small man wearing light blue striped pajamas turned to face them as they entered. Unruly strawberry-blond hair haloed his skull like spun sugar.

"You're back," he said.

"Mr. Payaso, this is that colleague of mine I was telling you about," said Frank.

The man thrust a hand in Charlotte's direction. "You can call me Felix. Frank says you're a detective?"

"Yes. Charlotte Morgan, nice to meet you." She declined to offer more specific information. She suspected Frank might have implied she was a *police* detective. He wouldn't have *lied* to the man, but he might have left out the part where she was a freshly-minted *private* detective in order to keep the homeowner from objecting and ruining her chance to intern.

"Here, let me show you," said Frank, walking toward

sliding glass doors leading from the living room to an enclosed lanai.

Charlotte followed. The smeary image of a face stared back at her from the glass.

She tilted her head. "Is that—?"

"A clown face?" said Frank. His tone implied he was locked in a losing battle against laughing.

Felix didn't seem to notice the sheriff's amusement. He pointed at the smear, with a furious expression on his red face, his hand shaking.

"This is how you'll get him," he announced, as if he were pointing to a captured man in handcuffs.

"You got him?" Charlotte asked Frank.

The sheriff shook his head, but Felix continued before he could speak.

"The man who *robbed* me. I woke up and caught him in the house. He tried to run, and his face hit the glass."

"What did he take?" asked Charlotte.

Felix seemed to deflate an ounce. "Nothing, in the end. But only because I woke up."

Charlotte moved in to take a better look at the smeary mess on the slider door. The image looked vaguely like a black cat's face, complete with whiskers. There were gaps in the pattern where the robber's cheek bones kept his eyelids from pressing against the glass. She took a couple photos with her phone.

"Why would a robber choose makeup over a mask?" she wondered aloud.

"Guess he was a cat burglar," said Frank, before looking away, clearly pretending to be interested in a stack of coasters to hide a grin.

"He had a tail," said Felix.

Charlotte's brow knit. "Like a cat?"

Felix nodded, sending clumps of his wispy hair bouncing. "Yes."

Frank snorted and cleared his throat. "Excuse me," he muttered. "I'll be back. I have to make a call."

Charlotte watched him go. "Um, sorry. So this robber was fully dressed like a cat, head to toe?"

"Yes." Felix pointed at the glass. "This is how you'll find him. Clown makeup is like a fingerprint."

"You think he was a *clown*? A cat clown?"

Felix nodded. "This wasn't run-of-the-mill Halloween stuff. This was professional clown stuff. I—I think, anyway."

"So you got a good look at him?"

"Yes and no. I was so..." Felix put his hands on his hips and sucked a tooth with his tongue. "I guess, you could say I was so *impressed* by the costume, I didn't notice much else."

Charlotte nodded. "I'm sorry to make you repeat what you already told Frank, but can you run through how it happened?"

Felix huffed a sigh. "I startled him. He ran and hit the window. In pursuit, I clipped my hip on the table. By the time I got going again, he was gone. I closed and locked the door and called the sheriff."

Charlotte scanned the living room. "Do you mind if I look around?"

Felix looked over his shoulder and down the hall where Charlotte assumed his bedroom lay.

"Sure, but you'll find the spare bedroom on the right locked to keep my mother from wandering. Dementia. If you could skip that room—" He pressed his lips together, clearly concerned. "—it would be upsetting for her to see a stranger. Might take me all day to calm her down."

"Oh, of course."

Charlotte strolled through the rest of the small house, finding more on the same theme—clean, neat and outdated. If something was missing, Felix would know. She returned to the living room to inspect the patio door and the front's knob and lock.

"No signs of a break-in. Do you have any idea how he got in?" she asked.

Felix hung his head. "I might have left the slider open."

"Ah. It happens."

Felix's eyes narrowed. "It won't again."

Charlotte glanced through the front window to find Frank standing with his thumbs hanging in his belt staring off into the distance. He apparently had no interest in returning.

"Okay. Thank you. I'm going to confer with the sheriff."

"No problem. If you need anything else just let me know."

Felix followed her to the door, and Frank turned to wave back at the man.

"I'll be with you in a second to wrap up."

Felix nodded and shut the door.

Frank's gaze shifted to Charlotte as she approached.

"I thought we had our man," he said.

"Who?"

"Wasn't obvious from the smear on the glass? The robber was the drummer from Kiss."

Charlotte laughed. "Somehow, I doubt that."

Frank shook his head. "That face on the window is like something out of a cartoon—*splat!*" He clapped one hand into the other to simulate how he imagined the scene, and then rubbed his nose. "Okay. Back to being professional. See anything I didn't?"

"I don't think so."

"He told me the clown was wearing gloves so no sense in dusting."

"We could look for traces of kitty litter."

Frank pointed a finger at her. *"Stop."*

"You started it." Charlotte glanced back at the house. "He said he might have left the slider open. I don't see any sign of a break-in. My guess is some drunken goofball wandered into the wrong house."

"I can hear it already," said Frank, holding up his hands to imply a headline. *"Florida man* dressed as cat terrorizes neighborhood."

"That just means it's Tuesday."

"True. I'll tell him we'll look into it, but I don't see spending a lot of time on a non-robbery by a kook."

Charlotte squinted at Frank. "You didn't really need me here, did you?"

He grinned. "No, it was just too funny. I needed to share it with somebody."

CHAPTER SEVEN

While the world rejoiced the death of its most prolific serial killer, Stephanie Moriarty sat at her law office desk staring at the wall, trying to decide how *she* felt about her mother's end.

On one hand, she hated the woman who'd abandoned her as a child. She despised Jamie Moriarty, who had run off to live the life of the world's most glamorous serial killer, jet-setting around the globe as an international assassin, earning notoriety for her clever Puzzle Killer murders, becoming a U.S. Marshall to hide in plain sight...

Sure, *Mom* had earned points for flair.

But did she have to leave her only daughter with a poor, alcoholic, adoptive mother? A woman who had only tolerated her for the checks Jamie sent?

Stephanie had fought her way out of Charity, Florida, and made a better life for herself—all the while wrestling with her own murderous urges.

She should have never talked to Jamie again. Instead, when Jamie showed up, she'd been star struck.

Awed.

Needy.

She hadn't realized how desperately she needed to connect with *someone like her.* Meeting Jamie Moriarty had explained so much about her own impulses.

And now, Jamie was dead. Stephanie knew she should be happy like the rest of the world was, but—

The feeling of the room changed, and Stephanie straightened, recognizing the pressure shift signifying the opening of her lobby door. She heard the bolt click shut, followed by footsteps in the lobby. A second later, a short, thick man wearing a gray suit appeared in the doorway of her private office.

"Can I help you?" she asked, standing.

He sniffed. "I'm Sidney Cantor, your mother's lawyer. I assume you've heard?"

She nodded.

He held out a square package wrapped in a large manilla envelope. "In the event of her death, I was instructed to deliver this to you."

Stephanie stared at the package. Her cheeks tingled. Part of her had assumed her mother was still alive and the reports were wrong. As Declan had pointed out, it wouldn't be the first time Jamie disappeared, only to resurface.

The presence of her mother's lawyer made everything feel more *real*.

She reached to take the envelope and then lowered her hand without touching it. She suspected whatever lay tucked inside would destroy all hope her mother had staged her own death.

I really am alone now.

"Ms. Moriarty?" prompted Sidney.

Stephanie swallowed, her hands at her sides as she nodded at the package. "What is it?"

Sidney set the bulky envelope on the desk. "I don't know. It's for you." He turned and started for the door.

Stephanie couldn't shake the feeling there should be *more*. Some speech, instructions, fanfare...

"That's it?" she called to him.

He paused in the doorway and turned to splay his empty palms. "That's it."

Stephanie searched for a way to delay his exit.

"How long did you work for her?"

"Almost twenty-five years."

"Can I ask you something?"

He shrugged. "Sure."

"Are you going to miss her?"

He laughed. Stephanie retracted her neck, shocked by the reaction. Sidney Cantor didn't look like the sort of person who *smiled*, let alone barked a laugh capable of blowing back her hair.

He seemed surprised by his own reaction and smoothed his jacket lapel as he sobered.

"Ms. Moriarty, your mother was a good payer and a snappy dresser. She could be a hoot when she wanted to be."

Stephanie watched his shoulders rise and fall as he took a deep breath. He locked his gaze on hers.

"But your mother scared the crap out of me. Last night, I slept through the night for the first time in twenty-five years."

She nodded.

I get that.

Without another word, he left. She heard the outer door open and close behind him.

Stephanie stared down at the package on her desk wondering if it was *safe* to open it.

What if she wants me to join her in the afterlife?

Doubtful. Why start longing for her daughter's company *now*?

She lowered her ear to it.

No ticking...that's a good start...

She put her hands on either side of the package, sensing some sort of flimsy box inside. Pulling a pair of scissors from her drawer, she cut the envelope and slid it away to reveal a shoebox.

A Louboutin shoebox.

She rolled her eyes.

Figures.

Stephanie lifted the lid.

It didn't explode.

Inside sat a small book, a diary, sealed with a combination lock. Stephanie removed it and searched the inside of the box for the code.

Nothing.

She turned her attention back to the book.

Hm.

The lock would be easy enough to break, but she wanted to figure out the combination—crack the Puzzle Killer's last puzzle.

Four numbers.

She chuckled to herself. If it had been three numbers, she would have guessed six-six-six...

She pondered the possibilities.

The package was for *her*. Her mother must have thought she'd know the combination.

Stephanie dialed her birthday into the lock and pressed the latch.

It snapped open.

Well, that was anticlimactic.

Stephanie flipped through the pages. The first eleven contained a continuous list of names and dates, one set per line. She recognized a few of them as victims of the famous Puzzle Killer.

A list of her kills.

Her mother kept tally.

Why give this to me? Is she bragging? Does she expect me to be jealous or impressed or—

Stephanie sucked in a breath.

Near the end of the list she spotted a familiar name: *Lester Swander.*

Stephanie gaped at it.

Her mother didn't kill *him*.

She knew that for a fact, because *she'd* killed Lester Swander.

Why would she—?

Stephanie realized what she held in her hand. If she turned

the diary over to the police all the deaths listed would be credited to her mother.

She recognized another name on the list, and knew it *had* to be.

Mom's claiming my kills.

The list was her mother's final gift to her.

She'd given her a curse. Now, she'd given her a way out from under it.

Her eyes watered with tears.

That was so *sweet.*

Stephanie slid the box to the side of her desk and tried to return to work, but something kept nagging at her heart.

So *sweet.*

Wait a second.

Her mother hadn't done a sweet thing in her life.

The truth hit her like a bolt of lightning.

The book wasn't a *gift.*

It was a *challenge.*

She could turn it in...

...or she could continue the list.

CHAPTER EIGHT

Darla jerked a shopping cart from the stacked row of them inside the food store. When it refused to release she yanked on it again and again until she was grunting with the effort.

"*Darla*," hissed Mariska. "Just pick a different one."

Roaring, Darla gave the cart a final wrench. It popped free and she stumbled back into Mariska's arms. Steadying herself against her friend, she raised one fist into the air.

"*Got it!*"

Eyes in the checkout area turned to gawk. An elderly woman looked up from her checkbook, frowning with what Darla could only interpret as disapproval.

Mariska pushed her back to her feet, looking every bit as judgmental. "What is *wrong* with you? You're acting like a crazy person."

Darla closed her eyes and took a deep breath. "I'm sorry. That curly-headed golf cart hag has me hotter than a two-dollar pistol."

Mariska shook her head. "I don't even know what that means." She hip-checked Darla out of the way and claimed control of the cart, rolling it toward the fresh produce section.

Darla hustled to follow, grumbling, her thoughts wandering to a mutual friend of theirs with a frightening talent for revenge. "I've got half a mind to get Gloria after that witch."

Mariska turned. "Are you out of your mind?"

"That woman deserves Gloria."

"Nobody deserves Gloria." Mariska huffed and started forward again. "You think so, until Gloria shows up with a nuclear bomb."

"That would work—hey, why are you going right?"

"*Everyone* goes right. First fruits and vegetables, then…"

"I always go left first."

Mariska turned to scowl at her. "You're so weird."

Mariska rolled toward the lettuce. "We need celery. We can stuff it with cream cheese…"

Her voice seemed to grow farther away until Darla didn't hear her anymore. Her gaze had strayed down the aisle, where she spotted her golf-cart-driving nemesis picking through onions.

Darla's eyes narrowed.

We meet again.

The woman's toady, *Tabby*, stood nearby, perusing the refrigerated salad dressings.

Darla saw Mariska had wandered from the cart to look at peppers.

Mine.

Darla grabbed the handle of their cart and shoved it down the aisle. She walked until her cart was a good half-length past her foe's, which sat on the opposite side of the wide aisle.

She pretended to study the organic asparagus.

Tabby turned with dressing in hand, her eyes popping wide as she spotted Darla peering at her from the veggies.

"*Gianna,*" she hissed, loud enough for Darla to hear her across the aisle.

Darla smirked.

Gianna. Now, I have a first name…

Gianna looked up. Tabby bobbed her head in Darla's direction.

The corners of Gianna's mouth drooped.

With a flick of her wrist, Darla tapped her cart a few more inches forward, to be sure it was ahead of Gianna's.

Gianna's scowl deepened. She pushed her own cart until it sat a foot ahead of Darla's.

Darla sneered.

What was that thing she'd heard Charlotte say?

It's on, like Donkey Kong.

Darla motioned at the containers of cut fruit at the end of the aisle with a bob of her noggin.

"Fancy a fruit salad?" she called across the potatoes.

Gianna glanced where Darla had motioned. Without another word, she dropped the onion in her hand and lunged for her cart.

Darla felt the adrenalin dump into her veins. She clamped both hands on her own cart and *ran.*

Running parallel tracks separated by stacks of apples, the women bolted for the imaginary finish line. They reached the refrigerated unit at the same time, their carts slamming into opposite corners hard enough to send clear boxes of cut melon tumbling into the premade salads. Gianna whirled left and pointed away from Darla.

"Seafood!" she barked.

"Sonova—" Darla jerked her cart from the case and spun it to point toward Gianna and the seafood section at the opposite side of the store.

Gianna took three long strides before turning her head to check on Darla's pursuit. As she did, a man appeared from a side door, and her cart slammed into his rolling metal tower of bread.

The man yelped as loaves of wheat exploded around them. Gianna stepped on one and wobbled into the wall. The bag popped like a gunshot. Somewhere in the cereal aisle, someone screamed.

"*Sucker!*" shouted Darla as she swerved left to overtake Gianna, nearly twisting an ankle on a loaf of six-grain.

Darla regained her balance as her cart hit what felt like a brick wall.

"*Oof!*"

She doubled-over onto the handle as the air left her lungs. Gasping for breath, she looked up to find a woman standing with her hands on her cheeks, gaping as if she were starring in *Home Alone: The Retirement*. Darla had slammed into her cart so hard a dozen tins of tuna fish still rattled against the wall of the wheeled metal cage.

"Sorry," said Darla, backtracking to dislodge herself.

She turned to see Gianna barreling toward her, teeth clamped and coral-painted lips leering. She clipped Darla's cart as she passed. Darla's hands ached with the reverberations. Desperate, she threw out her foot to hook Gianna's shin. Gianna stumbled and spun, bounced a thigh off the meat section's refrigeration unit, and landed butt-first in the chilled chicken.

Darla shoved Gianna's cart out of the way, making sure to spin it backwards. She weaved around a display of brioche hamburger buns and skidded to a stop in front of the sushi section. Snatching a family-sized package of California rolls, she held it above her head, triumphant.

"*Loser!*" she screamed back at Gianna, who, with Tabby's help, had lifted herself from the drumsticks.

Howling with rage, Gianna grabbed something oblong from the case and chucked it like a football at Darla.

Darla dodged. The pork loin landed with a *splat* behind her, as she stuck out her tongue.

"Missed me, you—"

Something wet dripped on Darla's head. She looked up as a waterfall of soy sauce poured from the sushi platter in her hand.

Gianna cackled.

Darla wiped her eyes. "You—"

"Ma'am," said a voice behind Darla.

She turned, blinded by the salty liquid in her eyes. Lids fluttering, she made out the image of a man in a tie.

"Me?" she asked.

"I'm going to have to ask you to leave."

The voice sounded *managerial*. She knew. She'd spoken to a few managers over the years.

She motioned back toward Gianna.

"But—"

"*Now.*"

Hands grasped her arm. Gentle. Feminine. Nothing like the managers she remembered.

"What happened?" asked Mariska, suddenly at her side, sounding out of breath. "What did you *do*?"

Darla jerked herself free of her friend's grasp.

"Grab the cheese. I'll meet you out at the cart."

She pounded down the pet food aisle, licking soy from her lips, headed for the exit.

"But *Darla!*" yelled Mariska behind her, "cheddar or Gouda?"

CHAPTER NINE

Charlotte left Frank at the scene of the attempted robbery and made it to the main thoroughfare of Charity before she realized she'd forgotten to tell him about her parents.

How is that possible?

Who knew a clown robbery was the perfect distraction?

She wasn't sure how much longer she could put off thinking about her growing family and dreaded heading home. What would she do all day other than fret over the approaching dinner? How was she supposed to feel? How many questions would Mariska think to ask her in the next five hours? What—?

Declan.

His name came to her like a motel's neon light blinking at the end of a long drive. Of course, her boyfriend could keep her distracted. She'd tell him about Shee and Mason, and then they'd move on to other things. Clown robberies, for example. He'd tell her about almost selling a stuffed iguana wearing a top hat and how many people tried to sell him used exercise equipment today.

As long as I'm not alone.

Problem solved.

She made a right and headed for Declan's store in the busy section of town. The Hock o'Bell Pawn Shop occupied the bones of an abandoned Taco Bell, not far from the larger stores in the area. She pulled into the parking lot and smiled at the sight of her tall, handsome man, standing in the doorway of his store as if he'd been expecting her. He wore his usual work clothes, khaki shorts and a polo shirt, his smile punctuated by double dimples.

"You look like you knew I was coming," she said as she approached him for a hello kiss. His green eyes remained looking past her, and she turned to see two elderly ladies arguing over who would drive their Cadillac.

"Oh," she said. "You're out here watching the drama."

He sighed. "They were in here about to free me from a few Josef figurines. That is, until Stephanie scared them away."

"Stephanie was here?" Charlotte sniffed as she walked inside. "Oh, yep. I smell sulfur."

Declan chuckled. "She had big news."

"She's moving?"

"No. Bigger. Her—"

Charlotte held up a palm. "Hold on. I bet I have bigger news."

Declan crossed his arms against his chest. "Not a chance."

"Let's bet." Charlotte hadn't played much poker, but how she felt had to be akin to holding a royal flush. There was no way Declan's news could be bigger than finding out she had living parents.

"Fine," he said. "The one with weaker news buys lunch."

He looked smug.

Poor guy.

Win or lose, she'd won. Lunch meant more time not alone and not thinking about how many ways she could put her foot in her mouth with her parents that night.

"Charlotte?"

She snapped back to the conversation at hand, embarrassed to find Declan staring at her.

"This is exactly what I came here to avoid," she grumbled.

"What?"

She waived him off. "Nothing. Deal. You go first."

He displayed his palms, fingers pointing to the sky like a magician readying a trick. "Ready?"

"Ready."

"Can I get a drumroll?"

She rolled her tongue to provide him a soundtrack.

He swallowed and began.

"Jamie Moriarty..."

"Yes?"

"The Puzzle Killer..."

"Yes? They caught her?" Charlotte felt a trill of excitement. It would be good news to hear the woman they'd sent to jail, the serial killer who wanted them dead, had been recaptured. She might finally get a good night's sleep.

Granted, even that news wasn't good enough to win the contest, but he'd come a lot closer than she'd imagined he would.

Declan closed and opened his fingers, simulating the pop of a flashbulb.

"...is dead."

Charlotte's jaw dropped open. "What? She's dead?"

"Officially."

"That's why Stephanie was here? To tell you her mother's dead?"

He nodded. "And to bleed me for sympathy."

Charlotte scowled. "She knows her mother tried to kill us, right?"

"Sure. But that isn't about her."

"Good point." Charlotte's brain swirled. So many questions were trying to push their way out of her mouth and only the smallest made it through.

"How?"

"Shot at a roadside motel."

"By whom?"

"They didn't say."

"Who's 'they'?"

"The FBI. They called her."

Something about Declan's information struck Charlotte as odd. "Wait. What was fancy Jamie doing in a motel?"

"Laying low, I suppose."

She nodded. Made sense. "Wow. That is pretty big news."

"See? I told you. I win."

She put a hand on his arm. "Hold it right there, partner. Don't start counting your sushi rolls yet."

"We're getting sushi?"

"Yep. It's expensive."

He squinted one eye. "Wait... You're saying you can beat that news?"

She shrugged. "It's true, any other day, you would have won."

"No way you have bigger news. Let's hear it, big talker. Shoot."

Charlotte took a deep breath. "I just had crackers and cheese with my parents."

Declan stared at her, seemingly stunned into silence.

"Well, they didn't actually eat any crackers or cheese," she added. "It was a dumb snack choice so early in the morning..."

Declan reanimated, measuring his response as if he were working out a math problem. "You said parents. Like a mother and a father?"

"Yep. Both. Double-barrel parents."

He shook his head. "I don't understand."

"Neither do I."

"You said your parents were dead—"

"I thought so. Turns out they were my adoptive parents—and my aunt and uncle. My real parents just showed up in my living room."

"So you've gone from orphan to having two parents and two aunts?"

She cocked her head. "Two aunts?"

"The one you thought was your mom and the one in Jupiter Beach?"

"Oh. I see your confusion. The aunt in Jupiter Beach is my

real mom."

Declan grinned and threw out his arms. "That's amazing. That's great. Right?"

"I think so."

"Where are they now?"

"I'm not sure. We're having dinner with them at five, though. Me, Mariska and Bob, Darla and Frank and you—assuming you want to go?"

"Of course. Gosh." He put his hands on his hips and stared at the floor. "I'm having trouble processing this. I can't imagine what you're going through."

"You have no idea."

He put his hands on her shoulders. "Are you okay? How do you feel?"

She sighed. "It's weird. I've gotten that far."

"I bet. Wow."

"Yeah, wow. So, do I win?"

He laughed. "Yes. You win. You definitely win."

Charlotte and Declan ate sushi rolls in the pawn shop while an elderly woman agonized over a wicker patio set. They searched online for more information on the death of Jamie Moriarty. The news had broken, but none of the reporting offered any more clues to the circumstances surrounding Jamie's death than Stephanie had shared.

One social media post claimed the Puzzle Killer had been executed by aliens who'd stowed away on a returning Mars rover, but they disregarded that one.

Charlotte wondered how Stephanie felt about the death of her estranged mother. She imagined discovering her estranged parent was dead was something like finding out her estranged parents were alive. Their parallel experiences *almost* inspired her to check in on her nemesis, but after talking through it with Declan, they decided the last thing she wanted to do was draw the attention of a potentially angry and confused Stephanie.

Declan's ex had too much in common with her mother.

After reorganizing the used comic book section of the shop, even Charlotte had to admit she couldn't kill any more time with Declan. A gaggle of old men arrived to pick out a new lounge chair for the one in a knee brace, and she sensed they would require her boyfriend's full attention.

"I'm going to hit the road," she said, pecking him on the cheek.

"Okay. I'll meet you at your house around three-thirty."

She nodded. The dinner.

Sigh.

Charlotte pushed open Declan's door to the tune of his shop bell, squinting under the late afternoon sun as she made her way to her Volvo. She hadn't driven three blocks toward home when she did a doubletake. The name on a road sign had caught her eye.

Big Top Way.

She knew the road. It led a few miles east to the Big Top Retirement community—known locally as Clown Town—a large and popular spot for retired circus performers.

Hm.

Could it be a coincidence?

Felix believed the robbery suspect wore clown makeup, and he lived a mile from Clown Town.

When looking for a clown, circuses—or places circus people gathered—made for good places to start.

It hadn't been much of a robbery. Frank wouldn't pursue it. But that didn't mean *she* couldn't do a little digging.

She looked at her watch.

She *did* have some time to kill...

She also had a picture of the painted faceplant. Maybe someone in Clown Town would recognize the pattern.

Charlotte made a U-turn and headed back to Big Top Way.

It couldn't hurt to check.

CHAPTER TEN

"I'm going to stick my foot in my mouth, I know it," said Shee as she and Mason walked into their beach hotel, overnight bags in hand.

She'd picked The Lanai, a hotel on the beach, instead of one closer to Charity. She didn't want Charlotte to feel crowded, and she'd figured if her daughter rejected her multi-leveled apology, from a beach hotel she could walk directly into the ocean and not stop until she hit England.

Mason chuckled. "You *should* stick your foot in your mouth. She should know the real you."

Shee shot him a withering glance.

"Can I help you?" asked a young woman behind a flesh-colored counter. The rest of the lobby looked as if Hawaii had barfed on it, featuring potted palms growing from pots in every available corner. Though Florida had its share of palms, for some reason this hotel had embraced a decidedly Pacific theme, complete with ukuleles and colorful fake flower leis around the staff's necks.

The check-in girl's nametag read *Jade* in gold letters. Despite her exotic name, Shee suspected she wasn't eager to stand out. She sported one piercing in each earlobe, had no visible tattoos, and her hair color appeared to be natural. Behind her, what looked like a textbook lay open on the counter.

Jade is a good girl and a student who—

Shee took a deep breath.

Stop it.

Old habits die hard. But she didn't need to break down the check-in girl. She'd been on the run for so long she'd forgotten what it was like to take a stranger at face value.

Jade is standing behind the desk. She is the desk clerk. That's all I need to know about her.

No one was lurking behind the giant, sour-faced tiki in the corner.

Jade wasn't going to report her location to her enemies.

Shee smiled.

"Hi, Jade. We have reservations under McQueen?"

A tiny shot of nerves strummed in her chest. Saying her real name out loud still made her uncomfortable.

Smiling, Jade tapped on her keyboard. "Here we are. King with balcony?"

Shee nodded.

"And...?" asked Mason beside her.

She swiveled to face him, and he stared back at her, eyebrows raised.

Oh.

Her cheeks grew warm.

Whoops.

"I only booked one room," she said.

Mason scratched his nose, blocking the view of his mouth from Jade. "Can I talk to you for a second?"

Shee smiled and held up her index finger for Jade. "We'll be *right* back."

The couple shuffled toward the middle of the room, and Mason turned his back to the counter.

"One room?" he asked. "One bed?"

Shee winced. "Sorry, I didn't think about it. I'm used to traveling alone. Habit. We'll get you another room."

Mason paused, appearing as if he hadn't expected her to give in so easily. Shee put a hand on his chest.

"I mean, I know you're not ready to forgive me. I apologize

for not thinking."

He cocked an eyebrow. "Why are you being so reasonable?"

"I'm always reasonable. And I don't want you to feel *helpless*."

Mason scowled. "What do you mean, *helpless*?"

"I mean, I understand you need your space to keep your hands off me—"

Mason barked a laugh. He glanced back at Jade and then leaned down to whisper in Shee's ear. "We both know *you're* the one who can't keep your hands off *me*. I don't want to put *you* under any undue strain."

Shee rolled her eyes. "Oh, *please*..."

"Did you, or did you not, steal my leg so I couldn't leave your room the other night?"

He spoke in a normal tone, and Shee turned to find Jade staring at them.

Taken out of context, that comment *had* to sound odd. She turned her back to the check-in counter to work on a witty retort slow to pop to mind.

Mason wasn't wrong. After a celebratory night of tequila shots, she *had* hidden the retired SEAL's prosthetic leg in the closet in an attempt to keep him in her room. Not her most dignified moment, but the chances of her admitting that *now* were about the same as the stuffed toucan in the corner taking flight.

She glanced at the bird and did a doubletake.

"Are there toucans in Hawaii?"

Mason frowned. "Don't change the subject. Tell me you *didn't* steal my leg."

"Sure. Yes. I stole your leg. Blah, blah, blah. *We were celebrating*. It was a *joke*. Sue me."

Mason crossed his arms against his massive chest. "Uh huh. I think we both know what was going on."

Shee glanced over her shoulder at Jade, who stood waiting, playing with her hair and pretending not to listen.

She turned back to Mason. "Look, I *swear* my reservation

wasn't an attempt to seduce you into forgiving me for Charlotte."

He snorted. "Like you *could.*"

"What? Seduce you?" She poked a finger in the divot between his pecs. "Oh, I *could,* mister, if I *wanted* to."

They glared at each other, eyes locked, cocky smiles on their lips.

Shee relaxed. "Look, this trip is about *Charlotte*, not about me leaving you a thousand years ago."

Mason held out his hands, bouncing one and then the other as if they were competing scales. "Leaving? Or *disappearing*? Breaking up? Or scuttling off with our unborn—"

"Yeah, yeah. I get it. I'm a *monster*. Do you want me to get another room or not?"

He seemed rattled. "I wouldn't call you a *monster*—"

"Do you want your own room?"

He sighed. "No. We'll make do."

"Then it's settled."

She'd already started back to the desk when he added, "But see if they have twins."

She turned. "What are we, two years old?"

"I'm pretty sure two-year-olds sleep in a *crib*. You'd know that if—"

"Shut it. *Fine.*"

Shee composed herself and approached the desk with a smile. "Hi, Jade. That King bed—would you happen to have doubles? Twins or—"

Jade nodded. "We have a similar room with double queen beds. Would that work?"

"*Perfect*," said Shee. "Our, uh, daughter might be stopping by." She looked away, mortified she felt the need to lie to Jade, a girl she'd probably never see again.

Jade winked. "It's double occupancy, but I'll pretend I didn't hear that."

Shee tittered, the sound of her own uncomfortable laughter grating on her ears.

I am an idiot.

Somewhere close behind her Mason snorted, and she turned to glare at him.

"Shut *up*," she mouthed.

He displayed his palms in *mea culpa*.

Jade programmed their key cards and handed them over. Avoiding further chit-chat, Shee grabbed her bag and headed for the elevator with Mason on her heels, where they rode in silence to the seventh floor. Traversing a floral-patterned carpet designed to hide stains and wear, they found their door.

The Lanai wasn't the most chic lodging, but Shee did find it nice to be in a *hotel*. The cheap *motels* she'd frequented during her time on the road paled in comparison to even a mid-level beach tower. The only busy patterns outside her door at motels had been left by the drunks the night before.

Shee raised a hand to shield her eyes as they entered their room. Sunlight streamed through the sliding glass balcony doors opposite the entry, making it hard to see, but also giving the room a pleasant, airy feel.

She dropped her bag and wandered to the window to peer down at the beach.

"Nice view," she said.

She turned to see Mason set his own bag on the end of the queen bed closest to the door. Unzipping it, he pulled out his shaving kit and headed for the bathroom.

She watched him walk by in the linen pants he'd chosen to wear, butt hopelessly wrinkled by the long drive from Jupiter Beach.

"You should take your pants off—"

"Already trying to get me naked?" he called back from the bathroom.

"—and put on *shorts*," she finished. "I don't know why you wore *pants*."

He strolled out to stand beside her at the window, his hands tucked in his pockets.

"I guess I didn't want her to know about the leg right

away."

"You think she'd like you less with one leg?"

He chuckled. "I dunno. I don't have a lot of experience reuniting with secret daughters. I'm feeling my way here."

"Fair enough."

Shee glanced back and noticed a minibar.

"Want to have a cocktail on the porch and come up with a game plan?"

Mason closed his eyes. "*Yes.*"

She moved to the fridge. "Tiny bourbon, tiny vodka, tiny rum, or tiny gin?"

"You choose. I'm going to change."

"Don't go changin'," she said.

He ignored her.

Shee rustled through the tiny bottles of booze. When Mason emerged from the bathroom wearing shorts and a tee shirt, she sent him down the hall for ice while she mixed two rum and Cokes and changed into a loose-fitting tank dress.

Ice added to drinks, they moved to the balcony, a soft gulf breeze fluffing their hair as they sat.

Shee took a sip and closed her eyes to enjoy the sun.

"This is nice," she murmured. "I might not even vomit from my nerves if this keeps up."

Mason nodded. "This might be the first time my shoulders have relaxed since you said we were coming."

Shee chuckled, "Tell me about it. I think—" She paused as her mind wandered to their meeting with Charlotte earlier. A thought had occurred to her then. Something important...

"What?" prompted Mason.

She remembered. "I think we have to stop thinking about the impact of all this on us and just concentrate on *her*."

"We are, aren't we?"

"Yes. I mean, I'm certainly thinking about how she feels, but mostly how she feels *about us*."

"Ah. I see what you mean. Good point. This has to be hard for her."

"Yes." Shee smiled. "Wasn't she *pretty*?"

Mason's eyes widened. "She's *gorgeous*." He shook his head. "I know where she gets her looks."

Shee blushed.

"Me," he finished.

She threw an ice cube at him, and he batted it away. He took another sip of his drink, and she watched his smile fade.

"What is it?"

He sighed. "We still have a lot to tell her."

"Yes." Shee held up her glass. "But so far so good."

Mason clinked her glass with his own. "Cheers. To our *daughter*."

"To our *daughter*." Shee took a sip and looked away so he wouldn't see her eyes tearing.

CHAPTER ELEVEN

From afar, Big Top looked like any other modular home retirement community. A wide grassy lot preceded it, where what looked like a town of booths had been built beside a huge building painted with red and white vertical stripes.

Charlotte recognized the building as the circus grounds Mariska and Bob had taken her to as a child. For decades, Big Top had held a yearly circus to raise money for charity, using its residents as performers. She imagined they brought in some younger ringers too, because she remembered an elaborate trapeze act she felt sure no retiree could have accomplished.

Other than the circus theme, she imagined Big Top was like any other retirement community...

Charlotte hit her brakes.

A woman walking a small, white Chihuahua eyeballed her from the sidewalk leading to the Big Top entrance. As she approached, the woman flicked her wrist, and a plume of smoke burst from the ground.

What the heck!

By the time the cloud dissipated, the woman and her dog had disappeared.

Charlotte twisted in her seat, trying to see where'd they gone.

She didn't see anyone.

Okay...

That didn't happen much back at Pineapple Port.

Maybe Big Top is a little different...

Charlotte rolled forward again and entered the community to cruise down what seemed to be the main drag. Spotting a second large vertically striped building with a red roof, she guessed it to be the community center and pulled into the parking lot surrounding it.

She made her way inside, directly into what looked like a large banquet room. Red silk drapes hung on the walls, covering the windows and fluttering beneath the air conditioning. The effect made Charlotte feel as if she'd stepped into the center of a living heart.

Not creepy at all.

Charlotte scanned the room.

She wasn't a huge fan of circuses. She had a mild case of *coulrophobia*—fear of clowns. The sight of a painted face and goofy shoes didn't send her spinning into a panic attack, but she headed in the opposite direction. She didn't appreciate anyone in a costume really. Maybe her aversion to disguises was the reason she'd become a detective—to *reveal* people hiding behind masks of any kind.

She'd never thought about it that way until now.

Charlotte giggled to herself.

Wow. Deep.

She returned her attention to the empty community center. A group of tables and chairs crowded one corner. An ornate black podium stood beside a bingo cage and what looked like a smattering of magicians' equipment, including the classic 'saw a woman in half' box. Three low round pedestals, like those an elephant might step on during its act, lined one wall, each painted with colorful polka dots, stars, and stripes. A large slab of wood painted black with the outline of a body chalked on it leaned against the far wall.

Yikes. What are their bingo nights like?

Above the elephant steps hung row after row of photos.

Charlotte moved to them, wondering if the trapeze artists and fire-breathers represented were current residents or past ones.

"Can I help you?"

Charlotte jumped. A man with an old-timey handlebar mustache had sneaked up behind her. Both the mustache and his blue-black pompadour shone beneath the ceiling's high-hat lights. Heavily tattooed arms poked from beneath a blue tee-shirt with *Circuses are In-Tents* blazed across the chest. She guessed him to be in his early sixties.

"You scared me," said Charlotte. She smiled. The man did not.

"Can I help you?" he repeated.

"I'm Charlotte Morgan. I'm—" She paused, knowing the rest of her sentence would sound odd. "I'm looking for a clown."

He frowned. "This is a private facility."

"I understand. I didn't mean to intrude—"

"If you need to hire a clown for your kid's birthday party, try the Internet."

"I don't want to hire a clown. I'm a detective looking for a clown who might have been involved in a robbery." She pulled her phone from her pocket and held up the photo of the sliding glass door smear. "He hit the window on the way out."

The man peered at the photo without reaction.

"You're a cop?"

Shoot. She'd been hoping he wouldn't ask her that *directly*.

"Private detective."

He seemed relieved. Leaning back, he scratched the back of his head. "Yeah, well, unless you're a cop with a warrant, I can't help you."

"Do you mind if I look around a bit?"

"Yes, I *do* mind. This is private property. We don't like people walking around, *gawking*."

"I understand. I—"

Movement caught Charlotte's eye, and she looked past the man at a woman poking her head from behind one of the red curtains. She pointed to the exit in an urgent, almost conspiratorial manner, and then disappeared behind the breathing fabric once more.

"Sorry," said Charlotte, refocusing on the man. "I'll go."

He turned to see where she'd been looking. Seeing nothing, he motioned to the exit with his arm.

"I'll see you out."

He followed her to the door and closed it behind her as she left. Through the glass she watched him disappear back into the bowels of the community center, before scanning the area for the blonde woman she'd seen motioning to her from inside. She was about to give up when someone hustled around the corner of the building.

"Hey. I'm Cassie," said the blonde Charlotte recognized as the same from inside. "Did you say you're here about a robbery?"

"I'm Charlotte."

They shook hands. The woman was curvy and cute, and Charlotte guessed her to be in her mid-fifties. She wore a cheery floral sundress that made her appear as light as the mustachioed man had felt *dark*.

"Someone in clown make-up broke into a man's house last night," said Charlotte.

"Ah. That explains why Stark didn't want to help." Cassie bobbed her head in the direction of the community center. "He's my ex-husband. He's a first-class jackass but very protective of the community. We need that sometimes." She tilted her head. "So you're a cop?"

"I'm a private detective."

"Really? How cool!" Cassie put her hands on her hips. "So, what'd he look like? The clown?"

Charlotte fished her phone from her pocket and held up the faceplant. "Like this."

Cassie peered at the image. "Hm. I don't think we have any cat clowns—"

"*Cassie*," barked a voice. Stark had reappeared at the door of the community center.

Cassie flashed a middle finger in his direction and grabbed Charlotte's arm, tugging her away.

"Come with me."

Charlotte allowed herself to be led as Stark glowered after them. Cassie looked over her shoulder several times as they scurried.

"He thinks he's big-man-on-campus." Cassie picked up speed until Charlotte nearly had to jog to keep up. "Which he *is*, but he doesn't have to be such a *jerk*," she added.

"Can I ask where you're taking me?"

They reached a modular home much like all the others, but for a large collection of gazing balls in the front. Cassie released Charlotte's arm to climb the stairs to the door and knocked.

"This is Baroness' house. She's the one who saw it."

"Saw what?"

Cassie leaned toward her and spoke in a hushed tone. "The *murder*."

Charlotte straightened. "What murder?"

Cassie knocked again and the door gave way, opening a few inches.

Cassie's brow knit. "That's weird. The door's open."

"Maybe call inside?" suggested Charlotte.

"I don't know. Baroness is *scary*. That might piss her off." Cassie frowned. "She's got to be here. She doesn't walk well—hardly ever leaves this place."

Looking nervous, Cassie poked her head inside. "Baroness?"

No one answered. Cassie took a few steps inside.

"Baroness?"

No sooner had she disappeared around the corner, than Charlotte heard her yip.

"Are you okay?" Charlotte entered. "Cassie?"

It only took Charlotte a few steps inside to find the cause of Cassie's distress. An old woman lay on the floor in the center of the living room, her long black hair spread around her head like octopus tentacles. She wore a ruffled, thin black robe.

It looked as if someone had shot a witch out of the sky.

"I'll call nine-one-one," said Charlotte.

Cassie dropped to her knees beside the body to touch the woman's face. She recoiled and looked at Charlotte.

"Tell them not to hurry."

CHAPTER TWELVE

Darla's mood hovered somewhere between dark and murderous as she and Mariska pulled into her driveway with two bags full of cheese, fruit, pepperoni, cookies, and some other unexplainable items. She'd sat in the cart sweating for a half hour, waiting for Mariska to finish. Without her in the store to help, her friend had panicked and bought everything she could fit into the cart.

"It's going to take us a week to unload this stuff," said Darla, parking Midnight. "You didn't have to get every snack food ever invented."

"Then maybe you shouldn't have gotten kicked out," said Mariska in a chastising tone. "Anyway, I didn't know what they'd like. For all I know, they might be German or Australian—"

"That explains the mini franks and vegemite."

"I could make schnitzel—" Mariska twisted in her seat, her brow knitting. "Hey..."

"Hm?"

"Look." She pointed down the street at a bumble-bee-striped golf cart sitting in the middle of the road, six houses down.

Darla's mood darkened another shade.

"*Gianna.*"

Mariska's eyes widened. "They followed us home?" She slapped a hand onto Darla's leg. "She's here to *steal her cart back*."

Darla clenched a fist around her key. "Over my dead body."

The bumble-bee cart rolled forward, picking up speed.

"She's coming," said Mariska.

Darla got out of the cart, braced and ready for a confrontation, shaking a raised fist in the air.

"You'll never get Midnight!"

Gianna blew by without so much as tapping a break. Behind her, Tabby's arm swung, and something flew from the cart.

Mariska yelped and ducked as the object hit the roof of the golf cart with a thud that made Mariska yelp too. It bounced off, hit the grass, and rolled back to Darla's feet.

"What is it?" asked Mariska, peeking out from under her arms.

Darla reached down to pick up an oval, paper-wrapped object. She peeled away the paper to reveal rough brown skin.

"It's a potato."

"Why would she throw a *potato* at us?"

"There's a note wrapped around it. She used the potato for the weight."

Darla removed the rest of the paper to read out loud the message scrawled on the note.

"Old Swamp Gas Trail. Friday at eight."

Mariska scowled. "What does that mean?"

Darla crumpled the paper in her hand. "It's a racing challenge. She wants to race me for the pink slip to Midnight."

"How do you know that?"

"I've raced on Old Swamp Gas Trail before."

"Really?" Mariska opened her mouth, closed it, and then shook her head. "Never mind. I'm not even surprised." Her head tilted. "Eight seems early for illegal street racing, doesn't it?"

Darla shrugged. "She probably goes to bed early like most of us."

"Hm. Do you think you can beat her by taking the mayor off of Midnight?"

"*Governor.*"

"Whatever."

"I don't know." Darla raised a pointed finger as an idea sprouted. "I might have another trick up my sleeve."

"What's that?"

"I bought this cart from a man who *obviously* knows how to beat her. I need to find out how he did it."

Mariska gasped. "Ooh, good idea."

"I thought so too." Darla's attention shifted to the groceries. "Let's get the damn cheese out of here before it turns to fondue, and then we can take the cart to him. He lives on the other side of the neighborhood."

Mariska nodded, and the two of them schlepped the bags into Darla's house to transfer the perishables to her refrigerator. They would have needed a crowbar to stuff them in Mariska's fridge.

Food tucked away, they took Midnight to the far side of Pineapple Port and pulled up outside a house with the garage door open. Inside sat four golf carts. A man puttered in the back.

"Wow, make sure you never race *him*," whispered Mariska as they parked.

"I won't. Unless I get addicted to the thrill of racing and become obsessed with winning to the ruination of my life and family."

Mariska scowled at her. "You think that will happen?"

Darla shrugged. "It's fifty-fifty."

The two of them walked up the drive.

"Hello, there," called Darla.

The man in the garage turned. "Oh, hello." He glanced into the driveway. "I sold you that cart. Is there a problem?"

"Not with the cart. I ran into a woman who claims the cart is hers. She's challenged me to a race to get it back."

The smile on the man's face dropped. "Oh."

"I figured you'd beaten her to get the cart in the first place, so I came to find out how you did it."

The man seemed to perk. Darla guessed it was because she hadn't asked for her money back.

"You don't want me," he said. "I'm just the salesman. You want my wife. Just a moment."

He disappeared into the house through the garage's side door.

A minute later, a petite woman wearing overalls dotted with what looked like golf cart racing patches appeared. She smelled like lily of the valley and grease.

"I'm Carolina," she said, holding out her hand. "I hear you got a Gianna problem."

"I do. I'm Darla. This is Mariska."

"Hi," said Mariska, waiting her turn to shake Carolina's hand.

"So you know Gianna?" asked Darla.

Carolina closed her eyes and nodded. "Well enough to know she's a terrible loser."

"I'm getting that impression. She challenged us to a race on Old Swamp Gas Trail. I figured you beat her once, so with your help I could, too."

Carolina grimaced. "You don't have to race her, you know. You bought that cart fair and square—same as I *won* it fair and square."

"Yeah, but I don't think she's going to let it go," said Darla. "And I kind of *want* to race her."

"Even though she's afraid she might get addicted to racing and ruin her family," added Mariska.

Carolina pulled at her chin and stared at Midnight. "Well, thing is, the way I beat her when I won your cart, she won't let happen again." After a moment, she motioned for them to follow and moved to a cart in the back left of the garage. She lifted the seat to reveal several batteries.

"I used Jessie here to win your cart," she said. "The key is Lithium batteries and lots of them."

"Lithium?"

"Yep. They've got less weight and more power than lead acid."

"So Midnight has lead acid?" Darla eyeballed her own ride. "Could you get me lithium batteries before eight o'clock tonight?"

Carolina sighed. "I could. But like I said, she's probably already figured out my trick and made the switch herself."

"But it would at least give me a fighting chance."

"Looks like you win every time," said Mariska, gaping at Carolina's collection of carts.

Carolina's shoulders slumped. "Not anymore. Now they have *rules* to keep me from racing with extra batteries." She said the word *rules* in a singsong, mocking tone. "You said you needed the batteries by tonight?"

Darla nodded. "Yeah. But if there are rules—"

Carolina shook her index finger back and forth like an inverted clock pendulum. "Ah, but that's just it. Official racing night is *Saturday* and it's *Wednesday*. She's going to break the rules with extra lithiums, I bet, so she's racing you off the record. She figures you don't know any better."

"She's right," said Darla.

"So this is *illegal* illegal street racing," said Mariska. She looked at Darla. "You'll *definitely* get addicted to this."

Darla grinned. "How much for you to trick out my ride so I can beat her?"

Carolina considered. "Tell you what. You give me her cart after you win it, and I'll set you up to win."

"Perfect," said Darla grinning. She thrust out a hand to shake. "*Deal.*"

CHAPTER THIRTEEN

"So you found her here?" asked Frank, standing over the body of Baroness von Chilling.

Charlotte nodded. "Cassie brought me here to talk to her, and we found the door open. Then I called nine-one-one and you."

She glanced out the front window at the people lining the curb behind the copious crime tape Frank's deputy, Daniel, had strung at the edge of the property. She'd seen plenty of gawking crowds during her time working with Frank, but none quite like Clown Town's. In the first two rows alone were at least four dwarves, a man with a beard down to his knees, and a woman with enough tattoo ink on her skin to write out the Guttenberg Bible in long-hand cursive. Deputy Daniel had his hands full talking to a woman with a giant yellow snake draped over her shoulders.

Frank wandered to the window and closed the blinds before strolling into the bedroom. Charlotte joined him, her eye falling on a fuzzy, circular bed on the ground beside the king mattress.

"Looks like she has a dog," said Frank.

Charlotte shook her head. "Probably a cat."

Frank scowled. "Bed's big. What makes you say cat?"

She motioned back to the kitchen. "There are containers of tuna fish in her refrigerator labeled *Kitty*."

"You looked in her fridge?"

Charlotte nodded. Unsure she'd get a chance to investigate once the police arrived, she'd walked the house after calling nine-one-one. Baroness' decorating leaned more tropical and cheery than she'd have guessed for a woman dressed in black. In the closet of the guest room, she'd found clothes a different size than those in the master bedroom. They felt younger, too, but there weren't enough to imply another full-time resident of the home. Several were medical scrubs. She guessed a part-time nurse sometimes slept there.

After spotting the fluffy bed on the floor in the main bedroom she'd wandered into the kitchen to search for dog food or treats. She'd wrapped her hand in a paper towel and opened the refrigerator to find a collection of the usual suspects: coffee creamer, cheese, fruit, lunchmeat, and a small stack of square plastic containers with *Kitty* written on the top in black permanent marker. Prying off a lid, she sniffed the contents to find it was tuna fish.

"If it's a cat, it's probably hiding. I'll make sure someone comes looking for it when we're done," she added.

Frank squinted at her. "What were you doing here, anyway?"

"A woman named Cassie brought me. She said Baroness saw a murder."

"*Another* murder? Who?"

"I haven't found that out yet."

"Where is this woman?"

Charlotte motioned to the front door. "She's waiting outside."

The local medical examiner, Rachel Abrams, appeared at the front door with a bag in hand. She was a tall, dark-haired woman with full lips and a personality cheerier than her job implied. Charlotte recognized her from another recent crime scene.

"That's quite a crowd," Rachel said, pushing her sunglasses to the top of her head. "Hi, Frank." She looked at Charlotte and pointed. "Charlotte, right?"

Charlotte smiled. "Yep. Hi, Rachel."

Rachel put down her bag and stared down at Baroness' body, her gaze tracking from the woman's head to a large, blood-smeared crystal ball sitting on the floor nearby. She squat down for a better look.

"You probably don't have to be *me* to see the blow to the head was the beginning of the end," she said, pointing to the wound there. "But the bruising here suggests she was choked as well. I'd bet dollars-to-cents her hyoid is broken, too. We'll know after the autopsy."

"Hyoid?" asked Charlotte. "Is that part of her skull?"

"No, it's the little u-shaped bone right here." Rachel pointed to Baroness' upper throat. "It holds up your tongue and helps your jaw work. We find it broken in about a third of strangulation cases. The percentage increases with age. She's what...? I'd say early eighties?"

Charlotte and Frank shrugged in unison.

"There's a neighbor outside who might know," said Charlotte.

Frank caught Rachel's eye and nodded to the body. "Keep an eye on her so we can go ask around a bit?"

Rachel nodded. "Sure, but I don't think she's going anywhere."

Frank turned his attention to Charlotte. "Let's talk to that girl you came with."

She nodded, and they walked outside. Cassie sat under the carport in a plastic chair staring at the ground.

"Miss? Mind if we ask you some questions?" asked Frank.

"Her name's Cassie," Charlotte reminded him.

The woman snapped out of her trance to focus on Frank. "Hm? Oh, sure."

"What did you say this woman's name was?"

"Baroness von Chilling."

"That's her *real* name?"

Cassie shrugged. "Oh, no, probably not. It's all I know,

though. She's a fortune teller. A lot of us have stage names. We're all retired circus."

"Right, Clown Town," mumbled Frank, jotting something on his notepad.

"We don't like being called *Clown Town*," said Cassie, visibly annoyed.

Frank blinked at her and then returned to writing.

Charlotte made a mental note of her own. She'd always heard the place referred to as Clown Town. She hadn't realized it was a local joke unappreciated by the residents.

"Did you know her well?" Frank continued.

"No," said Cassie. "She kept to herself, mostly."

A man bumped into Charlotte's shoulder, and she turned to see it was her ol' buddy Stark from the community center, moving to his ex-wife's side.

"Are you okay? What's going on?" he asked her, but his angry glare focused on Frank.

Frank frowned. "Sir, I'm going to have to ask you to stay behind the crime tape."

Stark shook his head. "I have a right to know what's going on."

"Sir, please step behind—"

Chest puffing, Stark poked a finger at Frank. "You can't come here and start ordering us around—"

Frank exploded. "The hell I *can't*. Now get behind the tape."

Charlotte had never seen him so angry. The two men glared at each other a moment before Cassie squeezed Stark's hand.

"Do what he says, Stark."

Frank cleared his throat, calming. "This is an *investigation*. Please move yourself behind the tape, and I will get to you as soon as I'm finished here."

Stark paused another second and then moved. "I'll be right over here," he said, heading for the tape.

Cassie looked at Charlotte. "I'm sorry. I really don't know how I can help. I didn't see anything you didn't."

"You said Baroness saw a murder?" asked Charlotte.

Cassie shook her head. "Oh. Not a *real* murder. Baroness got into it with one of the headliners. Told him he'd better watch out because she'd seen his murder."

"Who?" asked Charlotte.

"Scotty the Skyscraper. But they were always going at it."

"What kind of name is Scotty the Skyscraper?" asked Frank, sounding annoyed. Charlotte guessed the oddity of Big Top's residents had him feeling out of his element.

"He's a clown."

"You said they fought a lot?"

Cassie huffed a sigh. "We're split into groups here. It's like high school all over again. There are the talents and the freaks. The *talents* are like the cool kids—the aerialists, the animal trainers, the hoopers, the tightrope walkers. The freaks are the sideshow performers. There's infighting between the groups."

"Which are you?" asked Frank. He looked up from his pad. "I mean, if you don't mind me asking."

Cassie shrugged. "I'm a clown. Clowns are neutral. We don't get involved in politics."

Frank frowned. "Was Baroness considered a... um..."

Cassie guessed where he was headed. "A freak? You can say it. It's the accepted term, not a slur. From what I know she considered herself to be on Team Freak, yes."

"So you think Baroness was just trying to scare this Skyscraper fella with her murder prediction?" asked Frank.

Cassie nodded and turned to Charlotte. "I'm sorry. I brought you to her as a joke. Plus, I thought she might know your cat clown—she's been here forever and knows—*knew*—everyone."

"Cat clown?" Frank turned to glare at Charlotte. "Were you here looking into—"

Charlotte moved to change the subject. "Do you know anyone who'd want Baroness dead?" she asked Cassie.

"No—" She straightened. "Wait. Are you saying she was definitely murdered? For sure?"

"We don't know anything yet," said Frank in his usual brusque tone. He scanned the crowd. "Anyone in particular you think we should talk to next? Besides that guy?" He nodded toward Stark.

Cassie looked into the crowd and pointed. "That guy there, in the track suit, is Tony the Tiger Tamer. He's her neighbor." She motioned to the house next door.

"Okay, thank you," said Frank. He gathered her contact information and then moved past Stark to the man in the white, iridescent track suit.

"Sir, can you step inside the tape here for a second?"

Tony the Tiger Tamer seemed surprised he'd been noticed, but he stepped under the tape after a moment's hesitation. Though he appeared to be in his sixties, his hair shone blue-black without a hint of gray. A cloud of cologne followed him as he moved.

"How can I help you, Officer?" he asked. The glimmering fabric of his track suit shimmered through the color wheel.

"Can I have your name?" asked Frank.

"Antonio Leone." He grinned and winked at Charlotte. "But you probably know me as Tony the Tiger Tamer."

Charlotte shook her head.

Nope.

Her rebuff seemed to have no effect on Tony, who continued to stare at her like a hungry lion.

"Your eyes are very cat-like," he purred to her.

Charlotte didn't answer.

Ew.

"Did you know Ms. von Chilling?" asked Frank, leaning to put his head between Tony's eyes and Charlotte's face.

Tony refocused on him. "Yeah, of course. Everyone knows everyone around here."

"Do you get along?"

"Get along?" Tony snorted a laugh. "*No.* She's a *thousand* years old and a first-class b—" He stopped and cleared his throat. "Let's just say she's nosey and she's got an opinion for everything."

"With everyone? Or just you?"

Tony scowled. "Are you asking if I killed her?"

"I didn't say she was killed."

Tony thrust a hand toward Baroness' house. "It doesn't take a genius. You're out here interviewing people, and nobody's rushing nobody to the hospital." He scanned the crowd, and Charlotte watched as his eye fell on Cassie. "What's that clown filling your head with?"

Cassie sneered back at him.

"When was the last time you saw Ms. von Chilling?" asked Frank, pushing on.

He shrugged. "I dunno. Maybe three days ago." He poked a finger at Frank. "Listen to me. Let me tell you somethin'. I got nothin' to do with whatever happened to that witch. Me and her didn't see eye-to-eye on everything, but any beef we had was the usual neighbor crap."

"What would you consider usual neighbor crap?" asked Charlotte.

"Oh look, she speaks," said Tony, smiling. He shrugged. "Get off my lawn stuff." He sniffed. "Plus, she's wrapped up with the freaks."

The way he said *freaks* had sounded like an insult.

"Any in particular?" asked Frank.

"No. I dunno. The whole lot of them. The little people, Fat Frankie, the Devon Sisters." He chuckled. "They're Siamese twins, the Devon Sisters. Some might love the idea of two women in bed, but let me tell you, they don't mean *that* mess."

Frank recoiled. "I'm asking you nicely to watch your mouth in front of the ladies."

Tony blushed and glanced at Charlotte. "Sorry, honey."

Charlotte's lip curled. She turned away and caught the eye of a tall man watching them from the crowd. She guessed he had to be seven feet tall.

"Who's that?" she asked, nodding with her head in the man's direction. "The guy in the green running shirt."

Tony peered over the crowd as the man in green began to move away.

His expression darkened. "That's Scotty the Skyscraper. *Clown.*" Again, he managed to make a word sound like a slur.

A small young woman with mousy-brown hair appeared at Tony's side, pushing her phone toward Frank's face.

"Sheriff, can you tell me about the murder of Baroness von Chilling?"

Frank scowled and took a step back. "Who are you?"

"Lulu Trapping, Charity Gazette, online edition."

He shook his head. "No comment."

"I'm her neighbor," said Tony, smiling at the woman with every inch of his too-white-to-be-real teeth.

"Can I get your name?" asked the reporter, swiveling her phone from the sheriff to Tony.

"Sure." Tony looked at Frank. "We done here?"

"We're done," said Frank. "If you hear anything let us know."

"Sure, Officer." He gave Charlotte one last heavy eyeballing. "You let me know if *you* need anything."

Charlotte looked away.

"Where'd that guy go?" asked Frank.

She turned back and followed his gaze to see Stark had disappeared.

CHAPTER FOURTEEN

Stephanie lowered her head over her paperwork, but her eyes kept flitting in the direction of her mother's diary and the list of victims within.

It was typical of her mother to steal all the attention in the room.

Even *dead,* the woman was a narcissist.

Stephanie sat back in her chair and stared at the ceiling.

Why do I even think of her as my mother?

She knew her mother's murderous urges flowed in her own veins. She'd tried to ignore her own instincts to kill—she'd even become a criminal lawyer to live vicariously through her dirtball clients. Still, whenever she found herself in a pickle, she'd *killed* her way out of it.

Not a lot.

Less than six times.

She counted on her fingers.

I think...

She'd promised Declan she'd be good. She knew she had to be a *Girl Scout* if she was to have any chance of winning him back.

...and Charlotte needs to be hit by a bus...

She hadn't figured a way to point a bus in Charlotte's

direction without Declan noticing, though. The girl could be hit by lightning, and he'd probably blame *her*, so she couldn't carve a shortcut to his metaphorical heart through Charlotte's *actual* heart.

She'd even called off her mother when Jamie offered to help make Charlotte disappear.

In hindsight...

Stephanie sighed and picked up the book.

An hour later, Stephanie stood at the Sheriff's Department's front desk, waiting for the receptionist on the phone to notice her. When she finally coughed loud enough, the woman slapped a palm to her chest and hung up.

"Girl, you scared the life out of me. How long you been standin' there?"

Stephanie suspected the friendly thing to do would be to smile and chuckle, but she didn't feel like making the effort.

"I need to talk to Sheriff Marshall."

"Frank!" The woman yelled so loudly and so suddenly Stephanie jumped.

"Ruby, dammit, I told you not to scream for me like that. Use the damn phone!" returned a male voice from down the hall.

"There's someone to see you."

A moment later, Sheriff Frank Marshall appeared in the hall, grumbling toward the lobby. His gaze fell on Stephanie, and his stride lost steam.

"Whatcha say your name was?" asked Ruby before the sheriff made it to the lobby. He took another step and answered for her.

"*Stephanie.*" He said the word as if it tasted sour in his mouth.

"*Frank*," said Stephanie.

"Oh, you two know each other," said Ruby, swiveling back to her keyboard. "You shoulda said so."

Frank put his hands on his hips. "Come to turn yourself in for something?"

Stephanie offered him a tight, mirthless smile. "Close. I need you to help me get this into the right hands."

She held out her mother's book. Frank stared at it as if it were boobytrapped.

"What is it?" he asked.

Stephanie glanced at Ruby, whose curiosity had apparently been aroused by Frank's snide comment. The woman stared, her chin resting on her knuckles.

All she needed was a bucket of popcorn.

"Can we talk in your office?" asked Stephanie.

Frank shot a glare in the receptionist's direction. "Sure." He walked back down the hall in his bowlegged manner to enter his office with Stephanie close behind.

"Go ahead and shut the door," he said, sitting behind his desk.

She did and then took a seat across from him before placing the book on the edge of the desk.

Frank's attention dropped to it.

"So, what do we have?"

"My mother sent it to me."

Frank's spine straightened. "Your mother? You know where she is?"

"In a manner of speaking. She's dead."

"*Dead*? What makes you say that?"

"The FBI called and told me."

He scowled. "They didn't tell *me*."

"Well, you're not next of kin, now, are you?" She sighed. "You can call them to confirm. Or I'm sure it will be on the news. Whatever. Whether you believe me or not isn't the point."

Frank's shoulders relaxed, and he stared past her, a strange smile curling the side of his mouth. He seemed to have fallen into some sort of happy trance.

"Frank?"

"Hm?" He cleared his throat. "Oh. I'm, uh, sorry for your loss."

Stephanie frowned. "Sure you are. We don't have to pretend anyone is sorry she's dead." She slid the book closer to him. "She had her lawyer bring this to me on the event of her death."

Frank reached out, his hand hovering over the book.

"You already looked through it?" he asked.

She rolled her eyes. "It isn't rigged. It won't blow your fingers off."

He lifted the book and flipped through a few pages. After a moment, he looked up, seeming alarmed.

"Is this—?"

She nodded. "A list of her victims. I figured it might give the families some peace."

"Definitely." He flipped a few more pages. "This is it? Just the names and dates? No body locations or motives or *anything*?"

She shook her head. "Most, I imagine, were found right where she left them. She *did* like to take credit where credit was due."

As she said the words Stephanie felt a flutter in her stomach.

I didn't think of that.

Her mother had always left her bodies in the open, usually artfully arranged in a manner consistent with her sick sense of humor. But the names at the end of the list—Stephanie's kills— those bodies would never be found. She'd hidden them well. If those were the only two names with missing bodies, someone might realize the M.O.'s were totally different and suspect they weren't Jamie's.

Stephanie resisted the urge to snatch the book and run.

Calm down.

There were pages and pages of names. Some of those bodies

had to be missing—

"You okay?" asked Frank.

Stephanie looked up to find Frank scowling at her.

She sniffed. "I'm fine."

"You look a little pale all of a sudden."

"I'm *fine*."

"Okay." He closed the book. "So you want me to get this to the FBI?"

She nodded. "I wasn't sure who to send it to, and it's too important to drop in the mail."

He nodded. "Agreed. I'll get this taken care of for you. Don't you worry."

"Great." Stephanie stood and smoothed her skirt. "Well, have a good evening."

Frank stood. "I'll walk you out."

They headed down the hall.

"This is a good thing you're doing," he said.

She could hear it pained him to say something nice to her. She'd caused too much trouble for his precious Charlotte in the past.

As they moved into the lobby, the receptionist's attention snapped to the sheriff. "There you are. You better get hustlin', mister. You're gonna be late for Charlotte's special dinner."

"Special dinner?" echoed Stephanie, pointing her widest, most innocent eyes in Ruby's direction. "Is it her birthday?"

Frank seemed ruffled. "Uh—"

Ruby's eyes had closed, or she might have seen how desperately her boss wanted her to *shut up.* She shook her head. "Charlotte's parents are here. Isn't that something? After all these years."

"Her *parents*?" Stephanie scowled. She hated her ex-boyfriend's perfect girlfriend, but the one thing she appreciated was their shared orphanhood.

Did Goody Two Shoes lie? Did she lie to Declan?

Stephanie looked at Frank. "I thought Charlotte was an orphan?"

Frank stammered. "She is, er, was—"

Ruby held up her hands, palms to the heavens. "Turns out she's had parents all along. It's so—" She closed her eyes and grimaced as if she were trying to pass a bowel movement. "I don't know—*romantic*, but for families instead of couples." Her eye popped open again. "Is there a word for that?"

"Heartwarming?" suggested Stephanie.

She wanted to vomit all over the whole sugar-dusted moment.

Ruby pointed at her. "Yes. *Heartwarming.* That's exactly what it is. To think, after all—"

"Okay, Ruby," barked Frank. "I'm sure Ms. Moriarty needs to get on with her day."

"Ms. Moriarty?" Ruby scowled. "Why's that sound familiar?" She tapped her chin with her index finger and then bobbed in her chair. "*Oh,* I know. I just saw on Facebook they shot that serial killer lady—"

"My mother," said Stephanie.

"Your—" Ruby's eyes saucered. "Oh, my sweet baby—I am so *sorry*..." She looked at Frank. "I didn't know." She mouthed the words.

"Told you it would be on the news," deadpanned Stephanie to Frank.

He nodded and put a hand on her shoulder to guide her toward the door "Well, thank you for stopping by. I'll take care of everything for you."

Stephanie jerked her shoulder from his touch and strode to her car without looking back. She slid into her candy apple red Viper, shut the door, blasted the air conditioning and sat gripping the wheel with both hands.

Charlotte has parents now?

She gets everything? Declan? Parents?

She slammed her car into reverse and peeled out of the parking lot, bound for her office. She still lived there, tucked in a room in the back. She passed the sign for Pineapple Port and suffered another dark thought.

Charlotte has a house, too.

Something had to change. Life hadn't improved since she vowed to be a good girl for Declan. If anything, life had gotten *worse*. She still hadn't moved out of her office. Business was down. Her mother was dead. Granted, Jamie was the *worst*, but she was still an *ally* on some strange level.

It was almost as if denying her true nature had cursed her.

Stephanie pulled into her lot and shook the wheel as if trying to tear it free from the steering column. She screamed until her voice went hoarse.

I need to do something. I need to change the trajectory of my life—

Her phone dinged and she glanced at it, panting.

A headline alert from the local news glowed on the screen. *Does Charity Have a New Serial Killer?* it said, in classic clickbait fashion.

She clicked on it.

Call it irony or symmetry, but only a day after the death of Charity's most famous daughter, serial killer Jamie Moriarty, it seems someone has decided to fill her shoes.

Reports from Big Top, a fifty-five-plus community catering to retired circus performers, suggest someone is killing its residents. Fortuneteller Baroness von Chilling was found dead in her home of apparent strangulation, and the sudden death of another resident last week is now being reexamined as related—

Stephanie looked up from her phone.

That's it.

She could piggyback on the Big Top serial killings. It didn't matter if they actually had a serial killer in their midst or not. Any killing in Clown Town would be lumped in with the others. If they ever found a suspect and he denied killing one or two— who would believe him?

A strange calm came over her.

Her mother had taken credit for her most recent killings. Someone else could take credit for her future killings.

Declan would never know.

Stephanie smiled.

It would be good to let off a little steam.

CHAPTER FIFTEEN

Grin the Bullet-catcher stared into his bathroom mirror as he brushed his teeth. At seventy-one, he still had all his original chompers, a fact he loved to point out to the other residents of the Big Top Retirement Community—particularly the ones with dentures. He'd made his living 'catching bullets in his teeth', yet he still had his, and they didn't.

He never got tired of that joke.

Grin spat minty white foam, his hand fumbling in the drawer for the floss.

Sensing something behind him, he glanced over his shoulder.

Nothing.

He shrugged it off. The sensation was strange, but not unusual. Since the death of his wife four years before, he'd often found it unsettling to be in the house by himself. At night, he still stuck to his side of the bed, careful not to crowd hers. Sometimes, he pulled two plates down for dinner. He missed her, and he'd underestimated how much he needed companionship. He'd considered getting a dog but kept pushing it off. He'd joined the community's magic club, started a cornhole team with the tattooed man down the street, ran for—and won—a seat on the community board, and met an ex-knife thrower's assistant at the local supper club over grouper and rice pilaf.

Still, he felt alone.

He flossed.

Something *ticked* behind him—like two small metal objects clicking against each other. The sound rang familiar.

Returning from his drifting thoughts, he looked in the mirror.

Someone stood behind him, a gun in hand.

Grin whirled.

He didn't recognize the intruder's colorful Mexican wrestler-style mask, but the leather pants, the black cape, the vest hanging on the thin, almost waifish frame—those he recognized.

"That's my costume," he said. It was an odd thing to say to someone who'd broken into his house and walked unannounced into his bathroom, but in truth, he felt more surprised by the appearance of his old costume than he did by the person wearing it.

Lips encircled by the mask moved. They pursed, and something shiny and gold appeared between them before being spat to the floor.

The object pinged as it struck the ceramic tiles and Grin watched it bounce onto his shower rug, harmless, like a blown kiss.

A bullet.

"What are you doing here?" he asked.

Another bullet appeared between the stranger's lips before dropping to the ground. Another. The intruder took a small step forward with the appearance of each new bullet, pushing Grin tighter against the counter behind him.

Feeling cornered, anger built in Grin's chest. He pointed to the door and roared in his most commanding voice.

"You get out of here!"

Another bullet fell, but this one didn't ping. Grin glanced down to see if it had landed on his rug.

It hadn't.

It was the wax bullet.

There'd be no wondering where the trespasser had got the bullets now. They were Grin's—most recently stored in a wooden box beside his costume in the closet of his guest room.

Who but a bullet-catcher would have a wax bullet—the key to his bullet-catching trick?

There were other ways to accomplish the trick. He could have a beautiful assistant shoot blanks and then produce the real bullet he'd hidden earlier in his mouth. He could have a whole conversation with a bullet hidden in his cheeks and no one would be the wiser.

But toward the end of his career, Grin realized people weren't as gullible as they used to be when he started. Instead of blanks, he liked to load the gun in front of an audience with a marked bullet—someone he brought on stage could even get a close look as he loaded the weapon. By the time he loaded the gun, he'd swapped out the marked bullet with an identical one made of wax. When fired, the spray of wax broke through a pane of glass, giving the audience more *proof* he'd fired a real gun.

The original marked bullet was already in his mouth, of course.

Now, the wax bullet was on his bathroom floor.

Grin stared down at it.

Why?

"What do you want?" he asked.

Still pointing the gun at Grin with one hand, the intruder pulled off the sparkly yellow mask with the other.

Grin scowled.

"I know you," he said, though he couldn't place the face.

He heard the gun cock.

His own gun.

A *real* gun.

"See if you can catch this one," said the stranger.

CHAPTER SIXTEEN

Charlotte sat her computer on her lap and typed in *Tony the Tiger Tamer* after first pushing Abby's furry face off the keyboard a few times and erasing the gibberish she'd typed with her chin.

She found Tony's Facebook page. He was active on the site, posting new pictures of himself almost every day. Tony in a store, Tony playing bocce, Tony standing with a lion, Tony eating eggs, Tony standing outside his house—

Online, Charlotte looked past the grinning mug of Antonio Leon at a dark-haired woman wearing nurse scrubs. She appeared to be leaving Baroness von Chilling's house. She had her arms across her chest and her head down.

Baroness' nurse.

She'd been right to suspect a nurse owned the clothes in the spare room. She probably worked for a service.

I should find her.

Whoever she was, this woman knew Baroness well enough to keep a few changes of clothing in her house. They'd had to have been close. If anyone knew who wanted Baroness dead, it would be the nurse.

Charlotte looked at her watch. Somehow, it was already three and getting close to dinner-with-the-parents time.

It won't hurt to make a few calls first.

She searched online for the numbers of every nursing outfit she could find and called each, pretending to be von Chilling's niece doublechecking her aunt's appointment. She thought the ruse clever until she came up dry. No one had von Chilling on their schedule.

Shoot.

A search for *Baroness von Chilling* revealed nothing but a local news site's coverage of the murder. Charlotte recognized the bio pic of the writer as the rabid reporter Lulu Trapping from the von Chilling crime scene. *Amazing.* She'd already written up her story and published it online. Charlotte scanned the article, surprised to be *surprised*. For one, she didn't know Baroness' real name was Betty Romano, a child of Newark, New Jersey.

That might have been good information to have when she called the nurses. She'd probably been registered under her real name.

Charlotte rolled her eyes at her own stupidity and returned to the article to read another resident of Big Top had recently died—Bernard Teixeira, former bear trainer—and that while his death was originally thought to be a heart attack, now local authorities were reopening his case. The author mused a serial killer might be targeting Big Top.

Really?

Charlotte looked up.

That seemed like a stretch. And local authorities? Who? *Frank?*

She'd have to ask him at dinner.

She felt a tingle of nerves.

There's dinner again.

Another glance at her watch told Charlotte another twenty minutes had passed. She was about to close her laptop when something in another of Tony's photos caught her eye. She recognized the red drapes of the Big Top community center in the background of a photo of Tony hovering over a plate of bacon and eggs. A woman who looked like Baroness' nurse sat at a table behind him. He'd only captured the side of her face, so Charlotte couldn't be sure, but she wore scrubs.

The way he'd framed the photo, it was almost as if he'd been *trying* to get the nurse in the photo. His breakfast and own smiling face felt like an afterthought.

Charlotte ran through the rest of Tony's photos again, this time paying more attention to the backgrounds. Along with a disturbing number of women wearing bathing suits or sporting plunging necklines, she found the nurse in four more photos and possibly a fifth, though the last, poolside, was blurry. She couldn't be sure the bikini-clad dark-haired woman was the nurse, but she was definitely younger than the average Big Top resident.

Charlotte frowned.

This can't be a coincidence.

Did Tony kill von Chilling to get at her nurse? Did he already kidnap her? The idea was a *leap*, but she already knew Tony had a thing for younger ladies.

She returned to dialing nurse agencies, this time inquiring for Betty Romano. For her second attempt, she spoke with a slight British accent in the hopes no one would recognize her trying a second time.

She was still on the phone when her front door opened, and Declan poked in his head.

"Knock, knock," he said, entering. He stooped to say hello to a wriggling Abby while she finished up her call.

"Hey," said Charlotte, hanging up.

His brow knit. "Am I crazy or did you just sound like Mary Poppins?"

She giggled. "I was disguising my voice." She paused. "You know, they seemed more eager to help me, I'm guessing because of the accent. I might use it from now on."

"Whatever works. I'm early—" Declan seemed to see her for the first time. "Wait—you're not even ready?"

Charlotte looked down at her shorts. "No. I got waylaid—I think someone might have kidnapped a nurse."

"Might have? Or *did*?"

"Might have."

Declan looked at his watch. "In that case, I'd go get a shower. You're going to be late."

Charlotte sighed. Declan was right. She's put off dinner for as long as she could. She put her laptop aside to stand. "I need to tell Frank about the guy and the nurse—"

"Okay. Tell him at dinner."

"Yeah, yeah." She looked him up and down in his polo and khakis. "You look nice."

"Thank you. I figured this would work for anywhere around here. You never said where we're going."

Charlotte put her hand over her mouth. "Oh, Mariska called me an hour ago, and I didn't call her back. She was picking the place."

"You let Mariska pick the place?"

Charlotte nodded.

He grimaced. "Boy, you *really* didn't want to think about this dinner."

Charlotte smiled. "How do you know that's what I was doing?"

"You never spend this long at lunch with me, you let Mariska pick the place, and you're sitting here half an hour before it's time to go, obsessing on a *potential* case. Or just the fact that you invited everyone you know to go with you...Come here."

He opened his arms and enveloped her in them. Charlotte melted into him.

"Thank you. I think I needed that," she murmured. She closed her eyes and listened to his heartbeat.

"Are you okay? There's no shame in telling them you need more time to process."

She shook her head as well as she could with her ear pressed against his chest. "I can't. They came all the way over here to see me."

"They live on the east coast, not Timbuktu."

She sighed. "No. I want to go. It's just that a whole thing I thought I knew about myself is *wrong*."

"I get it. Just remember we're all here for you." He eased her away from him and held her at arm's length. "But not if you don't get a shower."

She chuckled. "*Fine*."

Charlotte schlepped herself to the shower and kicked herself for her late start. Luckily, she was *so* late, didn't have time to fret.

Time moved fast once Charlotte's shower ended. Still in her towel, she called Mariska to find out what restaurant she'd chosen. Given the option of Mariska's usual hangout and a more upscale location overlooking the water, Charlotte chose water view and texted Shee to let her know the spot.

She spent another fifteen minutes picking out an outfit and another five willing her heart to stop beating so fast. Another fifteen was eaten by the drive to the restaurant.

She and Declan arrived early to find Darla, Frank, Mariska, and Bob already standing in the parking lot, waiting for them.

"I thought we'd better wait here in case they came early," said Mariska, eyeing Charlotte's dress. "Don't you look beautiful?"

"Thank you." Charlotte looked down at the blue dress speckled with tiny pink shells, still wondering if she'd made the right choice. "You look nice, too."

"This them?" asked Mariska's husband Bob, pointing to a black F150 truck as it pulled into a space.

Charlotte nodded, her mouth suddenly dry.

The truck parked, and Shee stepped from the passenger side in a dress so similar to Charlotte's they both looked down at their own outfits. Mason walked around the truck to join Shee.

Charlotte noticed he limped as he approached.

Mason held out his large hand as he and the others took turns introducing themselves.

"What's your last name?" Mariska asked Mason.

"Connolly."

"Charlotte Connolly," she mumbled to herself.

"Charlotte was my mother's name," added Mason.

"Really?" asked Charlotte. She'd been trying to pretend she wasn't eavesdropping, but she'd been watching to see how everyone responded to everyone else.

Mason nodded, a stiff smile on his face.

Shee's head turned, her brow furrowing as she eyed Charlotte's car. She squatted behind it to place her hand on a torn and faded bumper sticker.

"Is this Grace's car?" she asked.

Charlotte nodded. "I bought it by accident. I didn't know until later it was hers."

"Really?" Shee gaped at her for a moment and then stood, looking as though she might cry. After a moment, she sniffed and seemed to shake off her pensive thoughts.

"I like your dress," she said to Charlotte, grinning.

"Let's eat," said Frank.

"Here, here," said Bob, leading the way.

CHAPTER SEVENTEEN

Charlotte's large table of friends and family had placed their drink orders with the server when a strange silence settled on the table.

With horror, Charlotte realized the problem.

No one knew what to say.

She'd never seen Darla and Mariska so quiet. Her own mind had gone blank as well. The harder she tried to devise a line of small talk, the blanker it became, until she feared she might manifest a black hole in the middle of the dining room.

Declan was a better chit-chatter than she was, but he'd run back to the car to get her sweater. Darla looked at her watch, smiled at Shee and Mason, and then mumbled something to Mariska. Mariska looked at her watch and nodded.

Why aren't they talking?

Any other day she could have stuffed a hundred grapes into their mouths, and they *still* would have found a way to babble.

Charlotte studied them from behind her water glass.

They're up to something.

Frank had his phone out, checking messages. Bob was busy stacking creamer cups into a small replica of the Great Pyramid of Giza.

This is going to be a long dinner.

Charlotte offered her parents a quick smile, listening to the airy silence in her head. Shee opened her mouth as if she was about to say something, only to be cut short by Darla.

"Bread?"

Darla thrust a basket of rolls under Shee's chin.

Shee nodded and took the offering, taking a slice of raisin bread before the table passed the collection from person to person as if it were a part of a solemn religious rite. Each person *oohed* and *hmm'ed* over the mundane collection of rolls and breadsticks, before their attention shifted to the sherbet-style scoop of rock-hard butter following.

The butter couldn't move fast enough. Bob and Frank at the end of the procession grew panicky, watching as the scoop of butter grew smaller. Charlotte knew they wouldn't eat bread without butter even if they'd been wandering in the desert for a week.

Declan returned with Charlotte's sweater and took his seat.

"What did I miss?" he asked.

"Absolutely nothing," Charlotte muttered behind her hand, as she pretended to scratch her nose. "That's the problem."

"Did they redo that bar area where we walked in?" asked Darla.

Charlotte perked.

Someone's talking!

Her glee proved short-lived. Darla had addressed *Shee*, who couldn't possibly know what the restaurant *used* to look like.

"Me? Um, I don't know," said Shee. "But it looks nice…"

"I think they retiled behind the bar," said Charlotte. Catching Darla's eye, she nodded toward Shee. "Shee's never been here before."

Darla nodded. "Oh, right." She turned her attention back to Shee. "What kind of name is Shee?"

In the middle of chewing, Shee choked down her bread. "It's short for Siofra."

"What kind of name is She-fra?" asked Bob, forty decibels too loudly.

"Irish. It was my grandmother's name," said Shee.

"Oh, that's nice," said Mariska.

"Kinda weird," muttered Bob.

"We can't all have a name as interesting as *Bob*," added Frank.

Bob sat up as if his engine had kicked on. "What do you call a man with no legs and no arms in the ocean?"

"*Bob*," said half the table by rote.

Bob chuckled.

Shee grinned and looked at Mason, who returned her amusement.

"Whew. I can lose three more limbs before I have to change my name," he said.

Charlotte's brown knit.

Hm?

Darla heard him, too. "What's that?"

Mason leaned down to tap on his prosthesis. "I'm a leg short."

Mariska gasped, her head swiveling to glare at Bob. "You and your stupid jokes."

Bob's eyes popped wide. "How was I supposed to know?"

"No offense at all," Mason assured them.

Charlotte lowered her head into her hand.

This was such a bad idea.

The server arrived with the drinks, effectively changing the subject from insensitive jokes to toasts. Mariska held up her glass of pinot grigio.

"Here's to Charlotte's parents—"

The others raised their glasses.

"—for finally showing up," finished Mariska.

Charlotte groaned.

The others clinked glasses and repeated.

"All one and three-quarters of them," said Bob, winking at Mason.

Mariska smacked her husband's arm with her free hand, causing the glass in her other to slosh pinot to the tablecloth.

"When someone says you haven't offended them, you *don't keep trying*," she hissed.

Charlotte took a long and large sip of her cocktail.

Bob ignored Mariska, his attention still on Mason. "Where you been all this time, anyway?"

Charlotte sucked in a breath that sent a scattershot of liquid down her air pipe. She choked, fighting to keep from spraying the table with every shade of tequila sunrise.

"Are you okay?" asked Declan, placing a hand on her back.

"I'm trying to kill myself," she croaked to him.

Shee turned her attention to Bob. "We, uh, didn't come sooner because of me. I put a very dangerous, very rich man in jail, and he put a contract out on me. I didn't want to endanger Charlotte, so I stayed away."

"A contract?" asked Bob. "Like a hit squad? Like the Mafia?"

Shee nodded. "Something like that."

"Your life is like a movie," said Darla, clearly in awe.

"You put a man in jail? You're a police officer?" asked Frank, ever the lawman.

Shee shook her head. "No. I worked with my father. He skip-traced for the military."

"Skip-traced?" echoed Mariska. "That doesn't sound like something that could get you in trouble. It sounds like hopscotch."

"It's like bounty hunting," explained Darla.

Mariska eyed her friend. "How do you know?"

"One of my husbands—"

Mariska stopped Darla with a raise of her hand. "Nevermind." She leaned toward Shee. "I swear, before Frank, I think Darla was married to every criminal in the country."

Frank cleared his throat, pretending not to hear Mariska's thunderous whisper. "So, what did he do?" he asked Shee. "This guy you caught."

"He killed a girl. Two, actually. Maybe more we don't know about."

"You said your dad was military? What branch?" asked

Bob.

"Navy."

Bob grunted and then puffed his chest. "I was a *Marine*."

The corner of Mason's mouth curled.

The waitress arrived and asked if they were ready to order. As a rule, at this point in the evening Charlotte and Mariska launched into a battle of wills—Charlotte liked to relax for a while before a meal, Mariska liked to eat as soon as possible. Charlotte imagined Mariska would call in her order on the way to the restaurant if given the option.

This time, Charlotte didn't say a word.

As the waitress reached Bob to take his order, he looked at Shee and Mason. "You said you're paying?"

They nodded in unison.

Bob smiled and looked up at the waitress. "I'll take the surf and turf with the lobster."

Mariska hit him again.

"*What?*"

Mariska steamed. Charlotte could feel the heat of her glare from the opposite side of the table.

Bob sighed. "Fine. Make it the *crab*."

Mariska put her hand on Shee's arm. "I'm so sorry. He's untrainable."

Shee snickered. "It's *fine*."

"Please, I want everyone to order what they want," said Mason.

Bob elbowed Mariska. "See?"

"I'll talk to you later," she muttered.

Orders in, Shee turned to Charlotte. "So, how did you decide to become a detective?"

Frank snorted a laugh before she could answer. "She had to become a detective. Once she figured out that mess with Declan's mom, I couldn't keep her away from my crime scenes."

Shee and Mason both turned to Declan, whose cheeks had flushed red.

"They found my mother in Charlotte's backyard," he said.

"Dead. Bones. She wasn't squatting back there," explained Frank.

Charlotte considered sliding under the table.

"Your *mother*?" Mason's eyes were wide. "How?"

Declan shook his head. "Long story."

"Like a whole book," agreed Darla.

Shee pointed from Charlotte to Declan and back. "Were you dating then?"

They glanced at each other and shook their heads.

"It's how we met," added Declan.

Shee giggled. "Wow. That's like the world's worst Tinder date."

Charlotte and Declan laughed.

"What's a Tinder?" asked Mariska.

Darla opened her mouth to explain, and Frank caught her eye.

"Nope," was all he said.

Darla shut her mouth.

The food arrived.

"Wow. That was fast," said Declan.

Charlotte nodded and leaned toward Shee.

"Um, maybe we could get coffee tomorrow morning, just us?" she asked.

Shee smiled and nodded. "Sure. That sounds great."

"I'm realizing now that maybe bringing everyone was a bad idea," she added.

"No, it's nice to meet everyone," said Shee.

Charlotte squinted one eye. "Is it, though?"

The table fell quiet as the group shoveled grouper, steak, and chicken into their maws. As Charlotte took her last bite of fish, she heard the familiar jingle of Frank's phone.

"Sorry," he grumbled, pulling it from his pocket. He answered, made a few grunting noises, and hung up before looking at Charlotte.

"There's been another murder at Clown Town."

Charlotte gasped. *"Really?"*

He nodded. "I'm sorry, I have to go."

Charlotte dabbed her mouth with her napkin. "I should go, too."

Frank frowned. "No—"

"You said I could help with this one?"

"Yeah, but—" Frank motioned to Shee and Mason.

"I'd like to come, too, if you don't mind," said Shee. Mason looked at her and she shrugged. "I'd like to see my daughter in action."

Charlotte straightened, feeling oddly *proud*.

Frank seemed as if he wasn't sure what to say. After a moment, he lifted his hands and let them drop. "Fine. Whatever. You can all come. I can't stop you. Just remember it *is* a crime scene." He looked at the others. "You coming too?"

"No. Leave money," said Bob.

Frank pulled out his wallet and threw several twenty-dollar bills on the table.

"No, it's our treat," said Mason, realizing what was happening.

Bob picked up Frank's bills and slipped them in his own pocket. Frank scowled, thanked Mason and Shee, and headed for the exit.

Charlotte and Shee stood to follow.

"Go in Charlotte's car. I'll get the bill and take Declan home," said Mason to Shee. He turned to Declan. "Unless you were going with them?"

"No. Thanks," said Declan.

Charlotte turned to Mariska and Darla. "I'm sorry to run out—"

Darla waived her away. "We have to go anyway." She poked Mariska and flashed her watch in her direction.

Mariska scowled at the time. "What about my dessert?"

Darla shook her head. "We have things to *do*."

Charlotte frowned.

They are definitely up to something.

CHAPTER EIGHTEEN

Mariska and Darla dropped off Bob, his doggy bag of steak and the remaining dinner rolls in hand, before starting down the driveway to pick up Midnight for their golf cart pink slip race.

As they hustled off, Darla glanced over her shoulder to see Bob had made it to the porch landing before he turned to watch them scamper away.

"Where you going?" he called after them.

Mariska turned. "Darla has a new canasta move she's going to show me."

Bob rolled his eyes and walked inside as their dog, Izzy, did her best to knock the leftovers out of his hand.

"He still hasn't figured out you have no idea how to play canasta?" asked Darla.

Mariska shook her head. "He only knows he has no interest in hearing about it."

They continued to Darla's.

"Oh good, it's there," said Darla as they reached the sidewalk. "Carolina said she'd drop off the new, improved Midnight while we were at dinner. And now with Frank off solving crimes with Charlotte, he won't know a *thing* until he sees the second cart in the driveway."

Mariska nodded. "Lucky for you someone got murdered in Clown Town."

"No kidding. What a break that was."

They slid into the cart.

"I feel overdressed for a drag race," said Mariska, fiddling with her long-beaded necklace.

Darla turned the key and shrugged. "We'll look classy. Like we can win these things in our *heels*."

Mariska giggled.

Darla pulled out of the driveway and started down the road, maxing out her speed on the straightaways. She was impressed with Carolina's upgrades.

"It's definitely faster."

Mariska agreed. "I'd say. That horrible Gianna doesn't stand a chance."

Darla beamed, imagining herself crossing the finish line. "That's what I'm thinking."

They found the entrance to Old Swamp Gas Trail and wove their way down the partially paved road until they spotted a collection of three golf carts clumped together. Two women sat in each. All six heads swiveled to watch them as they rolled around the curve.

"Ah, *there's* my cart. What took you so long?" asked Gianna from her seat.

Darla pulled up beside her. "Sorry, I was cleaning out my garage to make room for your *other* cart."

Mariska tittered.

Darla poked a thumb in the direction of the other two carts. "Who are these people? The Sharks and the Jets?"

Tabby scowled from her perch beside Gianna. "They're *witnesses*, so you don't try to run out on us."

Tabby had grown even more *sneery* since their last confrontation. Darla felt pretty sure she despised her even more than she did Gianna.

Compose yourself. Concentrate.

Darla took a deep breath.

"Let's get this started."

One of the other carts took off down the road, popping on its headlights and soon turning to shine them across what she assumed was the finish line.

She frowned and held up a hand. "Hold on. You didn't give me the option of bringing a judge. If there's a photo finish, we only have *your* friends here to weigh in."

Gianna laughed. "It won't be close. Don't worry about that."

Darla crossed her arms against her chest. "Oh, okay, I'll just take your word for it."

Gianna huffed. "Tell you what. If there's any question who crossed first, we'll run it again. How about that?"

"Yeah, would that make you happy?" asked Tabby.

"What would make me happy is if you'd shut your trap," snapped Darla. She tilted to look past Tabby at Gianna. "Any confusion and we rerun. I guess that's fine."

"Deal," said Gianna.

"Deal," echoed Tabby.

"Deal," said Mariska, her eyes narrowing on Tabby. Tabby stuck out her tongue, and Mariska returned in kind.

Darla maneuvered her cart to the starting line as one of the ladies in the remaining visitor cart stepped out to take a position in the middle of the wide dirt road in front of them. That woman's partner, still sitting in her cart, turned on the headlights. The thin-lipped woman in the road held up a white and red checkered dish towel. Her white tennis outfit glowed beneath the beams.

Gianna maneuvered into place beside Darla.

Tabby leered, so close Darla could reach out and touch her. *Punch her.* She gripped the wheel tighter and grumbled to herself.

"I'm going to kill this *loon*."

"On your marks..." said Tennis Togs, waggling her dish towel.

Darla glanced at Mariska. "Ready?"

Mariska hunkered down. "Ready."

Darla crouched low in her own seat, foot hovering over the pedal.

"Get set..."

Mariska grabbed the side bar and braced herself.

The dishtowel dashed to the ground.

"Go!"

Darla stomped her pedal. Dirt ground beneath the tires. Both cars leapt forward.

"Catch!" screamed Tabby.

Something round and purple flew into Darla and Mariska's cabin.

"Watch out!" yelled Darla.

Mariska yelped and ducked, arms rising to protect her head. The soft lavender orb hit the dashboard and burst with a loud *pop!*

A hundred tiny *things* exploded into the air, peppering their faces and bodies.

Darla and Mariska screeched, arms flailing to block the assault.

"Worms!" howled Mariska, smacking at the living confetti sprinkling her lap. She fell sideways and knocked hard into Darla's shoulder. The cart lurched to the left. Tennis Togs screamed and dove to avoid being flattened.

Something touched Darla's lip, and she squealed. Her foot slipped off the pedal, allowing Gianna to cement a lead. Darla's hand touched one of the creatures in her lap, and she realized it didn't feel wet.

"They're *dry*," she called out, slapping her foot back on the pedal. "They're *millipedes*." She glanced down to watch one curl into a spiral on the seat next to her, confirming her suspicions.

"That's worse—they have *legs*." Mariska flipped her shirt toward the right side of the cart, and a shower of millipedes flew into the air.

Darla swerved back on course, her body pressed hard against the seat as they picked up speed. Mariska threw out a hand to steady her shifting weight. Darla heard millipedes crunch beneath her feet.

"Oh, I'm going to *die*," moaned Mariska, clapping her hands together to rid them of millipede parts.

"Just keep it together for another minute." Darla gritted her teeth and hunched low over the steering wheel as they closed in on Gianna.

Hearing no response from her co-pilot, Darla glanced to her right to be sure Mariska hadn't toppled from the cart. She found her friend with her arms clamped to her sides, her mouth and eyes squeezed shut.

"We got her!" whooped Darla as they closed in on Gianna.

"Just hurry before I *freak out!*"

Tabby twisted in her seat to peer back at them. Darla watched her enemy's eyes widen as she spotted Midnight closing in. Then she did something Darla hadn't expected.

She *smiled.*

"Oh no," said Darla.

Tabby reached down and tossed something long and shiny from the cart onto the dirt road. Too late to swerve, Darla braced for impact.

"Hold on!"

She hit the object to the sound of an explosion. The cart jumped as if popping a wheely. Darla and Mariska squealed and held on to anything they could grab.

By the time the vehicle landed on all four wheels again, everything had changed. Darla hit the pedal, but instead of speeding off, the cart lurched forward a few feet with a painful flopping noise.

"What happened?" asked Mariska, panting.

Darla took a moment to catch her breath. "I'm not sure. It won't move, and it sounds like we have fish for tires."

Gianna sped ahead and crossed the finish line to the sound of cheers.

Darla swung out of the cart and circled behind. By the glow of the red parking lights she saw what looked like a large silver pointy snake flowing from beneath Midnight.

"They threw a spike strip at us," she said.

"A what?" Mariska stepped out of the cart and joined her in the back. Her gaze dropped to the chain. "What the heck is *that*?"

"A *tire shredder*. Those things cops lay out to stop runaway cars."

"What? That's not *fair*."

"No. It's *not*." Darla stormed the additional hundred feet to the finish line where Gianna sat high-fiving her friends.

"You *cheated!*" she barked, slapping at her chest where a millipede had found a home in her bra. Unable to pretend the creature wasn't freaking her out, she danced in place until she managed to scoop up the critter and dash it to the ground.

"What's the matter, got bugs in your bra?" taunted Tabby.

"*You.*" Darla poked a finger at her. "I've had enough of *you—*"

Darla started forward. Clearly alarmed, Tabby jumped out of Gianna's cart and skittered behind it to keep it between her and Darla.

"Now, now—no fighting," said one of the spectators.

Darla whirled on the woman. "No fighting? But bags of *millipedes* and *spike strips* are fair game?"

"I told you there are no rules," said Gianna, a smug grin on her mug. "And do you think I didn't notice how fast your cart was? It wasn't that fast when it was mine. You did something to it. *You* cheated."

Mariska arrived at Darla's side and put a hand on her arm.

"Come on, Darla, they're not worth it."

"You want to play like that?" said Darla, her eyes squinting until she felt as if she could shoot lasers through the remaining pinholes. "*Fine*. We can play like that. I challenge you *again*."

Gianna cackled. "With what? You're out of carts."

"You let me worry about that."

Gianna shrugged. "Fine. Your loss. Same time next week?"

"Fine."

"*Fine.*"

Tabby had sneaked around to Midnight and started sweeping away the remaining millipedes. "I'll get Henry to come change the tires," she called to Gianna.

Gianna glowered at Darla. "I should make *you* pay for the

tires, too."

"Oh, please," said Darla. "*Try*. You'll rot in your grave before you see a penny from me."

Gianna made a U-turn and drove past Darla and Mariska to pull up beside the flattened Midnight and pick up Tabby. The finish line cart followed her, leaving Mariska and Darla in moonlight and the faint red glow of retreating taillights.

"How are we going to get back?" called Mariska.

"Not my problem," answered Gianna over her shoulder.

Darla heard the others braying as they disappeared around the corner.

"It's a two mile walk back home," said Mariska, sounding defeated. "I'll call Bob and have him come pick us up."

Darla shook her hanging head. "He'll tell Frank."

"No, he won't. I'll tell him if he keeps his mouth shut, he can have bourbon this weekend."

Darla looked up. "Good idea."

Mariska huffed. "After his manners in front of Charlotte's parents, he's so far in the doghouse already, he should be happy I'm even *talking* to him."

Darla stood with both fists clenched at her sides.

"I'm going to *destroy* her next time."

"Let's get out of the forest first." Mariska pulled out her phone and started walking. "Keep an eye out for possums. They hate me."

"Heaven help the critter that messes with me tonight."

Mariska called Bob and told him where to find them. After a short argument, she hung up.

"He's coming?" asked Darla.

"Yes. He's already in his boxers, so he's not happy, but he's coming." Mariska slipped her phone back in her bag. "Hey, what are you going to tell Frank?"

Darla snapped out of her murderous thoughts. "Hm?"

"*Frank*. Isn't he going to wonder where his new golf cart went?"

Darla stopped and turned to stare at Mariska.

"Crap."

CHAPTER NINETEEN

Charlotte sneaked a look at Shee from the corner of her eye while driving to Big Top.

Should I apologize for the awkwardness at the restaurant?

She couldn't decide.

Maybe it would be better to let it go…

"I appreciate you letting me come along with you," said Shee.

Lost in her own thoughts, Charlotte jumped at the sound of a voice other than her own.

"Oh, uh, I hope you know they all mean well," she said out loud, though her mind had already decided not to bring up any improprieties at the restaurant.

Nice going. Smooth as always.

Shee looked at her. "Who?"

"Um, mostly Bob and his, uh, insensitive comments."

Shee chortled. "Oh, don't worry about that. No one was offended by anything. We understand how strange this is. I wouldn't be surprised if they're all angry at me. I wouldn't be surprised if you're—"

Shee faced forward again.

Charlotte couldn't shake the feeling Shee had spoken out loud something she'd sworn to herself not to mention as well.

Maybe the apple doesn't fall far from the tree.

"I'm not mad," said Charlotte, realizing as she said the

words that the statement was true. "I'm more...confused."

Shee nodded, looking grim. "You have every right to be either, or both."

"I don't think they're mad, either. The others." Charlotte ran through the evening's conversations inwardly, remembering with particular discomfort Bob's joke about Mason having three out of four limbs. "Mason's missing a leg?"

Shee nodded. "Below the knee."

"Bob handled that particularly badly."

"Pssh. You should hear how I tease him. He's used to it." Shee paused and then added, "I have a tendency to put my foot in my mouth when I don't know what to say."

Charlotte chuckled. "There's something we have in common."

"Ha. Sorry about that."

Charlotte grinned. "At least now I can blame you for it."

"There you go. And at least Bob the Marine didn't find out Mason's Navy."

Charlotte giggled. "What did he do in the Navy?"

Shee hesitated and then leaned in to speak in a hushed tone. "He was a SEAL."

Charlotte gaped. "Really? Wow... Is that a secret?"

Shee chuckled. "No. He doesn't mention it if he can avoid it, though, or people start peppering him with crazy questions: How long can you hold your breath, were you in SEAL Team Six, blah, blah, blah."

"I can imagine." Shee'd mentioned some of the questions that had popped to her mind.

My father was a SEAL. How cool.

She turned right to follow Frank's car into the Big Top neighborhood. "I guess that's how he lost his leg?" She hoped that wasn't a stupid question.

"Yes. Some sort of ambush. He can tell you more. I can tell you he got a cool dog out of it though."

"Oh, well, that's totally worth it then."

"Totally."

Frank pulled beside a Sheriff's cruiser Charlotte recognized as Deputy Daniel's, and she parked behind them. The Medical Examiner, Rachel, walked toward them as they got out of their cars.

"We meet again," said Rachel to Charlotte as she and Shee walked to the crime tape border.

"Hello again," said Charlotte. "Rachel, this is my, um, mother. Shee. Rachel is the medical examiner."

Rachel smiled and reached out to shake hands. "I was going to guess she's your sister."

Shee grinned. "Yeah, right."

Frank ducked beneath the crime scene tape, and Rachel turned her attention his way, eying him from head to toe.

"Don't you look dapper," she said.

Frank cleared his throat. "I was at dinner. What do we have?"

"Gunshot victim. Charles Grineau, A.K.A. Grin the Bullet Catcher. Single bullet to the throat."

Frank cocked an eyebrow at her, and she shook her head.

"No, it wasn't a joke. He was literally a bullet catcher—caught them in his teeth for a living."

"What were the chances?" muttered Shee.

"Better than you think," said Charlotte. "Yesterday's victim, Baroness von Chilling, was a fortuneteller hit in the head with a crystal ball."

Shee's eyes widened. "Wow. You get fun ones over here."

Charlotte nodded. "We have an unusual situation that causes...flare-ups."

"Flare-ups?"

"Hopefully, that's all over now," interjected Frank.

"What do you mean? What's over?" asked Rachel.

Frank's eyes slid in her direction. "Jamie Moriarty's dead."

Rachel straightened. "She is?"

Charlotte nodded. "Declan found out from her daughter."

"Whoa, whoa, whoa," said Shee, waving both hands in the air as if she were washing the side of a van. "Jamie Moriarty—

you mean the Puzzle Killer?"

"You know about her?" asked Charlotte.

Shee scoffed. "Yes. Angelina shot her."

Now it was Charlotte's turn to gasp. "What?"

"Who's Angelina?" asked Frank.

Charlotte turned to him. "Remember when I found that box of my grandmother's stuff in my attic and went to Jupiter Beach looking for my aunt?" She motioned to Shee and added, "...who turned out to be my mother?"

Frank's brow knit. "Yes..."

"Well, Angelina works at the hotel where I stayed. The one owned by my grandfather."

"My dad. Who dates Angelina," said Shee. "As best he can," she added.

"Do you mind if I go grab a chair and popcorn?" asked Rachel. "I can't get this kind of family drama on the Hallmark Channel."

Shee tilted her head. "But what does this murder have to do with Jamie Moriarty?"

Charlotte took a deep breath. "When Jamie worked as a US Marshal, she hid all her witness protection clients in Charity to keep them close and get them to do her bidding. Consequently, we have an unusually high number of shady residents on the lam."

Shee gaped and pointed to the ground. "I heard something about that. But I didn't know it was here."

"How did Angelina end up killing her?" asked Charlotte.

Shee shrugged. "Self-defense. Some mix-up over a man."

"I thought you said Angelina dated your father?" said Frank.

"I definitely need some popcorn," said Rachel.

"Do you people mind if I get back to the murder at hand?" asked Frank in his gruff voice.

"Awww..." moaned Rachel.

He turned to her. "Sorry. Tell me. Sign of a struggle? Robbery?"

Rachel huffed a sigh. "Every party has a pooper. No. No struggle, no robbery. Not that I noticed. He was in his pajamas, brushing his teeth when it happened, judging by the wet toothbrush on the ground next to him."

"Let's go take a look," said Frank.

Charlotte dipped to slip under the crime tape. Frank put a hand on her head to block her.

"Not you."

She backed up. "Why?"

"Because you're not a deputy, that's why."

"You could deputize me again," she suggested.

"Again?" piped Shee.

Frank pointed to the ground at Charlotte's feet. "Stay there."

Frank and Rachel headed for Grin the Bullet Catcher's house while Charlotte glared at their backs from behind the crime tape.

"Do you always help Frank?" asked Shee.

"When he lets me tag along. He sponsored me for my detective's license."

"That was nice of him."

She smiled. "I don't know if I gave him much of a choice."

Shee scanned the crowd. "Lot of people here. He probably felt a little self-conscious letting a girl in her night-out dress walk into the crime scene."

Charlotte glanced down at her dress. "Maybe." Glancing at the large crowd, she noticed the tall man she'd seen at Baroness' house. It seemed he saw her spot him. Ducking his head, he turned to stride away.

Charlotte touched Shee's arm. "I'll be right back."

Weaving her way through the crowd, she jogged after the tall man as he left the edges of the group and started down the street.

"Hello? Excuse me?"

She called twice more before he turned and placed a hand on his chest.

"Are you talking to me?" he asked.

"Yes, hi—I think I saw you at the last crime scene?"

His brow knit. "You're saying this was a crime, too? Grin is dead?"

"Uh—" Charlotte silently kicked herself for feeding him answers.

"Are you a cop?" he asked.

She shook her head. "No, I—"

"I saw you with the sheriff."

"Yes. I'm in training."

He slipped his hands into the pockets of his baggy shorts. The man had to be nearly seven feet tall, standing as skinny as a no-fat latte.

She could feel him readying to leave again.

"I'm Charlotte Morgan," she said.

"Scott."

"You live here?"

He nodded.

"What's your, uh, talent?"

"My talent? I'm a clown, if that's what you mean. Scotty the Skyscraper." He pulled his phone from his pocket and opened it to show her the lock-screen photo of a clown on the front.

Charlotte studied the picture of a clown in baggy gray pants speckled with white squares. His shirt and hat had the same pattern, and she realized the effect made him look like a giant skyscraper. His makeup was gray with square windows painted above his eyes as well as his cheeks.

"Neat," said Charlotte. "You must be the world's tallest clown."

"Maybe living." He slipped the phone back in his pocket. "But I'll always be second to Buck Nolan. He was seven-four. I'm six-ten."

A thought occurred to Charlotte. "Do you ever wear other costumes?"

He seemed insulted. "I'm Scotty the Skyscraper. That's my brand. Does Coke ever dress up like Pepsi?"

Charlotte chuckled. "No. I guess not. Do you know any cat clowns?"

Scotty's face twitched. "I, uh, knew a guy who worked with a capuchin monkey once."

"No, I mean a clown with makeup that looks like a cat."

"Oh. No." He looked at his watch. "Look, I have to get going. See ya."

He turned, and Charlotte had to jog to catch up to his long strides.

"Did you know Grin?" she asked, following him.

He shrugged, but continued walking. "Sure. Everybody knows everybody here."

"So you knew Baroness, too?"

He stopped and turned. "Are you saying I had something to do with killing them?"

"No, I'm—"

The tall clown's features scrunched to the center of his face as he leaned down to address her. "Look, I don't know who you are. I tried to be polite, because you're obviously trying to help the sheriff, but I can't help you. Good luck with your stuff."

Scotty whirled on his heel and left her standing on the sidewalk.

Charlotte sighed.

"Kitty," called a voice nearby.

She turned.

Kitty?

Charlotte scanned the area until she spotted Tony the Tiger Tamer standing in someone's yard.

"Kitty," he called again, opening the door of an outdoor shower. He closed the door, and, spotting her, froze as if she couldn't see him if he held still.

She strolled to him. "I imagine it makes people nervous when the Tiger Tamer loses a cat."

Tony didn't laugh. He looked irritated. "I'd never misplace one of my cats."

"So Kitty isn't yours?"

His jaw clenched. "No."

"Baroness'?" she guessed.

He seemed surprised. "Yeah. How'd you know?"

"I saw she had tins of tuna in her fridge marked Kitty."

He nodded, seemingly unsure what to say or do next.

"Are you planning to adopt it?" she asked. "Maybe for your girlfriend?"

He scowled. "I don't have a girlfriend." He grinned. "Are you fishing?"

"Huh? No." She didn't mean to be rude, but his comment had flustered her. "I thought maybe you and Baroness' nurse—"

"What?" Tony straightened as if he'd shoved a fork into a light socket.

"Baroness' nurse. You know her, don't you?"

He swallowed. "Why do you ask?"

Charlotte didn't miss that he hadn't said no. She decided not to admit she'd noticed the woman in his Facebook photos.

"Because you're her neighbor," she said instead.

"Yeah, but—" He ran a hand through his thinning hair and headed for the sidewalk.

"What's the nurse's name? I'd like to talk to her," said Charlotte, fearing she was losing him.

He seemed angry. "Why would I know? I'm trying to help out, looking for the old lady's cat, like you said."

"We're pretty far from Baroness' house. Did you see the cat around here?"

"No. I thought maybe because of the commotion. You know—thought the people might attract her."

"Aren't cats usually afraid of people?"

"Depends on the cat." He looked her up and down, leered a moment, and then headed off in the same direction as Scotty had.

Charlotte watched him go. She could have chased him, but she didn't want to be near him.

That dude is creepy.

She walked back to the crime scene to find Frank had

rejoined Shee.

"There you are. Who were you talking to?" he asked as she approached.

"Some guys I noticed at Baroness'."

"Anything promising?"

"Not really. They're both odd."

Frank grunted. "Everyone here is odd." He eyeballed a man with tattoos and a large, waxed handlebar mustache. "That's the guy who made me mad..."

"That's Stark," said Charlotte. "I think he's, like, the unofficial mayor of Big Top."

"The Ringmaster," offered Shee.

"Exactly. Any clues here?"

Frank shrugged. "No. Rachel said that bear trainer person they mentioned in the paper has been cremated, so there's no way to go back and double check if he's part of this string of murders."

"Convenient, huh?" said a young woman, appearing at Charlotte's elbow so suddenly it made her jump. She recognized her as Lulu, the reporter, appearing as if Frank had invoked her.

Lulu held her phone in front of Frank's mouth again. "Lulu Pendleton, Charity Dispatch, online edition. Do you think we have a serial killer, Sheriff?"

Frank's neck recoiled from the phone as if it carried typhoid. "Get that thing out of my face."

"You're the one who floated that idea," said Charlotte.

"And it looks like I was on to something," said Lulu, appearing happy with herself.

"But he died of a heart attack. What makes you think his death was related?"

"Did he die of a heart attack? Who knows?" Lulu turned back to Frank. "Fortune teller brained by a crystal ball, bullet catcher shot, think we should tell the knife throwers to hide their cutlery?"

Frank scowled. "Who are you? Get out of my crime scene."

Lulu ducked back under the yellow tape and moved into

the crowd.

"I'll let you know if I find anything useful," she called over her shoulder.

CHAPTER TWENTY

Declan waved goodbye to Charlotte as she and her mother followed Frank to his new Big Top crime scene. He knew better than to compete for Charlotte's attention against a juicy mystery. He'd joked that when he wanted her focused on *him*, he'd kill someone—like his pain-in-the-neck uncle Seamus, for example.

"My truck's over here," said Mason starting toward a black Ford.

Declan followed, sizing up Charlotte's father as they walked across the parking lot. The little old ladies in his pawn shop were always commenting on how big *he* was—now he knew how they felt. Mason stood only an inch or two taller than him, but somehow he *felt* about a foot taller. He'd like to get Mason and his employee, Blade, in the same room to compare them, like some kind of grizzly bear zoological experiment. Heck, he'd like to throw them into a ring, two-men-enter-one-man-leaves-style—

"Want to get a drink?" asked Mason.

Declan shook away his goofy daydreaming. He could feel his cheeks grow warm, embarrassed, as if Mason had heard his thoughts.

Turns out he hadn't dodged *making a good impression on the father*, after all.

"Uh, yes, sure."

"I mean, if you aren't doing anything," Mason continued as they climbed into the truck. "I don't know about Charlotte, but I know Shee well enough to know if there's trouble involved, she won't be back any time soon."

Declan smiled. "If you're looking for proof they're mother and daughter, *there's* something they have in common."

Mason looked at him. "Do we need proof? Does she *want* proof?" He seemed alarmed.

"Uh, no—I was just kid—"

"Maybe we should offer to get a DNA test?" Mason stared at his steering wheel, concentrating as if he were reading hieroglyphics. "I never thought about proof—I mean, I know what the results will be, but to make *her* feel more comfortable..."

Declan could almost hear the nerves twanging in the man's body. The mere mention of his daughter had instantly transformed the man from a big, tough sailor into a father on prom night.

"It's pretty obvious you're her parents," said Declan.

Mason turned to him and grinned. "She looks like her mother, doesn't she? Lucky girl." His attention drifted a moment before snapping back to Declan. "So, where should we go? It's your home port, so you lead the way."

Declan considered the local watering holes. The obvious choice would be his uncle's bar, The Anne Bonny, but introducing Seamus to people was like trotting past the monkey cage. Sometimes, the monkeys waved and performed charming tricks.

Sometimes, they shook their butts and flung poo.

Mason rolled to the edge of the parking lot and turned to him, waiting for direction.

Declan panicked. "We could swing by my uncle's bar?"

He tried not to groan aloud as he heard the words pass his lips. Mason cut too impressive a figure. Seamus would feel like he had to out-alpha-male him...

Such a bad idea.

"Your uncle owns a bar? Perfect. Left or right?"

Declan sighed. "Right."

Mason rolled onto the street. "Could you do me a favor, and let the girls know where we're going?"

Declan texted Charlotte their plans.

K, she texted back.

He chuckled. "I got the one letter answer, so they're already hip-deep into something."

"Told you," said Mason. "Like a dog with a bone if she's like her mother."

Declan's phone dinged with a second text.

Are you sure Seamus' is a good idea?

No, he sent back.

She wrote back.

Don't let Seamus try to wrestle him. Mason was a SEAL.

Declan gasped.

"Everything okay?" asked Mason.

"Oh. Yes. Just... —nothing."

He eyeballed Mason from the corner of his eye as he typed.

A SEAL. That explains a lot.

He looked up to see they were already close. "Left here and you'll see it on the left, halfway up the street. The Anne Bonny," directed Declan.

"Like the pirate?"

"Yes. I'd say he named it after her because he's Irish, but I think he just wanted an excuse to buy a busty ship's figurehead."

Mason laughed.

"You're Irish too, I guess with a last name like Connolly, but Seamus is one hundred percent *Irish*-Irish. Off the boat. Literally."

"Ah." Mason made the turn. "I'm not *that* Irish." He glanced at Declan. "So how long have you and Charlotte been dating?"

"Almost a year. Feels like ten though."

"Oh—"

Declan realized how his comment had sounded and rushed

to clarify. "I didn't mean it that way. I mean we've been through a lot since then. Her job keeps things lively."

"I bet. I'm getting that feeling with Shee. I think I've aged ten years in the last three weeks."

He pulled to the curb outside The Anne Bonny.

Declan hopped out of the truck, his feet dragging the moment he pointed them toward the bar.

"Before we get in there, I feel like I should warn you my uncle is a bit of a character," he said as they crossed the street.

The big guy shrugged. "Believe me—I've met them all."

Declan opened the bar door, and a blast of frigid stale-beer-scented air struck his cheeks. Chatting patrons and baskets of fried food filled most of the tables and chairs, but he spotted two empty stools at the end of the main bar.

Seamus was nowhere to be seen.

Declan smiled.

Looks like I lucked—

Before he could release a relieved sigh, Seamus popped up from behind the bar like a whack-a-mole. Without meaning to, Declan groaned aloud. No one could hear him over the Irish band playing *The Wild Rover* in the corner of the room.

Seamus displayed the rugged wooden shillelagh he kept behind the bar to a pair of giggling fifty-five-plus women. The ladies wore similar bright, floral-print dresses. Declan guessed the short glasses sitting in front of them filled with pink liquid to be 'sex on the beach' shots.

They'd made the common mistake of asking Seamus' advice on drink choice.

All of these clues meant his uncle was in the middle of his patented *"I'm Irish, want to see my shillelagh?"* pick up line.

Declan considered grabbing Mason's arm and dragging him back to the truck.

Seamus glanced in their direction, did a double take, and broke into a grin.

Too late.

Declan swallowed and leaned to speak in Mason's ear.

"Remember, I warned you. Please don't hold him against me."

Mason laughed.

Seamus threw out his arms. "Declan, how ye doin', *me boyo*?" His Irish accent had a habit of deepening whenever ladies hovered nearby.

Declan nodded his hello and motioned to Mason. "Seamus, this is Charlotte's father, Mason. Mason, this is my Uncle Seamus."

Seamus' eyes popped wide. "You were serious about her havin' parents?"

"Why would I make that up?"

Seamus shrugged and reached out to pump Mason's hand with overzealous vigor, clearly testing the man's strength. "My God, look at the size of ye. Ye need a whiskey."

Mason shook his head. "I—"

Seamus closed his eyes and cut the air with two small karate chops. "No, I insist. Don't move." He moved to the bottles lining the back wall and poured three shot glasses of whiskey before placing them on the counter in front of Mason, Declan, and himself.

"*Sláinte*," he said, holding one aloft.

The three drank them down. Seamus nodded at the main bartender, Stig, who grabbed the bottle and refilled the shot glasses.

"Whatcha say yer name was?" asked Seamus, squinting one eye at Mason.

"Mason."

"No, yer surname."

"Oh, Connolly."

Seamus clapped his hands together. "I knew it! Yer Irish. That requires a taste." Seamus raised the second shot, and Mason followed suit.

Declan pretended not to notice. He kept his eyes riveted on the band in the corner, like a rabbit hoping to avoid the attention of a predator.

When it felt safe, he turned and noticed Seamus' ladies eyeing Mason. Maybe it was the shot of whiskey seeping into his veins, but the women's shifting affections seemed to delight him to no end.

"What are your friend's names?" he asked his uncle, nodding at the women. "I think they'd like to meet Mason, too."

Seamus turned to see the ladies tittering, batting their eyes at Mason. He frowned.

"I think they were just leavin', weren't ye, lassies?" He motioned to the window. "To go to that fine table o'er there with the view. I saved it just for you."

The women seemed surprised. Flustered, one snatched her purse from the bar and dropped from her stool to move to the table by the window.

"What view? It's dark out," said the other, following.

Seamus motioned to the vacated chairs. "Here you go, gentlemen, two spots just opened up for you."

Declan grinned, feeling victorious. Not only had he foiled his uncle's flirting plans and caused him to lose round one to Mason, he'd knocked the ridiculous Lucky Charms accent right out of the Irishman.

"Where's the lovely Charlotte this fine evening?" asked Seamus.

Declan ran his finger around the brim of his still-full second shot. "Hm? Oh. She went to a murder scene with Frank."

Seamus glanced at the shot and then scowled at Declan. "Don't play with yer food."

"You don't seem surprised she's off to a murder scene," said Mason to Seamus.

Seamus laughed. "Oh, *no.* Your daughter's quite the detective." He cocked his head, his gaze locked on Mason's bulging biceps. His chest puffed.

Declan winced.

Here we go.

"So, how much do you bench, Mason?" asked Seamus.

Declan held up a hand. "*Seamus—*"

Seamus slapped his hand to his chest, acting as if his nephew had accused him of stealing the crown jewels. "What? It's a simple question."

Mason shrugged. "Maybe three-fifty, give or take."

Seamus whistled.

"But," added Mason, "boredom and other factors have meant a lot of arm-days lately."

Seamus' eyebrows slid to a jaunty angle. "Stint in the slammer?"

Declan choked. "Why would you think he's been in *prison*?"

Mason laughed. "No. Hospital. Lost a leg."

Seamus bellyflopped across the bar, grabbed the opposite side to slide himself forward, straining to see Mason's legs. "Oh yeah?"

Declan covered one eye with his hand. "*Seamus*—"

Seamus ignored him. "Come on. Give us a look. What you have there? A peg?"

Mason lifted his pant leg to flash the metal. "Titanium."

"Ah, fine bit o' hardware," said Seamus, dropping back to his feet. "I thought maybe I could slap an eyepatch on ye and have ye stand outside the bar." He laughed at his own joke.

Declan caught Mason's eye. "I warned you. He's completely untrainable."

Already chuckling, Mason patted Declan's shoulder, seemingly amused by all.

Declan relaxed a little and sipped his second shot. Seamus grabbed the whiskey bottle from the rack. "Let me refill the men's glasses." He hovered over Declan's mostly full shot, careful to be sure his nephew felt his disappointment.

"I wouldn't mind a beer back to slow this down a bit," said Mason. "I'm a not quite as big as I used to be."

Seamus looked confused and then roared with laughter. "Oh, the *leg*." He passed the order on to the bartender. Declan motioned that he'd prefer to downgrade to a beer as well. Stig nodded and poured a second from the tap.

Seamus tapped his fingers on the bar, staring dreamily

across the room. This meant the man was somewhere in his head.

Never a good thing.

His uncle jerked upward, as if he'd been toasting an idea that had popped.

"We should have a *decathlon*," he said.

Declan stopped his beer midway to his lips. "Hm?"

Seamus ignored him, musing a moment longer. "I'll lose the arm-wrestling portion of the evening to this great bear," he said, nodding toward Mason, "so I'll need a way to even out the score..."

"You want to have a competition?" asked Declan.

Mason shrugged. "I'm game. What did you have in mind?"

Declan hung his head. "Please don't humor him."

Seamus scanned the bar, pulling at his chin. "How about arm wrestling, and then a foot race?" he laughed and slapped Mason's arm. "Sorry, I'm pullin' yer leg." He laughed harder.

"Maybe we should *go*," suggested Declan.

"Relax," said Mason. "I've been in a hospital for months. A little friendly competition sounds like fun."

"*Friendly* competition does," muttered Declan.

"See? The man knows fun when he sees it," said Seamus. "How about arm wrestling, a round of darts and a round of pool?" He looked at Declan. "We could go to your house and swim laps in your fancy movin' pool—"

"Bad idea." Declan hooked a thumb to his right. "He's a SEAL."

Seamus blinked at Mason. "Really? He *looks* like a man. You're sayin' he's some kind of selky?"

"A *Navy* SEAL. He'd *kill* you at swimming."

Mason held up a hand. "Hey, now. I'm retired. I'm not allowed to kill anyone."

"And he's missin' a flipper," argued Seamus.

"Does that matter?" asked Declan.

Mason smirked. "Probably not."

"Fine." Seamus snatched Declan's shot from the bar and

threw it down his gullet. "Then it's settled. The First Annual Anne Bonny Arm Wrestlin', Dart Throwin', Pool Shootin' Decathlon is *on*."

Declan propped his chin on his palm. "A decathlon is *ten* things."

Seamus shook his head "That's way too many. Why would I have a decathlon with *ten* things in it?"

Declan sighed. "Right. What was I thinking?"

Mason held up his beer. "May the best man win."

Seamus' eyes glowed as if fueled by inner fires. "You've only got one problem now, boyo."

Mason's eyebrows raised. "Yeah? What's that?"

Seamus grinned.

"No one beats me in my own bar."

CHAPTER TWENTY-ONE

Stephanie parked her car down the street from Big Top's entrance and cut the engine. The large lot of land beside the retirement community contained a giant, permanent structure built to look like a big top tent, complete with red and white vertical stripes. It served as a practice area for residents who, even in retirement, performed in shows to raise money for charity a few times a year.

Stephanie remembered a guy in high school taking her to a Big Top charity performance for a date once.

Longest night of my life.

Scanning the border between the field and the neat rows of Big Top homes, she searched for an entry to the community from the lot. Avoiding the cameras at the gate would be ideal for her needs.

In the dark, it took a moment to identify a gate in the fence line. The back entrance had a keypad lock and a cheap camera on a pole pointed at the door, but a few hundred yards away the chain-link terminated at a clump of scrub pines.

Stephanie scoffed and headed for the forest.

They might be really good at acrobatics, but they suck at security.

Stephanie slipped around the end of the fence into the community. A string of modular homes ran left and right without fencing between them, making it possible for her to move through their back yards unhindered.

Strolling to the sage green home nearest the fence termination, she peered through a window. Inside, a dwarf sat in a miniature lounge chair watching television with a small dog in his lap.

Dwarf.

Hm.

She'd never killed a dwarf. She wasn't sure dwarf murder *should* make her bucket list. It seemed like cheating.

She still wasn't sure if she'd kill *anyone.* She likened sneaking around Big Top peering through windows, to a quitting smoker carrying one last cigarette in her purse. *Just in case.*

She liked to know she had the *option.*

She felt pretty giddy, though. She'd almost pushed the idea of tacking a murder on to the Big Top Killer's list out of her mind—then a story popped up online about a bullet catcher who'd been murdered by bullet. The fortune teller had been offed by crystal ball.

The killer had some *flair.*

It made her jealous.

Not only did the new murder cement the idea of a serial killer at Big Top, but the sick sense of humor also reminded her of her mother and made her feel nostalgic.

So she went window-shopping.

Could it be a coincidence such a perfect situation had fallen in her lap? It was as if her mother had sent her a gift from heaven. Or...well, probably not *heaven*, but the same theory applied.

Still, she felt a twinge of something comparable to *guilt.* She'd promised Declan she'd be good and make a clean break from her mother's evil legacy.

But...

She'd have to avenge her mother, anyway, right?

So far, the FBI had been tightlipped about who shot Jamie,

but she'd find out later. And wouldn't it be *wise* to get in a little practice first?

She peered through another window. An average-looking older couple shuffled around their kitchen, emptying the dishwasher.

Yawn.

They seemed even less of a challenge than the dwarf.

She was about to move on when she noticed the old man of the pair take a moment to juggle the cutlery before placing it in the drawer.

Kill a juggler?

She wasn't sure how to kill a juggler. Pelt him with beanbags?

That could take a while.

Chainsaw, maybe?

Ugh. Too messy.

Through the next window she spotted two women sitting very close together on a sofa.

Very close. Strangely close—

The pair stood and Stephanie gasped before covering her mouth with her hand.

Siamese twins!

Now, *there* was something for the record books. Two for one. How would she do it? Double knives? Double guns?

A movement caught her eye and Stephanie spun away from the window to flatten her back against the home. Two houses down, a figure rounded a corner. The stranger stood peering through a window, just as she had been.

Strange.

Peeping Tom? Or—

Could it be the real killer?

Stephanie felt a flutter of excitement.

What if I killed the killer?

She could get in a little practice *and* be hailed a hero.

That might impress Declan. He seemed dazzled whenever Charlotte went around saving people.

Stephanie crept back to the tree line and reached down to pick up a short stick about the width of a gun muzzle. Tiptoeing through the grass, she slipped behind the figure and poked the stick into the stranger's ribs.

"Hold it there," she said, quiet enough so the twins inside wouldn't hear.

Hands raised toward the sky.

She gave the stick an extra poke. "Why are you spying on these people?"

Even as she spoke, Stephanie realized she couldn't kill her capture. There was no way to prove the peeper *was* the killer—there wasn't a body at their feet. In addition, *she* was trespassing, too. How could she explain why she was lurking around the backs of modular homes?

Shoot. I should have thought this through.

She reconsidered her options, a smile curling on her lips as an idea percolated.

That's it.

Without waiting for the stranger to answer, she continued. "Nevermind. Tell you what. I'm going to give you my card. If you're caught—I don't know, let's say *murdering* someone—you give me a call. Stephanie Moriarty. I'm the best defense lawyer in town."

"Did you say *murdering*?" The stranger sounded confused.

Nice try.

She scoffed. "Let's not pretend I don't know who you are."

She tried to sound disgusted, but in reality, she couldn't stop grinning. She'd thought of yet another opportunity. Once the loser called her to *hire* her, she'd come back to Big Top and kill someone else *while her client was in jail.*

Bam. Innocent client.

How did I not think of this angle before?

I am a genius.

She pressed the stick harder. "You have to be *smart*, though. Don't get caught red-handed. I can't help you if they find you hovering over a fire eater with a can of gasoline and a match. Understand?"

The creeper nodded. She took the lack of retort as a tacit acknowledgement of guilt.

I knew it.

"Good. Now, get down on the ground and cover your head with your hands. Face down."

The stranger dropped to the ground.

Stephanie tossed her stick and ran into the trees to work her way back to her car, her body vibrating with giddy excitement.

A new business plan.

How exciting.

CHAPTER TWENTY-TWO

Shee and Charlotte were halfway across the street to The Anne Bonny to pick up Mason and Declan when the door to the bar opened, and a petite woman with white hair pulled into a ponytail walked out.

She wore purple scrubs.

Charlotte gasped.

The nurse.

She grabbed Shee's wrist to stop her progress, treating the nurse like a nervous animal who might skitter away if she spotted them. She'd seen the nurse in so many photos, but never in real life—catching her in the wild felt a little like stumbling upon Big Foot.

Shee looked at her. "What's wrong?"

"The *nurse*," she said, whispering.

"What?"

Charlotte continued forward, her pace quickening. The white-haired woman took half a step forward and then stopped, her gaze locked on Charlotte.

Any chance of a stealthy approach had been blown.

"Excuse me," she called, raising a hand and forcing a smile.

The woman's body tensed, and Charlotte could see the future.

She's going to run.

"Wait—"

The nurse bolted to her right to whip down an alley between the corner of the bar and the shop next door.

"Wait!"

Charlotte broke into a sprint. Behind her, she heard Shee call her name, but she didn't stop. Snagging the edge of the building with her fingertips, she sling-shotted herself down the alley. She felt bad leaving Shee behind, but she couldn't miss her opportunity to talk to the nurse. The woman *had* to be the key to everything.

"I just want to ask you some questions!" she called.

The nurse jumped over a broken crate and raced down the alley, deeper into the darkness. Charlotte had guessed her quarry younger than her snowy hair implied, and the gazelle-like way the nurse had vaulted the obstacle by two unnecessary feet confirmed her suspicions.

"Please, *wait*," she tried again.

Mistrusting her vision in the dim light, Charlotte dodged the crate in favor of leaping over it. An eight-foot-tall wooden wall, signifying the end of the alley, loomed into view.

The nurse had nearly reached it.

Dead end.

Charlotte slowed.

Gotcha.

She raised a hand, expecting the woman to stop and turn.

"Hey! It's okay! I just want to talk—"

The nurse didn't stop.

She didn't even *slow down.*

Without hesitation, the nurse leapt into the air like a kangaroo to bounce one foot off the brick wall of Seamus' bar. Using that contact, she propelled herself to the top of the fence, gripping the top with curled fingers before scrambling on top. She clung at the crest on all fours, balanced, looking down at Charlotte.

Charlotte thought she heard her *hiss.*

She stopped six feet in front of the wall, wondering if the woman was about to pounce on her.

The nurse tilted back...and disappeared. The sound of her landing on the opposite side made Charlotte wince. It hurt her knees *thinking* about dropping that far to the ground.

"Where'd she go?" said Shee, arriving behind her.

Charlotte pointed to the wall, still out of breath from her own run. "She bounced off that wall and propelled herself to the top of the fence."

"She *parkoured* herself up there?"

"Yep. And I think she *hissed* at me."

"Hissed?"

Charlotte nodded. "Then she dropped to the other side, and that was that."

Shee stared open-mouthed at the wall, scaling it with her eyes. "I think my knees would explode if I jumped from that height."

Charlotte laughed. "That's the same thing I thought."

"Do you have bad knees?"

"Not terrible, but I don't trust them."

Shee offered her a lopsided smile. "Sorry. That's probably my fault." She walked to the wall and tried to peek between the horizontal slats. "Who is she? Why did she run from you?"

"I think she's the fortuneteller's nurse."

"You think she killed her?"

"I don't know. The weird thing is, no one seems to know anything about her except the fortuneteller's neighbor, who can't seem to take a photo without her in it."

"And he won't tell you who she is?"

"She's in the *background* of all his photos, giving him plausible deniability."

Shee cocked an eyebrow. "Giving him plausible *creepiness*."

"Oh, I don't need the photos to confirm *that*." Charlotte glanced back down the alley. "She came out of Seamus' bar. Maybe he knows her. Maybe she's a regular."

They strode back up the alley to enter The Anne Bonny. The live band in the corner behind the pool tables played *The Wild Rover* as they entered. Declan, Mason, and Seamus sat at the bar, laughing as if they'd known each other for decades. Declan turned, looking past them as they approached, to focus on the band.

"Is that the only song they know?" he asked, frowning. His head jerked as he noticed Charlotte walking toward him.

"Hello, you," he said, looking happy and tipsy.

"Hello." She scanned the *very* relaxed faces of the men and held her downturned palm throat high. "I don't suppose any of you noticed a woman dressed in scrubs in here? Short? Long white hair in a ponytail?"

The three of them stared at her blankly.

Yeah, they didn't notice anything.

"Always such help," said Shee, winking at Charlotte before her attention returned to the men. "What are you three up to?"

"Tie breaker," said Seamus. "I'm winning The First Annual Anne Bonny Decathlon."

"I won pool," said Declan, beaming.

"Only because someone bumped into my stick." Mason sounded grumbly, but he smiled at Charlotte to let her know his sour grapes were faked before pointing at Seamus. "He won darts and I won arm wrestling."

"I think he broke my arm," said Declan, rubbing his shoulder.

"The tie-breaker is drinking," said Seamus, smiling so broadly Charlotte feared his face might tear.

She scowled. "Didn't I hear you say it was a *decathlon*?"

Declan shook his head. "Don't even bother."

"I'm thinking we should head back," said Shee, slipping an arm around Mason's shoulder. She said something in his ear, and he glanced at Charlotte.

"Yep," he said, standing. "Yep."

"Does that mean I won?" asked Seamus, a full shot in his hand.

Mason nodded. "You won."

"Yes," said Declan. "*Finally.*"

Seamus raised both hands in the air. "*Undefeated.*"

Mason pulled out his wallet and tossed money on the bar. "Good night, daughter." He turned and wrapped his arms around Charlotte, pulling her in for a hug. She laughed as Shee peeled him away and pointed him to the door.

"Bye, all," she called over her shoulder, adjusting her stance as Mason jostled her with his bulk and wobbly leg.

Charlotte waved goodbye. When her parents had made it safely out the door, she turned to Declan.

"Hey, handsome, give you a ride home?"

"Yes, please," he said. "You showed up just in time. Seamus started it, as usual, and then things snowballed. The gauntlet was thrown."

"Poor baby. That seems to happen to men a lot."

He nodded and positioned her at arm's length, staring deep into her eyes. "It's *hard* being a man."

Charlotte snickered. "It must be *terrible*."

Sliding off his stool, he glanced out the front window as Shee pulled away driving Mason's truck.

"Your dad is *cool*," he said.

"Not as cool as me," said Seamus, lifting his victory-hands into the air a second time.

"No, Seamus," said Declan. "*Never* as cool as you."

Charlotte spent the first part of the next morning staring at the wall, a dreamy smile on her face.

Parents.

I. Have. Parents.

Not only did she have parents, but she *liked* them. *Bonus.* She'd spent at least an hour talking to Shee about solving crimes, suspect interviewing techniques, skip tracing, martial arts, and a dozen other interesting things before they headed for Seamus'. She could have spent another *day*, but it was a good thing she hadn't. She would have missed her nurse sighting, and

Declan might never have recovered from saving face in front of two-clearly-more experienced drinkers.

She giggled at the memory of pouring Declan into his bed.

Poor guy. His head had to be *pounding.*

After her coffee, Charlotte hopped online to find more information about her two favorite suspects for the murders at Big Top—Scotty the Skyscraper and Tony the Tiger Tamer. She was halfway through Scotty's sparse Facebook page when something in one of his photos caught her eye.

A flash of white hair.

She gasped and flipped back to the previous photo.

There she was again.

The nurse.

Why would Baroness' nurse appear in both Tony and Scotty's photos? In the post, the nurse looked somewhere to the left, but Scotty had his attention on *her.*

Charlotte recognized the expression on his face.

Love.

Clearly, she needed to talk to Scotty again. He had to know at *least* the nurse's name, and hopefully, where she lived. Maybe the nurse would know what was so special about Baroness' cat that Tony was clearly obsessed with. Was it rare and valuable? Had it eaten a piece of incriminating evidence? Had it scratched the murderer? She didn't know if anyone had ever pulled DNA from beneath the nails of a house cat...

Charlotte researched, puttered around the house, and checked in on Declan. He'd survived the evening with only a small headache as proof of his poor choices, but he still remembered *nothing* about a small white-haired woman in scrubs.

Charlotte checked her watch. At nine, it was still too early to shake Seamus' memory again, but it *was* late enough to head for Big Top and look for Scotty.

She knew the general area Scotty's house *should* be, assuming he'd been heading home after their talk outside Grim's, but entering the retirement community, she realized she'd been optimistic to think identifying the clown's house would be easy. Most of the homes looked alike, and nothing screamed *a tall clown lives here.* No huge doors. No oversized shoes on a stoop. No lawn flamingos made out of balloons.

She was about to head back home when she spotted her helpful friend Cassie watering plants. She pulled over.

"Hi, Cassie," she said, getting out of the car.

Cassie spotted her approaching and smiled, putting Charlotte at ease. She'd worried she'd worn out her welcome with the good-natured clown.

"Find your cat-faced clown?" asked Cassie.

"No. I've been distracted looking into these murders."

Cassie turned off the water. "So you really think we have a serial killer?"

"Oh, I don't know. That reporter might be a little over-confident with that theory."

"But *two* people?" Cassie grimaced and shook her head. "Maybe *three*?"

"Would you say you know the people in the neighborhood pretty well?" asked Charlotte.

Cassie shrugged. "As well as anyone, I guess. We're easy to remember—we're all pretty *unique*." She tittered and then sobered. "Wait—why? Do you think the killer is one of *us*?"

"It's possible. Are there outsiders you'd consider more likely?"

"No. I mean, I hear stories about townie jerks picking on the dwarves and whatnot—the sideshow freaks get the worst abuse, as you can imagine—but I've never heard about anyone threatening to *kill* us."

Charlotte pulled her shades off the top of her head as the sun peeked over Cassie's roof and stabbed her retinas with laser-like beams. "Did Baroness and Grin know each other?"

Before Cassie could answer, the door to her home opened, and Stark walked out wearing shorts and no top, his black, handlebar mustache ruffled and unwaxed. Charlotte could see that the heavy tattooing on his arms stopped at his shoulders.

His chest and stomach glowed white as a fish's belly.

"You again," he said, spotting Charlotte. "What do you want *now*?"

"She wants to stop whomever's killing us," snapped Cassie. "Why don't you try to be helpful instead of being such a grump?"

Stark's gaze slid from Charlotte to Cassie and back again. "Got any leads?"

"Not really," said Charlotte.

"Did Baroness and Grin know each other?" asked Cassie, repeating Charlotte's earlier question.

"Of course. They're both on the HOA board." Stark sighed. "It's a nightmare losing them both. We're going to have to have elections again."

Charlotte's eyebrows bounced skyward. "Really? Is there any reason someone might be angry with the board?"

"There's always *someone* mad at the board. Couple months ago we told everyone they had to stop swapping out live oak trees with queen palms, and you'd think we'd told them they weren't allowed to eat anymore."

"I don't think anyone would murder someone over an oak tree," said Cassie.

"You'd be surprised," muttered Charlotte. "Are Scotty the Skyscraper or Tony the Tiger Tamer on the board?"

"No," said Stark, looking more annoyed.

Cassie snorted a laugh and elbowed her ex. "Did I tell you Tony hit on me at the pool the other day?"

"I'm surprised it took him this long." Stark scratched his little potbelly, squinting at her. "You nipped that in the bud, I hope."

"Oh, *immediately*." Cassie leaned toward Charlotte. "Tony considers himself quite the Don Juan."

"More like Don *Wan-n*a-be," grumbled Stark. "He gets *obsessed*. I've got ten written complaints from women he's harassed over the years."

"Is he dangerous?" asked Charlotte.

Stark scoffed. "No. He thinks if a woman is polite to him, they must *want* him."

"He sends gifts and calls and shows up until the women are ready to file a restraining order," muttered Cassie. "He's a menace, but more annoying than scary."

Unconvinced, Charlotte frowned, and Stark poked a finger at her.

"Look, there's a big difference between thinking Tony's a jackass and thinking he's a murderer. Don't come here asking us to throw our people under the bus."

"That's not my intention," said Charlotte. "He and Scotty both have a connection to Baroness' live-in nurse, and I can't seem to track her down."

"Her nurse?" Cassie looked at Stark. "Did you know she had a live-in nurse?"

Stark shrugged. "She could barely walk. It's not a big surprise."

Cassie's head tilted. "You know, I saw Tony and Scotty arguing the other day—screaming at each other, but I didn't hear about what."

Stark huffed. "This is starting to sound like gossip. For all we know, they were arguing because Scotty's dog pooped on Tony's lawn."

Cassie shook her head. "Scotty doesn't have a dog. He gave it to Teeny."

Stark seemed surprised. "Yeah? Why?"

She shrugged. "I don't know. I saw Teeny walking it, and he told me Scotty didn't want it anymore."

Stark grunted and glared at Charlotte. "We done?"

Feeling she wouldn't make further progress, Charlotte relented. "Yes. Thank you."

Stark stormed back into the house, letting the door slam behind him.

Cassie rolled her eyes. "He's a charmer."

"I'll let you go," said Charlotte. "Thanks for your help again."

"No problem. Sorry about *him*." Cassie jerked a thumb toward her house. "He shouldn't be here, but ex-husbands make the *best* boyfriends. They're already trained, and you can send them home when you're sick of them."

CHAPTER TWENTY-THREE

Darla held her breath as she sat in her kitchen chair, watching Frank through the window. He had one foot in his vehicle. He ducked inside the cruiser...his butt lowered to the seat...

A smile crept across on Darla's lips.

Looks like I made it—

Frank's head popped back up and out of the car as if his seat were made of lava.

Oh no.

He peered over the roof of his cruiser at the exposed driveway—the empty bit where the golf cart used to be.

Should be.

Darla squeezed her lids shut.

Don't come in. Don't come in. Don't—

She heard the car door shut and opened her eyes to find a scowling Frank striding back toward the house. She pretended to be engrossed reading the back of the powdered creamer cannister as he entered.

"Where's the golf cart?" he asked, screen door banging shut behind him.

Darla turned. "Hm?"

"*The golf cart.* Where is it?"

"Oh, I'm having it cleaned."

Frank's brow seized another notch tighter. "Cleaned? It was practically new."

"It had someone else's dirty paws all over it. I thought we'd get a fresh start."

"Do you spend your spare time *inventing* new ways to spend money?"

"It was full of millipedes."

"Millipedes?"

Darla grimaced.

Why did I say that?

She strained to think of a good reason why millipedes would take up residence in their golf cart.

She couldn't think of anything.

Let's try this again.

"Not *millipedes*. I said *a million peas*. Little pea things. Like off a tree."

The story sounded ridiculous, but for some reason, Darla felt much better about her new answer.

Frank hadn't finished his interrogation.

"Off what tree? We don't have a pea tree."

"I lent it to a friend. *She* has a pea tree."

"Who?"

"You don't know her. I play canasta with her."

Frank huffed and looked at his watch. "I have to go. Tell your canasta friend the next time she parks our golf cart under a pea tree, *she's* paying for the cleaning."

"Yep. Actually, she is. I made sure of it."

"Oh." Frank's expression relaxed. "Good. I'll see you later." He kissed her on the side of her forehead.

"See ya."

As Darla turned back to her coffee, she heard Frank excusing himself to someone. She turned to find Mariska standing in the spot Frank had occupied a moment before.

"Good morning." Mariska made a beeline for the coffeemaker to get herself a cup.

Darla ignored her to pop up and peer out the front window,

watching as Frank pulled away. When he was gone, she flopped back in her seat.

"Whew. That was close."

"What was?" asked Mariska, sitting across from her.

"Frank noticed Midnight is missing."

Mariska gasped. "What did you say?"

"I told him I'm getting it cleaned because it's full of millipedes, like an idiot."

"Oh *no*. Did he believe you?"

"Not for a second. So I told him I'd said *a million peas,* and that it was full of little pea thingies off a tree."

"Wow. Quick thinking." Mariska took a sip of her coffee and then scowled. "What tree?"

"That was the next problem. I told him a lady from canasta borrowed it and parked it under *her* tree."

"How many times can we pretend we play canasta before one of them figures us out?" Mariska clucked her tongue. "And this *cart racing*—I'm going to have to get you a ladder to get out of this hole."

"You can't," muttered Darla. "You're down here with me."

"Well, at the rate you're digging, we'll be able to pick up some Chinese food."

Darla slumped over to rest her forehead on her kitchen table. She remained that way for a minute before Mariska piped up again.

"What time are we supposed to meet Carolina?"

Darla sat up and looked at the clock on her microwave. "In ten minutes. We better get going."

Mariska took a few more gulps of coffee, and then they headed out the door.

"What did you think of Charlotte's parents?" she asked, as they walked to Carolina's side of the neighborhood.

"They seem nice, don't you think? I can see where Charlotte gets her looks. Shee is *beautiful* and that father of hers—" Darla whistled. "If I were a couple years younger, I'd eat him up."

"A *couple* years?" teased Mariska.

"Shut up."

"They *are* a good-looking couple." Mariska sniffed. "Not the greatest *parents*, though."

"You mean not like *you*."

Mariska side-eyed her. "I didn't say that."

"You didn't have to."

"I think it's nice she's getting to meet them."

"Yep."

Mariska sighed. "You don't think she'll move to *their* town, do you?"

"*No.* Why would she do that? Her life is *here*."

Mariska nodded. "Right. She wouldn't move."

"Of course not." Darla put her arm around her friend. "She loves you. She knows you love her."

Mariska's eyes rimmed with tears. "I'm being silly."

"You are. Everything's fine."

Mariska pulled a tissue from her cleavage and wiped her eyes as they arrived at Carolina's. The golf cart queen stood inside her open garage, her brow twisting a little tighter with each step they took toward her.

"The fact you *walked* here isn't a good sign," she said. "Where's my cart?"

"Gianna *cheated*," said Mariska.

"How?"

"She threw worms at us."

"*Worms*?"

"Millipedes," corrected Darla. "A whole bag of them."

"That's a new one." Carolina chuckled and then covered her mouth. "Sorry. That's awful."

"I'd think it was funny, too, if it hadn't happened to *me*," said Darla. "The worst part is we caught back up, only to have them toss a spike strip in front of us."

Carolina sucked in a breath. "A spike strip? Wow. She isn't messing around."

"Any idea how to beat her at her own game?" asked Mariska.

Carolina pulled off her Tampa Rays baseball cap and scratched the brown curls beneath it. "Well, for one, you're going to need a cart."

Darla frowned. "That would be the other reason we're here. We need the best cart *money-I-don't-have* can buy."

"I don't think it's that simple. The only way to make sure she doesn't spike you again is to stay in front of her..." Carolina squeezed her way between carts toward the back of her garage. "I have an idea, but you already owe me for the batteries in Midnight. If I give you another cart and you lose it—"

"That would be bad," said Mariska.

"*Real* bad," agreed Darla.

"And not to put too fine a point on it, you'd still owe me the cart you should have won the first time."

Mariska's mouth molded into a perfect 'O' of horror as she grabbed Darla's arm. "Even if you win this time, you'd have to give Midnight to Carolina for lending us the carts and batteries."

"Which leaves me cart-less again." Darla paced the garage entrance, tapping her fingernail on her teeth, deep in thought. "What if I told Gianna I wanted to race for *two* carts?"

"Why would she put up two carts against your one?" asked Mariska.

"The cart I'd lend you is worth two carts, but there's a Catch-22," said Carolina. "If she knows ahead of time *why* the cart is worth twice as much, she won't agree to race at all."

"Why's that?" asked Mariska.

Carolina patted the fender closest to her, grinning. "Come here, let me show you."

Mariska and Darla moved deeper into the garage as Carolina removed the seat cushion and opened the hatch of an evergreen-colored cart.

"Feast your eyes on that," she said.

Darla peered inside the green cart to gape at a shiny silver thing she'd never seen before. "What is it? It looks more like an engine than a battery."

Carolina grinned. "Exactly. It's an electric *car* engine."

Darla gaped. "You put a *Tesla* engine in a golf cart?"

"Not a Tesla, but same idea. Hit the pedal, and it'll peel the skin off your face."

"That sounds terrible," said Mariska.

Beside her, Darla clapped her hands together, giggling with excitement.

"How can we lose?"

Carolina closed the hatch. "In theory, you can't, but the fastest engine in the world won't fly you over a tire shredder."

Darla waved away her concerns. "Not a problem. She'll never be ahead of us." She punched her right hand into her left palm. "Here's the plan. We tell Gianna we want to race for two carts—hers and Midnight. If she wins, she gets my *car*."

"You mean Carolina's cart," said Mariska.

"No, my actual *car*."

Mariska gasped. "Your *car* car?"

"Yep. Then when we win, Carolina gets Gianna's cart, and I get Midnight."

"And if you lose? You'll be out a golf cart, a car, *and* owe Carolina for—" Mariska motioned to the evergreen cart. "What's this one called?"

Carolina shrugged. "The Mean Green Machine?"

She turned back to Darla. "—you'll owe her for the Mean Green Machine. It's too much. You have to know when to *quit*."

Darla grit her teeth. "I can't quit. I can't let her win." She turned to Carolina. "So it's a deal? You'll let me use Mean Green Machine?"

Carolina nodded her chin toward Darla's hand. "Sure. I'll take your ring as collateral."

"No problem." Darla twisted at her wedding ring, grunting.

Mariska sucked in a breath and Darla scowled at her.

"What?" she asked as the ring popped off her finger.

"You said you'd get obsessed..." said Mariska, shaking her head. "...and here you are."

CHAPTER TWENTY-FOUR

Charlotte knocked on Tony the Tiger Tamer's door. After chatting with Cassie, she'd decided to confront him about the nurse. He *had* to know something. It couldn't be a coincidence she'd ended up in so many of his photos.

And if he was obsessed with her...

The horizontal blinds in the window to Charlotte's left split open, an eye materialized, swiveled in her direction, and then disappeared as the blinds snapped shut.

The door remained closed.

"Hello?"

She leaned down to peer through the warped louvers. Inside, a figure in gray sweatpants retreated from the door, hustling toward the back of the house.

"Just a second," called a voice.

Two minutes later, the door opened to reveal Tony in leopard-print joggers and a loosely tied short black kimono. Reddish-blond chest hair spilled from the gaping front of his robe like wrestling goldendoodles.

Charlotte coughed as a cloud of pungent cologne enveloped her.

"I thought you'd be back," Tony purred the words.

Charlotte struggled to keep from coughing again. She took a step back and sucked in a fresh breeze as it bumped against Tony's fog and tried to make a run for it.

"What can I do for you?" asked Tony.

Charlotte cleared her throat. "Um, I had some questions I wanted to ask you about Baroness."

"Of course. Come on in." He stepped back, making way for her to enter.

Crap.

Charlotte took a deep breath and stepped into the main living area of Tony's house, her gaze slowly sweeping the room as he closed the door behind her.

Sweet mother of pearl...

A lamp on a tawny-colored table had been draped with a gauzy leopard-print scarf, casting spots across the wall and ceiling. An enormous fuzzy tiger print blanket lounged across the back of a large black leather sofa. In the corner sat a round platform with a giant, life-sized stuffed tiger balanced on it, its enormous paw raised as if it were waving at her.

At that point in her self-tour, Charlotte's brain seized, refusing to catalog any more animal prints. She found herself unable to pull her attention from the stuffed tiger staring back at her with glassy amber eyes. It was the only thing in the room she felt sure wanted to be there even less than she did.

"I see you're admiring Delilah," said Tony.

"It looks so real."

"Because she *is*." He put his arm around the cat's shoulders. "She was my best girl."

Light glinted off Tony's tight joggers and Charlotte realized they had to be made from some kind of *pleather*.

She knew she'd never be able to *unsee* Tony and his humble abode. She wondered where *Dateline* would set up their cameras after she went missing.

Probably over by the black fur-covered lounger so they can get a good shot of poor Delilah...

"Can I get you something to drink?" he asked.

Charlotte's eye fell on a yellow bottle of cologne with a tiger image on it, tucked behind the leopard-covered lamp.

"Um..."

Before she could answer, Tony slipped into the kitchen and returned a *second* later to push a long-stemmed wine glass into her hand.

"This is a playful little merlot," he said, leering.

He released it with a flourish, and she snatched the glass to keep it from dashing to the ground. The stem felt cold.

Did he have this pre-poured?

She glanced at the tiger-themed clock on the wall, its paws pointing at ten and two like a careful driver.

"Come, sit down," said Tony, moving to the sofa and motioning for her to follow. She sat, setting her wine on the sofa table. Instead of legs, the glass tabletop sat snug on the back of a ceramic black panther.

Tony reached to the table next to him and produced a plate of cheese, meat and crackers.

"Charcuterie?" he asked, sliding the platter a few inches below her chin as if he expected her to graze across its surface like a horse.

She raised a hand to create a wall between herself and the snacks. "Uh, no, I'm good."

"I was going to call you, you know," he said, lowering the platter to the panther table before turning to smile at her.

He looked...*hungry.*

Charlotte squinted.

Are his eyeteeth a little too sharp?

Words failed her as he continued.

"I got information I think could blow this case wide open."

"Really?" She felt her pocket for her phone as he nodded. "That's great. Um, you should tell the sheriff directly. I could call him—"

"No, no." Tony leaned forward and placed the tip of his finger on her knee. "I feel more comfortable telling *you.*"

She glanced down at his hand, and he slid it back to his own lap.

Tony's creep-factor had reached Charlotte's breaking point. *Time to go.*

"Mr., uh, Tiger Tamer, I'm thinking—"

"Have you looked into Scotty the Skyscraper?" he asked.

Charlotte blinked, shocked to hear him mention her *other* favorite suspect. She pushed aside her nerves for a moment.

"Who?" she asked, deciding to play dumb.

He frowned. "I saw you talking to him."

"Oh, *right*, the tall clown."

"Right. He's a clown, all right," muttered Tony. He leaned forward to take a sip of her wine as if it had been his all along.

"Why do you think we should look into Scotty?" she prompted him, as he lingered over the merlot's bouquet.

He scoffed. "Well, first off, he's a *creep*."

Charlotte barked a laugh.

Tony's brow knit. He seemed confused by her reaction.

"Sorry," she said. "Why, uh, why do you say he's a creep?"

"He's just *weird*."

Charlotte bit her tongue.

Tony continued. "I think he has *reasons* for wanting Baroness gone."

"Like what?"

"Like, they didn't get along."

Charlotte shrugged. "Lots of people don't get along. It doesn't mean he killed her. What about Grin?"

"I don't know how he felt about Grin. But if you can kill one person, how hard is it to kill another?"

"Pretty hard, I'd hope," said Charlotte. "So you think Scotty is a serial killer, but you don't have any proof or—"

Something moved outside the window across from them, and both their eyes slid in that direction.

A face stared back at them through the glass.

A cat face, complete with ears.

Charlotte gasped.

"Kitty!" yelped Tony, jumping to his feet.

Charlotte looked up at him.

Kitty?

By the time she looked back at the window, the face had

disappeared.

Shoot!

Scrambling over the sofa arm, Charlotte bolted through the front door. She rounded the side of Tony's house as a figure wearing what looked like white dance tights climbed over the fence separating Big Top and the field next door. The peeper darted across the field toward the simulated big top tent, long white tail flapping.

Charlotte ran to her left to use the gate. She wasn't sure if chasing the stranger was the best idea, but it seemed more appealing than returning to Tony's creepy big cat wonderland. Anyway, if she chased one more fence-climbing suspect this month she'd certainly fill her foot-pursuit punch card.

The cat ran past the big top tent and down an alley lined with small, colorfully painted sheds. Charlotte remembered the area featured games of skill and other sideshow attractions during Big Top's charity circus events. When she was young, a man wearing a tall hat there had guessed Darla's weight, and Darla had plotted his death for a week afterwards.

Charlotte closed ground, galloping down the sideshow area's center lane. The cat dodged into one of the side buildings. Charlotte followed, tripping over the threshold and stumbling to catch her feet before plowing into a wall. She hadn't expected the flooring to be so uneven—the cat seemed to glide across any surface.

Peeling herself off the paint, she spotted a thin hallway heading left.

What the heck?

She took a step outside to check the signage she hadn't bothered to read on the way in.

House of Mazes.

Charlotte frowned.

Great.

On the upside, she didn't see how the maze could work to the cat's advantage. Maybe it would level the playing field.

Unless the cat *knew* the maze.

Charlotte reentered the building and started down the skinny hallway. The world around her grew dimmer as she moved from the entrance, until the last of the light disappeared. Blind, she slid her hands along the walls as she moved.

I hate this.

Charlotte stopped and glanced back the way she'd come. A small person with a painted cat face didn't seem particularly dangerous—it could be a *child*, for all she knew.

But it could also be the killer.

Charlotte was still trying to decide whether to go forward or turn back when she heard manic laughter up ahead. She was halfway back to the entrance when she realized the laughter sounded vaguely *mechanical*.

Weren't there always mechanical monsters in mazes like these, triggered by motion to move, like Mariska's jolly Santa Claus? Santa had shaken with laughter at people, dogs, and birds, until Bob threw it out and told Mariska kids must have stolen it.

The circus laughter hadn't sounded far away.

The cat had to be working through the maze.

What the heck.

Charlotte continued deeper into the maze, working her blind way around a ninety-degree turn. The laughter burst again, this time close and *loud*. Charlotte grabbed her chest as a spotlight on the floor flickered to illuminate a tall, toothy clown.

She closed her eyes, panting.

I hate clowns.

The light snuffed out, leaving her with spots before her eyes as the hall fell dark once more.

Please let this end.

She inched forward again, triggering the clown a second time. This time, she appreciated it for the light and sped her chase.

More laughter echoed from up ahead.

The cat woman had triggered another motion sensor.

Fingers dragging along the wall, Charlotte worked around

another corner to come face-to-face with a cackling witch, a green light glowing at its feet.

Dangling rubber spiders and three screechy yips on her part later, the maze spat out Charlotte. She cringed, giving her eyes a chance to adjust to the sunlight. When she could see again, she saw only trees and the backs of houses.

The white cat was gone.

"Half a heart attack for *nothing*," she grumbled, following a waist-high makeshift fence back around the maze building to the main drag of the sideshow village.

"There you are," said Tony, walking towards her. His ridiculous outfit looked even more horrific in the sun.

"Did you catch her?" he asked.

Charlotte arched an eyebrow.

Her?

She'd guessed the figure to be female, but he seemed to *know*.

"Catch *who*?" she asked.

He sniffed. "Whoever it was looking through my window."

She shook her head. "Let's stop the games, Tony. You said *her* and you called her *Kitty* back at the house."

He turned his palms toward the sky. "I call *all* cats Kitty."

"Fess up. Who's the cat?"

Tony stared at her a moment longer before his shoulders slumped.

"Fine," he said. "She's Kitty the Cat Girl."

Charlotte waited for more. "*And*?"

"And what?"

"What does she have to do with you? With the murders? Why did she try and rob someone's house?"

He seemed shocked. "*What?* Whose house?"

"That's not important. The reason I came to Big Top in the first place was to find a cat-faced clown who'd broken into a home."

"She's not a *clown*, and Kitty wouldn't rob *anyone*."

He looked upset and Charlotte believed *he* believed his

statement to be true.

"So tell me why she ran," she said.

Tony chewed his lip as if considering the pros and cons of sharing more. Finally, he closed his eyes and hung his head. "She's shy. She's had a hard life."

"How so? Who is she?"

He touched his upper lip with his index finger. "She was born with a partial cleft lip. The effect makes her look a little like a cat. She was billed as Kitty the Cat Girl."

Charlotte nodded. The story explained her presence in Big Top, except—

"She didn't move like a fifty-five-plusser," said Charlotte. "She lives here with her parents?"

He shook his head. "Her parents were killed by a drunk driver when she was young." Tony's expression grew dark. "Baroness took her in, but for her own selfish reasons. Made her sleep in a bed on the floor. Treated her like a—a—" He choked up and pressed the side of his fist to his lips.

"A cat?" said Charlotte, guessing the end of his sentence.

He nodded, looking pained. "Baroness wanted to keep her from becoming independent. She hid her from everyone. Wanted to keep her like a *slave*. Especially when she got older. The witch needed someone to take care of her for free."

"Take care—" Charlotte gasped. "She's the *nurse*."

Tony nodded. "Baroness made her wear scrubs to go food-shopping and run errands so people wouldn't know she lived with her." He leaned forward to whisper, "It's illegal to have young people living here."

"I know something about that," said Charlotte. "She must have hated Baroness."

Tony shook a finger at her, his eyes wide. "No, no—I see where you're going with this. She didn't kill her."

"How do you know?"

"Because I know."

"But *how* do you know?"

Tony sobbed and dropped his face into his open palms.

Charlotte felt her skin tingle.

He's going to confess.

It all made sense. Clearly, he had feelings for Kitty. Baroness had mistreated her. So he killed Baroness. It didn't explain what happened to Grin, but she could get to that later.

First, she needed to hear him say the words.

"Tony," she said softly as he continued to sob into his hands. "How do you know *for sure* it wasn't her?"

He looked up, his eyes red and swollen, and curled his fingers into fists.

"Because I love her!" he wailed to the heavens.

She nodded. "So *you* killed Baroness to save her?"

"*What?*" He lowered his chin to gape at her. "Are you out of your mind? I didn't kill Baroness."

Charlotte used her most soothing voice. "It's okay. People will understand—"

Tony took a step back. "You hold on one second there, missy. Kitty is the woman of my dreams, but I wouldn't kill *anyone* for a woman. Not even her."

Charlotte felt the excitement bleed out of her.

Not a confession.

Tony wiped his nose on the back of his arm. "Especially not now," he added.

"Why?"

He huffed an angry grunt.

"Because *she* loves that stupid Skyscraper."

CHAPTER TWENTY-FIVE

With Tony the Tiger Tamer anxious to rid himself of his competition for Kitty's affections, it didn't prove difficult for Charlotte to finagle Scotty the Skyscraper's address out of him. She even got the information before they arrived back at his doorstep, while circumventing any need for her to step inside Casa Stuffed Tiger again.

Score.

She skittered back to her car as fast as her legs would take her, fought the urge to run home and get a second shower, and rolled through the neighborhood until she spotted Scotty's house number on a light blue home across from Cassie's.

She rolled her eyes.

I was right here all along.

Maybe that's why Stark had reacted so angrily when she asked about Tony and Scotty—he clearly wasn't a fan of Tony, but Scotty was Cassie's neighbor.

Feeling flustered after fighting off Tony, chasing a cat woman, and working her way through a creepy maze, Charlotte took a moment to take a few cleansing breaths before heading up the stairs to Scotty's door. She let her knuckles hover over his door with her eyes shut and said a silent prayer.

Please be normal, calm, and helpful. Please don't have stuffed former pets in the living room. Please don't wear cologne that doubles as tear gas...

She knocked.

Scotty answered, frowning down at her from his impossible height.

How's the weather up there?

"You again," grumbled the clown.

"I know about Kitty," she said.

His eyes widened as he opened his screen door. "You found her?"

Charlotte suffered mixed emotions. It relieved her to hear him admit he knew Kitty, but she'd been hoping he knew where she was. His concern and confusion seemed genuine.

Shoot.

"I was hoping you knew where she was," she admitted.

He hung his head. "No. She's been missing since they found Baroness." He ducked his head to walk outside and motioned to one of the two tall bar chairs beneath his carport. "Have a seat."

Charlotte hoisted herself into a seat. He joined her, the two of them separated by a tall glass table. Her feet dangled two feet from the ground. His nearly touched the cement.

"Are you and Kitty dating?" she asked.

Scotty's face twitched as if she'd slapped him.

"How did you know?" he asked.

Charlotte couldn't think of any downside to revealing her source. "Tony."

"Tony." At the sound of the tiger tamer's name, darkness settled on Scotty's expression.

"He thinks he loves her," he said, his tone belying what he thought.

"He says he does."

"He's obsessed with cats. Were you in his house?"

Unfortunately, yes.

She tried to remain tactful. "He, uh, definitely likes cats."

"He's got it into his head that she was made for him because of the way she looks."

"The cleft lip."

He seemed surprised. "You know?"

She nodded. "Tony again."

He sighed. "She was going to live with me."

"But you don't have any idea where she is?"

"No. She ran away the night Baroness died. I've seen glimpses of her a few times since, but I need to find her and get her here where she'll be safe from people like Baroness and Tony. She was making such great progress—"

He rubbed his face with his hands.

"Who do you think killed Baroness?" asked Charlotte.

"I have no idea. She wasn't a nice lady. Could have been anyone."

"You know what it looks like, though, right?"

He looked up. "Tony?"

"Tony wanted to get her away from Baroness, but so did you."

"Me?"

"Or maybe Kitty ended her indentured servitude herself."

"Kitty would never kill someone—" He huffed. "I know she's different, but she's not crazy. She's sweet, caring, wonderful—"

"Hey!"

Someone had barked the word from across the street. Scotty and Charlotte swiveled their attention to find Stark storming toward them. He'd taken the time to don a tee shirt this time.

"I told you to leave my people alone," he said, waving his arms.

"It's okay, Stark," said Scotty. "She knows about Kitty."

Stark looked at Charlotte. "You found her?"

She shook her head. "No. Maybe I would have if you'd told me about her sooner."

Stark put his hands on his hips and hung his head. "I didn't agree with how Baroness treated her, but I didn't want her homeless either. Then when Scotty and she started spending time together..." He looked up. "People should mind their own business."

Charlotte chewed her lip. "Believe me, the last thing I want to do is cause trouble for an orphan secretly living in a fifty-five-plus community, but we need to figure out what happened to Baroness, and she could be the key."

Scotty looked at Stark. "She says me, Tony, and Kitty herself are suspects."

Stark's eyes popped wide. "For Baroness? What about Grin? Why would any of you kill him?" He turned to Charlotte. "I thought you people thought it was a serial killer?"

Charlotte shook her head. "A reporter started that rumor." She slid off her chair and pulled a couple business cards from the back of her phone case. "If you have any more information or see Kitty, could you let me know?"

Scotty took her card. "You're a private investigator? Who hired you?"

"No one. I help the sheriff sometimes."

He hooked his mouth to the right. "What if I hired you?"

"Huh?"

"I'll hire you to find Kitty. I need to find her before someone railroads her for Baroness."

"She'd die in a cell," muttered Stark.

"Um…" Charlotte struggled to find the downside. She'd be working on the crime either way—this way, she'd get paid for it.

"Sure. I can do that."

"Great. Great."

Stark remained silent, staring at Charlotte through squinted eyes.

Charlotte wrapped up the details of her retainer with Scotty. Since Frank hadn't been quick to deputize her, being hired to find Kitty was perfect. She'd always suspected she wouldn't get far investigating the murders without Kitty's input anyway.

When the details of her employ had been ironed out with Scotty, she skirted around the glaring Stark and headed for her car, brainstorming how to find Kitty.

That's when it hit her.

What I need is a professional tracker.

CHAPTER TWENTY-SIX

Shee and Mason spent the morning pretending they weren't single-minded.

"We shouldn't bother her."

"Absolutely not."

"We'll just have a little vacation. We deserve a vacation."

"No kidding. What are you getting? Eggs?"

"Probably... I wonder if Charlotte likes eggs?"

"I wonder if bananas make her mouth itch like mine? Should I warn her?"

"About bananas?"

"About any genetic stuff."

"I don't know...maybe we should make a list. Do you think she'll call?"

"I don't know. Should we call her?"

By lunch, they'd run out of things to talk about to distract them from talking about Charlotte. Instead, they defaulted to staring at their phones, jumping whenever one of them pinged or buzzed.

After lunch, they moved onto the balcony of their oceanside hotel room, staring down at the beach-goers as if there would a be a quiz later. Shee flipped through the hotel's collection of magazines a third time. When her phone rang, she leapt from her chair as if it were spring-loaded.

Snatching her phone from the table, she looked up to find

Mason staring at her.

"It's her," she said.

"Well, answer it."

"I am." Shee cleared her throat and hit the green button. "Hello?"

"Hi. Um, what are you guys up to?" asked Charlotte.

It's her, it's her, it's her, it's her...

"Not much. How about you?"

"Funny you should ask. I just got a job. Well, it's the same job, but it's a person hiring me to do it instead of Frank putting up with me while I beg him to let me do it."

"That's good, right?" Shee wasn't sure it was good. She worried this was Charlotte's way of telling them she'd be too busy to hang out with them anymore.

"Paying jobs are always a good thing," Charlotte chuckled.

All Shee could hear was Mason hissing in her ear. He'd sat up and moved to the end of his chair to be closer to the phone, in no way hiding his attempt to eavesdrop.

"Tell her about the bananas," he whispered.

She put her finger to her lips. "Shh."

"Does she need money?" he asked.

Shee blinked at him.

That was a pretty good idea.

We'll bribe her to spend more time with us.

"Do you need money?" she asked, giving Mason a thumbs up.

What did kids want from their parents more than money?

They should have arrived with paperwork for a trust or something—except, after decades on the run, she was next to broke. It was hard to amass a fortune moving from town to town volunteering to locate and capture bad guys.

She wasn't sure how much Mason had squirreled away.

"No, I'm good," said Charlotte. "I still have my mother's— uh, I still have the money, um—"

"Your mother's inheritance," said Shee, letting her off the hook. She didn't expect the girl to start calling her half-sister,

Grace, aunt, when up until a few days ago, Grace was the only mother Charlotte had ever known.

"I'm good," repeated Charlotte.

Shee nodded.

Maybe I should be asking to borrow money from her.

"What'd she say?" asked Mason.

She waived him off. He grimaced and sat back an inch.

"Um, so, this job…" started Charlotte.

Shee bit her lip.

Here it comes. She's going to tell us to go home. She's too busy. She's—

"It's a tracking job."

Shee perked. "Tracking?"

"I have to find a woman. A cat woman."

"Like Batman's Catwoman or like an old lady with a lot of cats?"

"Like the first kind. She's a sideshow performer, Kitty the Cat Girl, only all grown up."

"Oh. That sounds like fun."

"I was wondering if you'd be interested in helping me?"

"Me?" Shee straightened. Mason dodged to avoid her skull as it whipped at his jaw.

"That's your thing, right? Tracking people?"

"It is. That is my thing," said Shee, feeling giddy. "When do you need me?"

"I don't know. We could make some progress today, but I know it's late notice—"

Shee stood. "No, no, not a problem at all. I'll be there in half an hour, okay?"

"Okay. Great—I'll get together what leads I have so far."

"Sounds like a plan. See you in a bit."

"See you."

Shee hung up, grinning at Mason. "She needs a tracker."

"I heard that."

"I'm a tracker."

"I know that."

"I'm going to go help her—" Shee gasped and covered her mouth with her hand. "I didn't ask—do you want to go?"

He shook his head. "This is all you."

"Are you sure? You won't be bored?"

"I'll be fine. I'd only get in the way. After all, what's more traditional than a mother and daughter tracking criminals together? This is like a Hallmark movie."

Shee threw her arms around him. "Thank you."

"No problem. I'll wait until we have a son."

Shee pushed him to arm's length.

"It was a joke," he said.

She nodded. "Duh."

Shee arrived at Charlotte's house in record time. She made her way into the house as her daughter hip-checked Abby out of the way.

"Have a seat," said Charlotte, motioning to a standalone chair. "If you sit on the sofa she'll sit on you."

"I don't mind," said Shee. "One of the hardest things about being on the road was not having a dog. For now, I'm living vicariously through other people's dogs."

Shee sat on the sofa, and as promised, Abby crawled into her lap.

Charlotte sat beside them and picked up a notepad from the sofa table. "Can I get you something to drink?"

"Nope. I'm good. Let's get started."

Charlotte took a deep breath. "Okay. So, you know about Baroness, the fortune teller who was killed?"

"With her crystal ball."

"Right. Well, it turns out she had a young woman living with her, Kitty the Cat Girl, who ran away the night Baroness was killed."

"You think she's on the lam?"

"Not exactly. She's been seen around town since."

"You think she murdered the fortune-teller?"

"It's possible. Or, at the very least, she must know something."

"So, this young woman is the cat-faced burglar you were looking for, for the robbery you told me about?"

"Yes. And she's also the nurse I chased out of Seamus'."

Shee perked. "Ooh, the fence hopper. That makes sense. Go on."

"It turns out Kitty has a couple of admirers. One of them, Scotty the Skyscraper, hired me to find her."

"Scotty the—?"

"Tall clown."

"Ah. Got it. So, where's she been spotted so far, besides Seamus'?"

"Well, at the robbery, Seamus' bar, and then today. I chased her into a funhouse maze after I caught her peeking into Tony the Tiger Tamer's house. She was wearing a white cat costume, from ears to tail."

Shee giggled. "I'm sorry. I'm starting to think your life might be even stranger than mine."

Charlotte laughed. "This is *nothing*."

"So who's Tony?"

"He's one of my suspects. Quite the character. I'll tell you more about him later."

"I can't wait."

Shee slid from beneath Abby and stood to pace, tapping her chin with her index finger. "I can't say I've ever tracked a cat girl before. Could we start at the beginning? Could we get into Baroness' house?"

"Depends..." Charlotte opened a drawer to retrieve a set of lockpicks, holding them aloft for Shee to see. "Are you a stickler for doing things strictly legally?"

Shee smiled.

"That is not a problem I have."

CHAPTER TWENTY-SEVEN

Stephanie clicked through a website-based gallery of the previous year's Big Top charity event. The photos featured people gathered in fancy clothes, milling around the fake Big Top tent with cocktails in hand. She looked past them, studying the performers tumbling and grinning in the background.

She'd decided rather than creep around the grounds, she'd shop online.

This is like Amazon for murderers.

She felt strangely *liberated*. Maybe because in the past she'd always had a good reason to kill someone. This time it was about *opportunity*. Trying to be good all this time had her feeling like a bird in a cage.

A gorgeous, *murderous* bird.

A Cassowary, maybe.

Clicking through a few more photos, she stumbled on the image of the conjoined twins.

Two for the price of one.

Still, very tempting.

Of course, she had questions. Did the twins have two hearts or one? How many lungs? They seemed to be connected near the hip—maybe they shared a liver? What if one was a drinker and the other wasn't?

The bell of Stephanie's entry door dinged, and her gaze rose to the clock on the wall.

Seven p.m. Little late for a walk-in client.

She'd forgotten to lock the door. Standing from her desk, she strolled the five feet to the lobby.

"Hello?"

A short, dark figure stood inside her front door, backlit by the streetlights outside.

Stephanie reached for the light switch.

"I'm closed—"

Her fingertips grazed the switch as a powerful jolt of electricity shot through her body. For a moment, she thought some faulty wiring in the wall had caused her pain.

Then, *no.*

Not the switch.

Taser.

Am I being arrested?

The overhead lights flickered on and then steadied. She'd managed to hit the switch before the shock. Falling forward like a felled redwood, she caught a glimpse of her attacker.

Not a cop.

She'd been a predator for so long it hadn't occurred to her the killer she'd interrupted while victim-shopping at Big Top might not appreciate her attentions—that maybe *she'd* be the next victim of the Big Top Killer.

She rolled to her side, back to her attacker, as the electricity gradually released its hold on her muscles. She curled a finger to activate the phone on her watch.

"Hello?" said a voice.

"Declan, hel—"

A second jolt surged through her body.

"Stephanie?" said a tinny voice.

She couldn't reply.

No sooner had the shock ended than she felt a prick on her arm.

"That's not good," she murmured, as the world spun.

CHAPTER TWENTY-EIGHT

Charlotte raised her picks to work on Baroness' back lock. Her gaze dropped to a blue plastic square at the bottom of the door. Poking it with her toe, she watched the hanging panel rock back and forth and looked at Shee.

"Pet door," she said. "Even easier."

"For you maybe," said Shee.

Charlotte put away her lockpicks, bummed she wouldn't have the chance to demonstrate her skills for Shee.

For *Mom?*

Nope. Still sounded too strange.

"Beauty before age," said Shee, motioning to the door.

Charlotte dropped to shimmy through the square. "I don't think that's how that saying goes."

Shee smiled down at her. "The beauty is that age gets to decide."

Charlotte shimmied into the house and popped to her feet to help Shee through.

"You have to be nuts to have a pet door in Florida," said Shee, standing to swipe the dirt from her knees. "Good way to wake up with an alligator in your bed."

Charlotte chuckled. "You take the back bedrooms. I'll look around out here."

Without further comment, Shee headed for the master bedroom and disappeared.

Charlotte took a few steps into the kitchen. Her nose wrinkled.

Ick.

Something smelled *awful.*

She glanced into the living room to confirm no body parts had been left behind and then moved deeper into the galley kitchen. The smell grew stronger. She opened the refrigerator to find a sparse array of groceries. A half-empty milk gallon sported an expiration date a week in the future.

Brand new, yet half empty.

Two six-packs of tuna lined one shelf.

Charlotte realized that was the stench she smelled—spoiling fish. She pulled open a cabinet to reveal a sliding trash can containing six empty and unrinsed tuna cans inside.

Ah ha.

Someone with a penchant for milk and tuna was squatting in Baroness' home.

Gosh, who could that be?

Shee appeared. "Nothing unusual," she said, entering the kitchen. "I'd say there were two people living here, though. Did they have a dog? Seems strange a cat girl would own a dog, but there's a dog bed in the master."

"I think that's where Kitty sleeps. Baroness treated her, well, like an animal, apparently."

"Yikes. No wonder she's a little off." Shee winced, her expression then shifting to disgust. "What's that *smell*?"

"Tuna in the trash."

Shee peered into the opened trash can.

"There's a new gallon of milk, half empty, too," added Charlotte. "It's safe to say the cat's been living here. All we need to do is stake out this place."

Shee nodded. "Since she takes this cat thing to the nth degree, she probably sleeps here during the day and roams at night. Explains why there haven't been more sightings of her, too."

Charlotte looked out the window at the dying light. "She's

probably out for the night now."

Shee frowned. "There's got to be a faster way to find her than sitting here until morning. Maybe we could call animal control for some tuna-baited traps…"

Charlotte laughed as an idea germinated. "You know, I *might* have an idea. We know she's been sighted in the area. We know she's up to something, though I don't know what."

"Robbing people, apparently," muttered Shee.

"What about a drone?"

A grin leapt to Shee's lips. "I *love* drones. Do you have one?"

Charlotte shook her head. "I don't, but we've got a nerd in the neighborhood who has *all* the toys. Unfortunately, he likes to charge me top dollar for borrowing them."

Shee sniffed. "That's not very nice."

"Gryph considers himself a sort of elite hacker-spy. Outside of his imagination, though, he's a retired IT guy for some pharmaceutical company."

"Typical NSA-wannabe," said Shee. "Drone it is. Don't worry about the money."

She opened the back door so they could exit like civilized people.

"I can't let you spend money on my case," said Charlotte locking the door behind them.

Shee snorted a laugh. "Who said I was going to spend money?"

Charlotte drove them to Gryph's as they plotted places to look for Kitty.

"He lives in your neighborhood?" asked Shee.

She nodded.

Shee pulled out her phone and dialed. "Dad?" Charlotte

heard her say. "Hey. I need information on someone. A Gryph—"

She looked at Charlotte, covering the mic on the phone with her hand. "Do you know his last name?"

Charlotte grimaced. "No. I know his cats are Chip and Java..."

"Not helpful."

"I didn't think so." Charlotte frowned, trying to remember everything she could about Gryph. It hit her the most obvious information might be the most useful. "Oh, I know his *address*. Sea Oat Drive, number..." She pulled outside Gryph's house and read the numbers from the wall. "302. Does that work?"

Shee nodded. "*Perfect.*"

She relayed the information to her father. There was a pause and then she said, "Something you couldn't easily find on the Internet. Something he'd be surprised to hear come out of my mouth." Another pause and she shook her head. "Very funny."

"What did he say?" whispered Charlotte.

"Unrepeatable."

"Tell him I said *hi*."

Shee nodded. "Charlotte says *hi*." She covered the phone again to report he'd returned the greeting and then returned to her call. "I don't know, Dad, ask Croix to do it. Or your cop friends..."

Shee lowered the phone to her lap. "It's so hard to get good help."

Her father said something on the phone and Shee returned it to her ear.

"Uh huh. Oh. *Perfect.* Thank you. Hm? Oh. Okay. Soon. I don't know. Okay. Bye." She hung up and looked at Charlotte.

"We're in business. Let's go."

"What is it?"

She grinned. "You'll see."

They walked to Gryph's door and Charlotte used the dragon-shaped door knocker to announce their arrival.

No one answered.

"He might be out walking his cats," said Charlotte, trying again.

Shee squinted at her. "Walking his—"

The door opened and a heavy-set man with a scruffy beard stood before them, a saucer-eared cat perched on each shoulder.

"Can I help you?" he asked, eyeing Shee.

"I need one of your drones again," said Charlotte.

Gryph pursed his lips. "I told you before; I'm not a *rental* service. These are very delicate pieces of machinery." He turned his attention back to Shee. "Who are you? You look like an old version of her."

Charlotte thought she heard Shee growl.

She tried to move things along. "This is—"

Gryph cut Charlotte short, all six eyes, man and cats, glowering at her. "You know, I'd appreciate it if you didn't spread information about my drones to everyone you know."

"You don't have to worry about your secrets," said Shee.

Gryph cocked an eyebrow. "Oh I don't, do I?"

"I'm NSA."

Gryph scoffed. "Sure you are. Let me see identification."

Shee shook her head. "Deep undercover. Can't carry it on me, but take my word for it, Mister Orville Owsinski, DOB July 11, 1961. Gryphon's your gaming handle."

Gryph blanched.

Shee plowed on. "Now about that drone. I need it fast, and I'm not close enough to an office to requisition one, so if you could help I'd greatly appreciate it. Unless, um...you'd rather talk to my sister?"

"Your sister?"

"She works for the IRS. She *loves* unregistered home businesses."

Gryph took a step back. "Uh, *no*. I mean, yeah, of course I can help. Come to the garage."

He shut the door and Charlotte looked at Shee.

"That was amazing. Where did you get all that information?"

"Your grandfather has his contacts. Croix—the girl at the front desk—is a wiz on the Internet." She chuckled and added, "—but don't tell her I said so."

They walked around the side of the house to find Gryph already there, sans cats, his garage door opened. A fleet of drones sat on shelves lining the wall.

"Wonderful, Mr. Owsinski. We're going to need one with night vision."

"You can call me Gryph." He walked down the line of drones and chose one. "This is a good one. Excellent range. Night vision, heat signature—"

Shee held up a hand. "Great. I need you to operate it for me. Time is of the essence. We're looking for a fugitive."

"A fugitive?" Gryph carried the drone to the driveway and returned to grab the controller. He seemed excited.

"Where to?"

"The area between Big Top community and the Albacore," said Charlotte. She leaned to Shee. "That's where the robbery happened."

Gryph gaped. "I used to live in Albacore."

"I know," said Shee. She pointed to the controller. "Go. You're looking for someone moving through the yards, avoiding streets and sidewalks. A woman. She, uh, might be in costume."

Gryph looked up from the controller. "In *costume*?"

Shee nodded. "I can't say any more."

Gryph raised the drone into the air, four propellors whirling. Shee and Charlotte moved to stand behind him so they could view his screen over his shoulder.

After five minutes of sweeping through the sky, Gryph zeroed in over an area.

"Hold on. I've got a bogey at three o'clock," he said.

Shee looked at Charlotte, and she looked away, afraid she'd laugh.

"What are we looking at?" asked Shee.

"Big Top, just like you said," said Gryph.

Charlotte leaned in for a better look and pointed to a figure moving through someone's back yard.

"Look—I think she's headed home."

"Do we have time to beat her?" asked Shee.

"Maybe. If we hurry."

"Let's go." Shee jogged down the driveway.

"That's it?" asked Gryph.

Charlotte patted him on the shoulder. "That's it." She took off after Shee.

Shee stopped and turned, poking a finger back at Gryph. "Just remember, the next time Agent Morgan needs something, you must be helpful."

Gryph locked on Charlotte, his chin dropping.

"You're an *agent*?"

With a quick nod, Charlotte turned to catch up to Shee, who'd reached the Volvo. She jumped into the car, giggling.

"That was *awesome*."

Shee grinned. "I don't think he'll charge you again."

CHAPTER TWENTY-NINE

Declan saw Stephanie's name pop up on his phone and rolled his eyes.

Now what?

"Hello?"

He heard his name, followed by a string of agitated grunts.

"Stephanie?"

The line went dead. Huffing a sigh, he put down the phone to return to work, but couldn't shake an uneasy feeling.

Had there been another word after his name? Before the grunting started? Something like...help?

He walked back to his phone and dialed back. No one answered. Huffing a sigh, he put down the phone.

What is she up to now?

The grunts—they could have been anything. Probably, she'd tried to call him in the car and dropped the phone.

But why did he think they'd sounded pained?

Normally, in a situation like this, he'd call Charlotte to discuss the pros and cons of being nice to Stephanie. There were usually more cons than pros. Whoever penned *no good deed goes unpunished* had definitely known his ex.

He knew Charlotte was busy running some clandestine mission with her mother and didn't want to interfere with their bonding time. Knowing Stephanie, she probably had Charlotte under surveillance—knew she was away for the evening—and was trying to trick him into coming to her office.

Still...

Something didn't feel right.

He pushed his uneasy feelings aside and finished closing up shop before hitting the road. Sitting at the traffic light at the end of Charity's main street, he found himself faced with two options: Turn right to head home, or turn left to swing by Stephanie's office.

He dialed Stephanie again.

No answer.

Crap.

When the light changed, he turned left.

A little wellness check couldn't hurt. After all, someone had killed her mother. He didn't know the details, but maybe someone was hunting down the whole homicidal family.

Two miles down the road, Declan slowed to pull into Stephanie's parking lot. The lights glowed, both in her office and the main lobby.

So there you go. She's up working late.

He swung around, planning to head back out, and then decided to park.

I've come this far.

He got out of the car and pushed on her office door, expecting to find it locked.

It gave.

Hm.

Late meeting, maybe?

He opened the door far enough to stick his head in and called her name.

"Steph—"

Declan's gaze settled on an overturned sofa table. Reading materials lay spread across the floor like a rug made entirely of outdated People Magazines.

Uh oh.

Slipping inside, he locked the door behind him and

surveyed the lobby for additional clues.

Nothing other than the upturned table seemed amiss. He crept to the entrance of Stephanie's inner office to take a quick glimpse inside. Seeing nothing strange, he gave the room a thorough scan.

Everything seemed normal.

His attention drew to the weapons Stephanie kept displayed as decoration on her wall. She used them as a show of strength for her crime syndicate clients, but a machete on a wall was still a machete. He pulled down the weapon, felt its heft in his hand, and headed back to the lobby to work his way deeper into the bowels of Stephanie's small office.

The bathroom in the hall held no surprises. He reached the makeshift apartment Stephanie had set up for herself in the back, wondering why she hadn't found a real apartment yet.

It didn't matter. Her inability to commit to a living space was not his problem.

The apartment held no sign of trouble.

He lowered the machete, thinking.

If she'd been robbed, he would have expected to find the apartment turned over. A thief would have snatched a few weapons from her power wall, too.

He chucked the machete on her bed and tried her phone again.

A phone rang somewhere back down the hall.

Following the sound, he traced his way back to her office to find her phone under papers on her desk.

Not a good sign.

Declan strode back into the lobby and stood with his hands on his hips, staring at the overturned table. He couldn't think of a single logical reason why the furniture would be flipped. Certainly, she wasn't cleaning. He wasn't sure she knew what a vacuum was.

Something silver poking from beneath the scattered magazines caught his eye, and he bent down to pull Stephanie's watch from the mess.

Okay. We officially have a problem.

His own phone rang, making him jump. Jerking it from his pocket, he glanced at the screen.

Charlotte.

"Hello?"

Charlotte sounded chipper. "Hey—"

"Hey, two seconds—not to interrupt, but you haven't heard from Stephanie, have you?"

"Stephanie?" echoed Charlotte. "Why would I hear from her?"

"It would be weird, I know, but I got a strange call, and now it looks like maybe something happened to her."

"Why do you say that?"

"I swung by her office and her lights are on, some furniture is flipped, and both her phone and her watch are here."

"Oh. That doesn't sound good."

"No."

"Do you need us to come help look for her?"

Declan sighed. "No. Finish up what you're doing. You know Stephanie. This could be some elaborate ruse. I'll poke around a little more, and we'll see."

He hung up and stepped outside to survey the area.

Nothing amiss.

He decided to head home and try her phone again in a little bit. Hopefully, she wasn't already at his house, lying in wait, with some made-up tale of woe.

That would be classic Stephanie.

CHAPTER THIRTY

"Should I get my gun?" asked Charlotte, as they pulled away from Gryph's house.

"You have a gun?" Shee seemed surprised.

Charlotte nodded. "I do, but I don't like to use it."

"Good for you." Her mother sighed. "No, I'm thinking a gun isn't the way to go. From what you've told me she's skittish at best, unstable at worst. She'd probably run anyway—which would leave us holding a gun and feeling stupid."

"So we corner her in the house?"

"Exactly."

Charlotte pressed on the pedal as they sped to Big Top. They parked several houses down and ran through the neighbors' back yards to reach the pet door.

"You think we beat her?" whispered Charlotte as they climbed the back porch stairs.

"I'm not sure it matters. Let's go."

Shee dropped and pulled herself through the door with Charlotte tight on her heels.

The house was quiet.

Shee put her finger against her lips and crept to the bedrooms. She returned a minute later with two long scarves draped around her neck.

"She's not here."

Charlotte released the breath she'd been holding and cocked her head to the side. "What's with the scarves—"

Shee pointed and Charlotte turned to the shadow of someone moving outside. They hustled to stand beside the pet door.

"I'll go first, then you," whispered Shee.

Charlotte nodded, her nerves vibrating.

The pet door flap swung inward, and two hands reached inside, the nails on each finger long and filed to a point.

Shee pounced. She grabbed the wrists and shuffled backwards, dragging the thrashing Cat Girl into the house.

"Get her feet!"

Charlotte snatched the cat by the ankles as they appeared, struggling to hold them down and avoid being booted in the chin. Kitty felt as if she were made of taut steel wires.

The Cat Girl howled, hissing and spitting, twisting as she tried to bite Shee's hands. Charlotte guessed she weighed a hundred pounds, but it took all her strength to keep her from breaking free.

"We're not here to hurt you!" screamed Shee.

"We're taking you to Scotty!" added Charlotte.

As quickly as the tornado of nails and teeth had started, all fell silent. Kitty lay still, panting, staring at the ceiling.

Charlotte kept her hands on Kitty's ankles, catching her own breath. Trying not to stare, she sneaked her first look at the wily Cat Girl.

The repaired cleft lip *did* make the woman's mouth look cat-like, but even under makeup Charlotte could tell the scar wasn't as pronounced as she'd imagined.

Kitty wore a black, long-sleeve body suit with what looked like fur hot-glued to it. Her white hair had been tucked beneath a black cap with cat ears poking from the top.

Shee pressed Kitty's left wrist down with her foot and whipped one of the scarves from her neck. Easing the now peaceful hellcat to a seated position, she tied her hands behind her back. When she finished, she pulled off the other scarf and tossed it to Charlotte.

"Tie her ankles."

Charlotte frowned. "Are you sure? She seems calm."

"Better safe than sorry. Take my word for it."

Charlotte tied Kitty's ankles.

They stood as Kitty sat staring at them.

"You want to ask her questions now?" asked Shee.

Charlotte shook her head and whispered her answer. "Let's get her to Scotty while she's calm."

Shee nodded. "Good idea."

They propped open the back door.

"We're going to have to carry her," said Charlotte.

Shee nodded. "Move fast in case the neighbors are watching."

Shee grabbed Kitty's arms and Charlotte took her feet to carry the cat to the car. Kitty remained limp, swinging between them like an Easter lamb. When they reached the Volvo, they sat her on the curb, opened the back hatch, and slid her inside.

She remained quiet during the short drive to Scotty's and, when they arrived, Charlotte hopped out to get him while Shee remained behind with the prisoner.

"We have Kitty," she said when Scott answered the door to peer down at her.

A smile leapt to his face. "You do? Where?"

Charlotte led him to the car where Shee had already opened the back.

Scotty leaned down to peer inside the car. "Kitty!" he scowled. "Why is she *tied*?"

"She put up quite a fight," said Charlotte. It felt tacky to mention Kitty still might be a murderer. Instead, she added, "until we mentioned you."

That made Scotty blush.

He leaned in and untied the scarves. Freed, Kitty threw her arms around his neck so he could lift her from the car.

"Why did you *run*?" he asked her. "I was so worried."

Charlotte heard Kitty *purr*. It looked as though the Cat Girl couldn't wipe the smile off her own face.

Scotty carried Kitty inside with Shee and Charlotte following.

He placed Kitty on his sofa, where she pushed herself into the corner, her knees pulled to her chest. She watched them with large blue eyes.

"Thank you. Thank you so much," said Scotty, turning back to Charlotte to wrap her hands inside his own giant mitts.

"I'm glad I could help," said Charlotte. "But now that she's here, we really need to ask her what she knows about Baroness."

Scotty grimaced. "Now? Can you give her a day?"

"We need to know," said Shee. "To help clear *her*."

Scotty sighed and squat down beside Kitty.

"Kitty, do you know what happened to Baroness?"

Kitty blinked at him and then looked away.

"Kitty, please. These people are trying to help."

She shook her head.

Scotty sighed and looked at Charlotte. "I don't think she's going to talk."

"She *has* to."

He fidgeted. "She gets like this. She won't. I'm telling you."

He straightened and moved to them to speak softly behind his hand. "Let me work on her. I'll get the story out of her. You can trust me. I want to clear her, too, you know."

Charlotte sighed. "Fine. I'll come back tomorrow, but remember, I'm going to have to tell the police we found her, too."

He nodded. "Let me get your money."

Scotty paid Charlotte, and then Shee and Charlotte headed for the car.

"My shoulder is killing me," said Shee, rubbing it. "Cat Girl? More like *Tiger* Girl."

"Don't tell Tony that," said Charlotte.

"Tony who?"

Charlotte laughed. "Oh boy. Wait until I tell you about *this* guy."

CHAPTER THIRTY-ONE

Charlotte waved goodbye to Shee and headed home, her mind swirling with questions about Kitty. She couldn't imagine the shy, slight woman murdering two people. Why would she spend all those years with Baroness only to kill her *now*? Had she reached the end of her patience? Did her love for Scotty inspire her to break free from Baroness? Hate and love were both motives for murder, but neither explained Grin. Why would she kill *him*? And why was she trying to rob Felix Payaso? Why was she at Seamus' bar—

Wait a second.

Why was she at Seamus' bar?

She seemed so shy—it would be out of character for her to be at the bar alone.

Charlotte looked at her watch. She'd planned to find Declan and see what he'd discovered about Stephanie.

Maybe, first, a quick stop at The Anne Bonny.

Charlotte drove to Seamus' bar to find Declan's uncle in his usual spot behind the bar, holding court.

"Charlotte!" he called out, as she approached. All heads turned to watch her enter, and she felt her face warm with embarrassment.

A woman sitting at the bar near Seamus pulled her attention from him and scowled.

Charlotte chuckled to herself.

Don't worry, honey, I'm not your competition for Seamus' affections. Seamus is.

"Can I get you a drink?" asked Declan's uncle, rapping the bar with his knuckle. He leaned to the woman at the bar and nodded in Charlotte's direction. "This lass is my nephew's girlfriend."

The woman seemed relieved and nodded a greeting. Seamus had shifted to his flirting accent but didn't seem as far into his cups as the last time she'd seen him.

"No bar decathlon today?" she asked.

"Nah. Only special occasions. How can I help you? Where's my nephew?"

"I imagine he's on his way home from work," said Charlotte. "I'll probably go see him, but I have a question for you first."

He made a gun with his finger and popped it in her direction. "Shoot."

"Remember last night I asked if you'd seen a woman dressed like a nurse in scrubs?"

Seamus grimaced. "Last night...?"

"Yes. That's the same look you gave me then, too."

"Sorry. Not ringin' any bells. I may've had a wee bit too much to drink last night."

"Really. I couldn't tell." Charlotte laughed. "But I have an additional piece of information now that might jiggle your memory."

Seamus shot her with the other hand. "Shoot."

His bar friend giggled into her cocktail.

"Have you ever seen a woman who looks like a cat in here?" asked Charlotte.

His brow knit. "An actual cat? Because we get our fair share of leopard print—"

"An actual cat. A woman wearing cat makeup or a cat costume. She has a mouth like a cat, with a scar running down the center."

"You mean the nurse with the lip?" said a voice to Charlotte's left. She turned to see Stig the bartender walking closer, drying a beer mug with a white cloth as he moved.

"Yes—you saw her?"

"Last night, like you said. She was tiny, thin, cute, but—I know what you mean by cat woman—she had a scar or something here." He touched the spot beneath his nose.

"Was she here with anyone?"

Stig nodded. "That's the thing. It wasn't even the lip that caught my attention. She wasn't drinking, she was just sitting in the corner over there alone, staring."

"At what?"

"I think at a guy sitting two tables over. He was by himself, too. It was weird, but it was busy, and I didn't think much of it."

"Did you recognize the guy?"

"He's been here before—" Stig poked Seamus' arm. "Hey, what's the name of that guy who wears that funny hat? You made a comment about it once."

Seamus sucked on his tooth, scowling. "Funny hat—Oh, the wee one? Felix?"

Charlotte straightened. "Felix Payaso?"

Seamus shrugged and held a flat hand perpendicular to his chest. "Don't know his last name. Little guy. Little hat."

Charlotte nodded. Felix Payaso was a small man, so it could be the same person. *First Kitty shows up at his house, now she follows him to a bar.*

Charlotte turned her attention back to Stig. "Did they talk?"

He put the dry mug on a shelf with the others. "Not that I saw. When you came in, I noticed she was gone. Pretty sure he was gone by then, too, but I'm not sure."

Charlotte walked to the table where Stig said Kitty had been sitting. From there, the woman would have had a clear view of the street.

Did she recognize me from Big Top, hanging out with Frank? Did she leave because she saw me coming?

She clucked her tongue as she moved toward the door,

frustrated anew she hadn't pulled more information out of Kitty.

"Thank you, Stig. That was a lot of help."

He shrugged. "No problem. I'll keep an eye out for them, if you want."

"That would be great." Charlotte waved to Seamus, who'd returned to beguiling the woman at the bar. "I'm going, Seamus."

He glanced up. "May the road rise to meet ye, lassie."

Charlotte rolled her eyes as his lady friend burst into coquettish giggles. Seamus winked.

Outside the bar, Charlotte paused to retrieve her phone. Kitty and Felix had her mind chugging along, and Declan made a great partner for working through a puzzle. She wanted to make sure he was home before she headed to his house.

He answered after one ring.

"Hi—are you home yet?" she asked.

"Yes. Are you coming?"

"Yep. Did you find Stephanie?"

He sighed. "No. Who knows what she's up to? I'm not my ex's keeper."

"I'm sure tomorrow she'll be back at her desk, plotting world domination."

"No doubt," he said, but he sounded unconvinced.

"Okay, well, I wanted to make sure you were home—I'm leaving The Anne Bonny."

"You stopped for a drink?"

She laughed. "This case is enough to drive me to it, but no. I think I've identified that cat thief, though. It's a woman who actually looks like a cat."

"Really? From Big Top, I'm guessing?"

"Yep. I thought Seamus might have seen her, but he didn't remember much—"

"Shocker."

"—Stig said he saw her staring at the same guy she tried to rob. None of it makes sense. I need you to help me work through my clues."

"Okay. I'll be here. Be careful."

"Always. See ya in a bit."

She hung up, smiling to herself, realizing she should have told him to be careful. He was the one looking in on Stephanie.

Before she could take another step, her phone rang and she answered, assuming it was Declan calling her back about something.

"Forget something, sexy?" she asked instead of saying hello.

"Um...Charlotte? It's Daniel."

Charlotte felt her cheeks grow warm when she realized it was Frank's deputy. "Oh, jeeze, I'm sorry Daniel, I thought you were Declan."

"I figured." Daniel sighed. "Anyway, Frank's out of town, and I thought you'd want to know. There's been an attempted murder in Big Top."

"Just now?"

"Yep."

"Attempted? Did they see who it was?"

"Victim's on his way to the hospital, unconscious. Took a bullet to the torso."

"Who was it?"

"A clown...funny name...I wrote it down, hold on..."

Charlotte heard Daniel flipping through the little booklet he always kept on hand.

"Here it is. Neighbor said his name is Scotty Skyscraper."

Charlotte gasped. "Was the cat woman there?"

"The what?"

"I just saw Scotty. I brought—" Charlotte stopped, feeling as if she were incriminating herself to say she'd brought Kitty to Scotty right before he ended up shot. She'd also have to explain why she captured her in the first place.

She chose a new tack.

"When I was there, he was with his girlfriend. Kitty. In the circus she was a cat girl. You'd know her if you saw her."

"No one else was here. For sure, nobody said anything about any cat girls."

"Okay. Okay. I'm coming. I'll see you in a sec."

"I figured. See ya."

Charlotte hung up, stunned.

Did I get Scotty killed?

She was about to step off the curb when she heard the call.

"Meow."

Charlotte spun on her heel to face the alley she'd chased Kitty down the night before.

"Kitty?" she called.

"Meow."

Charlotte scowled. Had Kitty followed her? Maybe she had something to say now. Maybe she hadn't wanted to talk in front of Scotty.

Maybe she was lying in wait with a gun.

"Kitty?" she called again, walking to the alley. Something rustled behind the large trash bin sitting against the wall.

"Kitty?"

A flash popped in the dark. Before she could refocus, something sharp pierced her stomach.

"Ow—"

Charlotte's muscles seized. Crackling filled the air. She collapsed to her knees on the broken cement, struggling to move as someone ran toward her.

Something small and sharp stabbed her arm.

CHAPTER THIRTY-TWO

Declan looked at his watch for the fifth time in as many minutes. It had been an hour since Charlotte said she was on her way. While he knew she could have been distracted by her case, it wasn't like her to make plans and then blow them off without a call.

He tried her phone. It went to voicemail.

He paced a bit.

She said she'd been looking into something at The Anne Bonny, so he tried Seamus' phone.

"Hullo," said his uncle, answering. "How can I help you this fine evening?"

"Is Charlotte there?"

"Charlotte? No. Earlier, looking for some cat lady, but she left maybe an hour ago."

"Can you go outside and see if you see her car?"

"Sure, *boyo*. Gimme a sec."

Declan heard Irish music swell in the background and then fade as Seamus made his way outside.

"Volvo's here," he said after a moment. "Parked across the street. Locked. I don't see her, though."

Declan felt a wave of nerves.

"You're sure she's not in the bar?"

"You think I'm hiding her from you?"

"No, Seamus. But she said she'd be here an hour ago, and she never showed up. Check your cameras?"

"On it."

Seamus hung up, and Declan peeked out his front window.

Nothing. Of course not. Her car sat at Seamus'—did he think she'd be arriving on foot?

He called Mariska.

"Hi, Mariska, it's Declan. Is Charlotte there?"

She hemmed. "Uh, I'm not at home..."

She sounded strange, almost...*guilty*?

"Are you okay?" he asked.

"Yes. Of course. I'm, uh, playing canasta."

Declan thought he heard *wind* on the phone, which seemed odd for an indoor canasta game. Whatever she was up to, there was no point in sending her into a tizzy over what was hopefully nothing.

"Okay. No problem. I was just having trouble reaching her."

"She food-shops at night sometimes to avoid the crowds," said Mariska, her voice shaking as if she were bumping along on a horse. "That place is a cell phone dead zone, except between the bagels and the ice cream in the bakery."

"That's probably it. No biggie. Thanks."

"No problem, sweetheart."

He hung up.

Now what?

Declan made a mental list of things capable of distracting Charlotte enough she'd forget to touch base with him.

Short of personal tragedy, he couldn't think of any.

Wait—her parents.

They were still in town, and they'd definitely sent her into a tailspin.

That had to be it.

Maybe they'd shown up unexpectedly? Maybe they'd whisked her away for a late dinner?

He scrolled through his phone to find the number Mason had shared with him at The Anne Bonny and dialed.

A woman answered.

"Shee?"

"Yep. Hey, Declan. Mason's out on the porch, and I saw your name pop up. I'll get him—"

"Is Charlotte with you?"

"No. Why? Is something wrong?" Shee's tone shifted from cheery chit-chat to an officious monotone.

"She called to say she'd be swinging by but never showed. I can't get her on the phone. Seamus says her car is parked outside the bar, but she's not there. I don't mean to panic, but this isn't like her. I thought maybe she was with you."

"Does Seamus' bar have cameras?"

"He's checking them as we speak," said Declan.

"Any idea why her car is there?"

"She stopped to ask Seamus about the cat woman. Apparently, she was there last night staring at the guy she robbed?"

Shee grunted. "Do me a favor—text us your address. We'll meet you in fifteen."

"I didn't mean for you—"

Shee cut him short. "It's not like we had plans beyond seeing Charlotte. Her *missing* goes right to the top of our to-do list."

"Okay. Will do. Thanks."

Declan hung up and texted his information to Mason's phone. When he finished, he remained staring at the screen, working through his mixed emotions. If Charlotte walked in the door now, he'd feel silly for bothering her parents. At the same time, he felt grateful they were on their way to help.

Something Shee had said echoed through his head.

Missing.

Was Charlotte *missing*?

He hadn't allowed himself to think of her that way.

He tossed his phone at the sofa, his fingers curling into a fist of frustration as it bounced from one cushion to another.

He couldn't sit and wait for Shee and Mason. Where else

could he look? Who could he call—

Frank.

He retrieved the phone and called Frank.

"Hello?"

"Frank? It's Declan. You don't happen to know where Charlotte is, do you?"

"Home, I assume." He cleared his throat. "Why?"

"She was on her way here but never showed. Her car is outside Seamus' bar, but she's not there. I'm a little worried."

"You think something happened?"

"I don't know. It doesn't feel right, though."

"Hm. I got called to Tampa, but it shouldn't take long. I'll be back in an hour, two at the most. Unless you think I should turn around now?"

Declan grimaced. "No. It's probably nothing. She maybe got distracted working on a case."

"Sounds like her."

"One thing you could help with, though. She was at Seamus' asking about a cat woman. Do you know where to find her?"

"A cat woman? You mean the robbery? The makeup on the window?"

"I think so, yes."

Frank grunted. "I didn't even know it was a *her*. Charlotte doesn't always fill me in on everything she's doing for fear I'd stop her."

"How about the guy she was robbing?"

"Felix something."

"Right. You wouldn't happen to have *his* address? She said the cat was watching him at Seamus'."

"Hm. Give me a second, and I'll find it and text it to you. Keep me in the loop on Charlotte."

"Will do."

Declan hung up and tried Charlotte's phone again. This time, someone answered.

A man's voice said *hello*.

Declan straightened. "Who is this?"

"It's Seamus, *boyo*."

"Oh—you scared me. You found her?"

Seamus' pause made Declan's stomach sour.

"The camera showed her walking into the alley," said his uncle.

Declan heard him take a deep breath before continuing.

"That's where I found her phone."

CHAPTER THIRTY-THREE

Darla leaned against the tarped golf cart in her driveway, watching Mariska toddle down the sidewalk toward her. Carolina had dropped off Mean Green Machine only an hour before, and she'd spent the next half hour covering the speed demon with a tarp in case Frank came home early expecting to see Midnight.

In another hour, she'd be behind the wheel racing Gianna. An hour after that, she'd either have her cart back and her debts to Carolina paid, or she'd be packing to move to Mexico, so Frank didn't kill her.

"Hurry up," she urged her friend, looking at her watch.

Mariska started shaking her head at the halfway point between her house and Darla's and didn't stop until she arrived at Darla's driveway. "I can't believe Gianna agreed to another race *already*."

Darla scoffed. "Why wouldn't she? She wants my car, and she doesn't think she can lose. Help me get this tarp off."

Mariska positioned herself to tug at the nylon sheet covering Mean Green Machine. "I can't believe you're risking your *car*." She paused and lolled her head to the left. "Wait, why is this covered?"

"So Frank wouldn't see it isn't Midnight."

"Ah. He'll be livid if he finds out about *any* of this."

"Yep, and he'll be home soon, so let's speed it up there,

sister."

The nylon slid to the ground, and the pair took a moment to admire their new wheels.

"Here goes nothin'," said Darla, balling the tarp and tucking it between a bougainvillea and her house. She returned to drop into the driver's seat.

"Let's see how she purrs."

Mariska climbed aboard. They pulled out of the driveway to the steady beeping of the back-up alarm, and then pointed the cart down the road.

Darla took a deep inhale and looked at her racing partner.

"Ready?"

"As I'll ever be," said Mariska, wrapping her fingers around the cart's handles.

Darla faced forward, knuckles turning white as she gripped the wheel.

She raised her right foot and *stomped* the pedal.

"Holy—"

The car leapt forward like a jungle cat, the women's heads whipping back as if they'd just been rear-ended by an eighteen-wheeler.

"Daaarrrlaaa!" wailed Mariska.

Darla slid her foot from the pedal and eased down on the break.

The cart rolled to a stop.

The two of them sat, panting.

"Well, that was something," said Darla.

Mariska grabbed her neck. "I think you broke my spine."

"Gianna is *not* going to beat this sucker."

"No, but I don't see us surviving, either."

"It's okay. I'll practice on the way there. I just wanted to simulate race conditions that time."

Mariska rolled her head counterclockwise and then back the other way. "Right, but maybe you could simulate warning me first next time."

Darla motored forward at a smoother pace, stopping and

starting several times as they made their way out of the neighborhood.

"I think I've got the hang of it now," she said as they pulled onto Old Swamp Gas Trail.

"It's darker than last time," said Mariska, peering up at the towering pines. "I hate this place."

Darla popped on the headlights. Ahead of them, a pair of glowing eyes disappeared into the underbrush. Mariska pointed.

"That was a Florida panther."

"Pssht. It was a *possum*. Calm down."

"How can you tell?"

"It waddled. Panthers don't *waddle*."

"Maybe she's fat. Maybe she ate a bunch of idiots racing golf carts."

Darla sniggered. "Maybe she ate Gianna. Either way, you're fine—she's full."

"I don't know. She would have spat out Gianna. Too bitter."

They cackled until Mariska's phone rang, and they both nearly jumped out of their seats.

"It's Declan," she said, looking at her screen.

"Don't tell him what we're doing," said Darla. "He'll tell Charlotte, and Charlotte—"

"I got it, I got it." Mariska answered and had a quick conversation before hanging up.

"He was just looking for Charlotte."

Darla nodded. "We're almost there. Ready?"

Mariska put a hand on Darla's shoulder. "Do me a favor. *Don't kill us.* Bob would starve to death waiting for dinner to appear. The man thinks the microwave is a clock."

Darla grinned. "Don't worry. Frank always said I'd die doing something stupid, and I can't let him be right."

The paved portion of the road turned to dirt as they came around a dogleg left.

Mariska pointed. "There they are."

Ahead on the road a collection of golf carts waited with lights glowing in various directions. At the starting line, Gianna and Tabby sat in the same cart they'd used to win Midnight. Another pair of women sat in Midnight.

Darla growled.

"Ready to lose again?" asked Gianna.

Darla sniffed. "My back hurts from clearing space in my garage for your cart."

"Get up to the line," said a cherub-faced woman as she maneuvered her basic white cart out of the way. She angled until her headlights spanned across the starting line. The woman next to her snapped her fingers as if urging Darla to hurry.

"Hey, Snappy—are you on the Sharks or the Jets?" asked Darla, scowling at her.

"They're *witnesses*, so you don't try to run out on us," spat Tabby from her shotgun seat in Gianna's cart. She'd grown even more sneery since their last meeting.

Darla ignored Tabby's comment and leaned forward to peer around her. "Gianna, could you ask your toady to quit croaking?"

Mariska tittered, "*Toady*," she echoed.

The women in Midnight jetted down the road, U-turning to position their lights at the finish line.

"Ready," one of them called back.

Darla motioned to them. "Great. If there's a photo finish, how convenient you have your *friends* here to decide the winner."

"Oh, it won't be *close*. Don't worry about that," said Gianna. She and Tabby laughed like cartoon villains.

"*Idiots*," muttered Darla.

Darla maneuvered Mean Green Machine to the starting line. One of the ladies in the starting cart hopped out to take a position in the middle of the wide dirt road. She held up a white dish towel for the racers to see.

"On your marks..."

Darla looked at Mariska. "Is she serious with this?"

"Get set..."

Darla crouched low in her seat, tucking in her neck, her foot hovering over the pedal. Mariska grabbed the sidebar and braced herself.

"Don't forget your neck. I'm going to stomp it," whispered Darla.

Mariska tucked her chin.

The starter paused, clearly for dramatic effect, and then dashed her dish towel to the dirt.

"Go!"

Something flashed in the corner of Darla's eye as she stomped on the pedal.

Not again.

Tabby had thrown something.

"Not today, Satan!" screamed Darla, throwing out her hand to block the object. She didn't care if she ended up with a fistful of one-eyed newts; she was *not* going to let Gianna win.

Something round and pliable molded itself around her hand, feeling both heavy and soft. Before her mind could flip through a mental Rolodex of possibilities, the round thing exploded with a loud *pop!* and Darla instantly knew what it had been.

Water Balloon—

Liquid showered the side of her head and inside the cart.

Mariska howled. Darla wiped her face, finding the liquid too viscous to be water.

"Oh no, *what is it*?" she screeched.

"Put us down!" screamed Mariska.

"What?" Darla had no idea what Mariska was talking about, as the liquid in the balloon had left her temporarily blinded. "What? I can't see!"

"Put us down!" repeated Mariska.

Darla wiped the liquid from her face and opened her eyes to find herself staring at the starry sky. No road. No trees...

What the—

She looked down and realized on takeoff Mean Green Machine had reared back like an angry stallion. They wheeled forward balanced on two back wheels. Darla twisted her neck to find sparks shooting from the back of the cart as the metal bumper scratched over rocks like a Boy Scout's flint.

On the upside, Gianna still remained beside them, but not for long.

Darla gripped the wheel tighter. "On three, lean forward: One, two, *three!*"

Mariska and Darla lurched forward like synchronized swimmers. The cart dropped to the ground, bounced once, and then tore forward like a rocket.

"Stop!" screamed Mariska after what felt like a second.

"Are you crazy? They'll catch up!"

"No, we *won* already. *Stop!*"

Darla realized she hadn't opened her eyes since the cart landed. When she did, she saw nothing but darkness. She hit the brake and Mariska threw out her hands to brace herself against the dash.

"*Warning!*" she barked.

"You told me to stop!" Darla wiped her face again and twisted in her seat. Through her squinted eyes, she saw the glow of the finish line behind them.

"We won?" she asked.

"By a *mile*. How do you not know this?"

"My eyes were closed."

"While you were driving?"

Darla whooped. "We won!"

"I think I sprained my wrist," moaned Mariska.

Darla smacked her lips. "Olive oil. They threw a balloon full of olive oil. I can taste it now." She made a U-turn to return to the finish line where the starting cart had joined the group. Gianna sat with her hands still on the wheel, staring out into the darkness with such intent Darla wondered if she was working up the power to shoot lasers from her eyes.

Doesn't matter. I won.

She pointed at Midnight and then Gianna's cart.

"That one's mine, that one's mine..." She pointed at the

plain cart. "You can keep that mess."

The woman behind the wheel scowled.

"You cheated. That's not a golf cart," said Tabby, pointing at Mean Green Machine.

"Oh shut up, Tabby," said Gianna.

Tabby's head snapped back, and she gaped at her friend. "But—"

Gianna climbed out of her cart and marched to the white one. "Move over," she snarled at the driver. The woman shifted to the middle of the bench seating and Gianna took the driver's seat.

Tabby, still gawping, returned her attention to Darla. "But—"

Gianna turned to leave, sidling beside Tabby. "Get in or get left."

Tabby found a spot hanging off the back of the white cart.

Gianna twisted to glare at Darla. "I expect a rematch."

Darla hooted. "I expect to lose twenty pounds eating ice cream and donuts. Not gonna happen."

"*Donuts*," echoed Mariska.

Gianna hit the gas.

"Have fun getting three carts home with two people!" She called over her shoulder as she wheeled away.

Darla and Mariska surveyed the two carts in front of them.

"I didn't think of that," said Darla. "I don't want to leave one here."

"No. They'll come back to steal it."

"Exactly. That would be just like them."

They sat a moment in silence.

"Isn't there a puzzle like this?" asked Mariska after a minute. "One of us takes a cart and comes back with a car—no, both of us take a cart and—"

"Just call Bob," said Darla.

Mariska scowled. "But then we'll have three carts and a car and three people…"

"He can watch a cart while we take two carts back and then

come back with one and—" She waved at Mariska. "We'll figure it out."

Mariska nodded.

"Yep."

CHAPTER THIRTY-FOUR

Is someone kicking me?

Charlotte felt the steady thud of something striking her shins.

Is the world rocking?

She struggled to open her eyes. Upon succeeding, she found another pair of eyes staring back at her.

"Glad you could join us," said a muffled voice.

It took a moment, but Charlotte realized she recognized those eyes, and the voice, as muted as it might be.

"Stephanie?"

Something impeded her own speech. Working her jaw and tongue, she explored what felt like a fabric gag in her mouth. Stephanie wore one as well.

Uh oh. This isn't good.

The gravity of the situation seeped into her fuzzy brain.

She and Stephanie both lay on their sides, arms tied behind their backs, ankles bound together with duct tape.

She squinted at Stephanie. "What did you do?"

Stephanie cocked an eyebrow. "What did *I* do?" Face contorting, she shoved the gag out of her mouth with her tongue. It dropped against her chin and lodged there.

"That's a little better," she said.

Jealous of Stephanie's uncovered mouth, Charlotte worked at removing her own gag.

"Where are we?"

"On our way to our deaths, I imagine," said Stephanie.

Charlotte glared, and Stephanie rolled her eyes.

"Fine. Here's what I know. Guy came into my office and hit me with a Taser, twice. I think he shot me up with something after the second zap."

"Scream," said Charlotte, still working on her own gag.

"What?"

"Scream."

"Oh. No point. Look around. Soundproofed. Plus, we're clearly on the road."

Charlotte scanned the box in which they lay. They were moving—every bump clunked her head on the carpeted floor. She guessed they were in some sort of van, but a wall of the same low-pile carpet stood where she, otherwise, might have been able to see the driver. Above their heads, a small round moonroof provided enough light to see.

"Hold on." Stephanie shimmied closer. "Give me your face."

"What?"

"I'll help you get the gag off."

Charlotte stretched forward to let Stephanie bite her gag—and a bit of her cheek.

"Ow."

"Sorry. Hold on."

Stephanie repositioned to drag Charlotte's gag down.

Freed, Charlotte took a few deep breaths. "Thank you."

"Any time. Hey, let me ask you something. Do you think Declan will ever fall in love with me again?"

Charlotte blinked at her. "Are you kidding me right now?"

"What?"

"Well for one, Declan's *my boyfriend.*"

"Yeah. But he was mine first—"

"Two, don't you think we have more pressing concerns at the moment?"

Stephanie rolled her eyes. "Oh, you have no idea."

"What's that supposed to mean?"

"The guy who Tased me is the Big Top Killer."

Charlotte gaped. "*What?* How do you know that?"

"I caught him."

"You *caught* him? Really? Is he in your pocket?"

"I didn't *keep* him. It was catch and release. It's none of my business if he wants to kill circus freaks."

Charlotte closed her eyes, fighting back the urge to *headbutt* the monster lying next to her.

Wait—

Charlotte opened her eyes.

"You said *him*—It was a man?"

"Yep."

Charlotte didn't know if Stephanie was right or telling the truth, but if she was both—Kitty wasn't her killer.

"Who is he?"

"I have no idea."

"Then how do you know—" Charlotte took a deep breath. "You know what? Never mind. We have to get out of here."

"Agreed. But really quick, about Declan—"

Charlotte grit her teeth. "Stephanie, for the love of all things holy, *forget Declan*. We—"

Stephanie shook her head. "But I *can't*. I'm trying to make a decision, and I need input. We don't get chances to chat like this that often."

Charlotte stopped struggling against her bindings. "*Did you stage this so you could ask me about Declan?*"

"Pssht. *No.* Don't be ridiculous."

Charlotte sighed. "Fine. You want input? *No.* I don't think Declan will ever be in love with you again. Okay?"

Stephanie scowled. "Why?"

"Why? Where should I start? For one, you caught a killer and let him go because he has *a right to kill circus folk.*"

"Well, he *does*—"

"No, he *doesn't*. And it's—" Charlotte struggled to find the words. *Sociopath* seemed applicable, but Stephanie would take it as a compliment. *Bloodthirsty* seemed harsh…

"—it's your complete *lack of a moral compass* that will always keep Declan from ever considering you girlfriend material again."

"He loved me before."

"Maybe. Or maybe he was just trying to *save* you."

Stephanie barked a laugh. "*Save* me? I don't need saving. *You're* the one who needs saving. *Look at you.*"

"You're tied up right next to me!" yelled Charlotte.

"Give me ten minutes." Stephanie glanced at the wall separating them from the driver. "I'll be free, and he'll be dead."

"Whatever. You're going to do what you're going to do. But for now, yes, please get free. Make it *five* minutes."

Stephanie nodded. "So you're a *no* on the Declan thing."

"I'm a *no*, but, by all means, feel free to try."

Stephanie chewed her lip, staring at her. "You're probably right. Between you and me, I'd probably break up with him again anyway. Half of me only wants him to piss you off."

Charlotte strained against the bindings around her wrist. "Awesome. Could you maybe turn that spite *on the guy who's kidnapped us?*"

Stephanie ignored her and shifted to gazing through the moonroof as she mused aloud. "Sometimes, I think Declan might be more of a symbolic goal for me..."

"Fascinating. *Really*. I'd love to read your therapy transcript some time. But right now—"

Charlotte stopped struggling as the van slowed and then stop. The women hushed, staring at each other, listening. A door opened and shut, the force of it rocking the vehicle. Charlotte heard two voices speaking outside, both male.

"Welcome to your final destination," said Stephanie in an ominous voice.

Unbelievable.

"We're about to die, and you're still cracking jokes," hissed Charlotte.

"Life sucks anyway."

"Maybe for *you*. *I'm* pretty happy."

Stephanie scoffed. "You would be."

The voices outside moved to the back of the van, outside the double doors.

"Maybe we should pretend we're still out," suggested Charlotte.

Stephanie didn't appear to listen, but a moment later she closed her eyes and tucked her chin to make it appear the gag was still over her mouth. Charlotte did the same as the doors of the van opened. She cracked open an eye to steal a peek.

A clown wearing a tiny bowler hat stared back at her, an artificial red smile circling his otherwise downturned lips. Black spots covered both eyes, stark against the white face paint smeared across his cheeks and forehead. Printed on his white tee shirt were buttons and a collar, giving it the appearance of a more formal work shirt. His baggy pants were four sizes too large and held up by suspenders. They appeared to be crafted from a thousand tiny fabric scraps sewn together.

Other than the makeup and ridiculous clothing, he seemed *familiar*.

The clown placed a small tackle box in the van and opened it to retrieve something. He held up the object, red parking lights glinting against its metal tip.

A syringe.

He reached forward to wrap his fingers around Charlotte's ankle.

"Needle!" she yelped, kicking out with her bound legs. The clown jumped back as she knocked his tackle box to the ground.

"I thought we were playing dead?" asked Stephanie, opening her eyes.

"He has syringes. He's going to knock us out again."

Frown growing deeper, the clown called out.

"Colossus!"

As he turned, Charlotte read the words stamped on the back of his tee.

Felix Funnypants: World's Greatest Clown

Charlotte gasped.

Felix!

The robbery victim.

An enormous man appeared beside Felix, standing a good foot taller than the clown.

"Is that a man or a trained bear?" asked Stephanie.

The clown focused on her, syringe still in his hand.

"Pull them closer," he barked.

The giant grabbed both Charlotte and Stephanie's ankles to drag them closer to the back edge of the van.

Felix raised his needle.

CHAPTER THIRTY-FIVE

Declan climbed into the back seat of Mason's truck.

"Seamus found Charlotte's phone in the alley next to the bar."

Shee twisted in her seat to gape at him. "Her phone?"

Declan nodded. "Frank's on his way back. He doesn't know where the cat woman lives, but I got the address of that Felix person from him. The guy the cat woman robbed."

Shee looked ashen. "I know where the cat is. We took her to her boyfriend's house today."

"So you want to try her first?" asked Mason.

"Yes. We couldn't get her to talk this afternoon," she turned forward, "—but we will this time."

"Yes, we will," muttered Mason, roaring forward. He followed Shee's directions to Big Top, but they didn't get far into the community before Sheriff cruiser's lights appeared, blinking against a small crowd of people gathered behind crime tape.

"That's the clown's house," said Shee. She reached out to place a hand on Mason's thigh. "Charlotte—"

"Charlotte's not hurt," said Declan.

Shee turned. "How do you know?"

"There's too much crime tape. That means Deputy Daniel secured the scene—he never knows when to quit. If Charlotte was hurt he would have called. We'd know."

Shee nodded, grim, clearly not totally convinced. Declan

clung to his assessment, willing himself to be right.

They pulled to the curb and piled out. Declan spotted Daniel and the deputy strolled toward him, his thumbs hanging in his belt.

"Hey, Dec, is Charlotte with you?" Daniel asked, straining to see past him.

"No. We thought maybe she was here?"

"Nope. Not yet. She's gonna miss it."

"Not *yet*?"

"I called her, but I haven't seen her."

Declan's shoulders slumped. Charlotte might have been on her way to Big Top when something happened.

"What happened?" asked Shee, motioning to the house.

Daniel glanced over his shoulder. "We're not sure. Someone called in a gunshot. We found a guy inside with a chest wound, but they already took him to the hospital."

"Tall guy?" asked Shee.

"His feet were *hanging over the gurney*." Daniel snickered and then sobered. "Wait—do you *know* him?"

Shee shook her head. "No. Did he say anything? Was there anyone else here?"

"Just him. No sign of a break in. We got nothin' so far."

"Thanks, Daniel," said Declan. "Hey, have Charlotte give me a call if you see her."

The deputy tipped his hat and strolled away.

"It's got to be the cat girl," said Shee. "Either that or she bolted at the first sign of trouble."

"Neither option gets us to Charlotte," said Mason.

She pointed down the road. "The cat's house is around the corner."

"Let's check it out. Lead the way," said Mason.

They drove to Baroness' house, and Shee spilled out of the cab before Mason fully stopped.

"There's a pet door in the back. I can crawl in," she said, breaking into a sprint.

"Wait," said Mason. He opened his center console and

pulled out a gun. "Take this."

She turned and jogged back to grab the weapon.

Declan opened his own door and put a hand on Mason's shoulder.

"I'll go with her. Someone should keep an eye out here for the cat."

Mason nodded. "Be careful. I don't have another weapon."

Declan jogged around the modular home, following in Shee's path. By the time he caught up, only Shee's feet were poking through the pet flap at the bottom of the back door.

He squatted and whispered through the door.

"Let me in?"

"Wait there. Watch the door for me," she whispered back.

A few minutes later, Shee's head reappeared, poking through the pet door.

"She's not here," she said, shimmying out. "Nothing's changed since Charlotte and I were here earlier."

"Now what?"

She put her hands on her hips. "Should we check your uncle's?"

Declan shook his head. "Seamus is a pro. If there'd been any clues, he would have found them."

Shee's attention pulled to the house next door. "Tony the Tiger Tamer lives there. Charlotte said he gave her the creeps. Worth a stop while we're here."

They walked out front to motion to Mason to wait and then approached Tony's front door to knock.

No one answered.

Declan frowned. "Should we try the back? Maybe there's an unlocked window?"

"Nah. Let's take the path of least resistance." Shee broke the glass of Tony's front door with the muzzle of the gun and reached in to unlock it.

"That works, too," said Declan.

They entered to make a quick sweep of the house. Declan ogled the giant, life-sized tiger statue, touching its fur only to recoil at how real it felt.

Shee reappeared from her inspection of the back rooms.

"Anything?" he asked.

"I can tell you this freak has jumped a few notches on *my* suspect list," she said, tucking the gun in her waistband. "But no. No sign of Charlotte."

"Maybe we should try Felix's?" asked Declan as they headed back to the truck.

"We're running out of other options."

Mason glowered at Shee as she entered.

"Was breaking and entering at the neighbor's house necessary?" he asked.

Shee shrugged. "Ultimately, no. Declan has the directions to our next stop."

Mason shifted into drive, and, using the address Frank had texted, Declan directed him to Felix's house. They parked two houses down from the address.

"Give me my gun," said Mason, holding out his hand.

Shee frowned but handed over the weapon before they headed toward Felix's house.

No lights glowed inside.

"Doesn't look like he's home," said Mason.

"Good." Shee motioned to the side of the house. "He's got a lanai. Let's go through there."

Mason shook his head. "We've got no good reason to break into this man's house."

"Last one, I promise," said Shee. "You have to turn every stone, or when you get to the end, you have a bunch of stones you have to go back and turn."

Mason squinted at her. "I'm sure that made more sense in your head." He motioned to the lanai. "After you."

Shee and Declan split to try the windows, while Mason tugged on the door.

"Locked," he said.

"Got one," said Declan, sliding open a side window.

She pushed past Mason. "Boost me." She thrust her open

hand at him. "And give me the gun."

He grimaced. "Shee—"

"Are *you* going to crawl through this little window? Give me the gun."

Mason muttered something Declan couldn't hear and surrendered the weapon. Bracing his artificial leg, the big man stooped to boost her. Shee folded herself through the opening and slid inside. She unlocked the slider.

"I'm not hearing anything," she said, as Mason and Declan stepped inside. Mason eased the gun from her hand.

"I'll take this."

They moved into the living room with the SEAL in the lead. Declan scanned the living room and kitchen, finding nothing but predictable decorating and neat housekeeping. Mason checked the bathroom in the hall and then tried the door across from it.

"Locked," he said. "Stay here while I clear the back."

Shee nodded, and Mason disappeared into the master bedroom only to reappear a minute later.

"Clear," he said, staring at the locked door. He eyed Declan.

"So how tight are you with the local sheriff?"

"Very."

Mason nodded. "That's good. We might need a favor by the end of this." He took a position with his gun pointed at the locked door. "You've got two legs. Want to do the honors?"

"My pleasure." Declan took a step back and then kicked the door to the left of the knob. The flimsy wood exploded. The door flung open, bounced off something, and swung back.

Mason stepped forward to ease open the door with the tip of his gun. After a second, he flipped on the light.

"Holy circus, Batman," muttered Shee.

Circus posters and memorabilia covered every inch of the small room, most of it clown-related. A handprinted banner strung along the top of the northern wall declared, *Felix Funnypants: World's Greatest Clown.*

"She's not here," said Mason, lowering the gun.

Shee entered the room, stepping over a collection of juggling balls in a netted bag.

"Let's go. We don't have time to pick through this guy's obsession," said Mason.

"Why is the door locked?" asked Shee.

"Because he's embarrassed?"

She studied a lined essay book sitting open in the center of the desk. "Or he's hiding something—" She flipped through the pages. "Hey. There's a list here with two names crossed out. *Baroness von Chilling* and *Grin the Bullet Catcher.*"

"So?" asked Mason.

"They're the murders Charlotte's investigating," explained Declan.

Shee held up the book for Mason and Declan to see. The page's title was scrawled in thick black ink, perched above a list of six names.

BT BOARD

Shee poked at it with her index finger. "Felix clearly considers himself the greatest clown in the world." Shee gestured to the banner on the wall. "Yet he doesn't live in Big Top. Why?"

Mason's eyebrows raised. "Because he's a wackjob?"

"No. Well, yes, maybe, but who would have actually blocked him?"

"The HOA Board," said Declan, following her thread. "*Big Top* Board. He's killing off the current board so he can get a fresh vote."

Mason scratched at his hairline. "Clowns sure have changed since I was a kid."

Declan scanned at a collection of photos on the wall. "Shee, look at this."

She moved to Declan's side to study the framed photos. Circus clowns grinned and tumbled in each picture, each shot seemingly taken from the bleachers. On each clown, a tiny face had been glued. The same face each time.

"I'm going to go out on a limb and say that's Felix," said

Shee.

Declan's gaze swept over the room, clocking every photo of Felix in face paint.

"That's it. He's not a *real* clown," he said.

"How do you know that?" asked Mason.

Declan gestured to the images of Felix stationed around the room. "Look at the photos. They're all staged. Not one shot of him working in a real circus. That's why they didn't let him into Big Top."

Mason scowled. "And Charlotte figured out his secret?"

Declan nodded. "She does that."

While they were talking, Shee had been flipping through the notebook. She held it out for the two of them to see. "What do you make of this?"

The men moved in to get a better view. Shee'd opened the book to a crude drawing of two stick figures with circles for breasts and *X*'s for eyes. The figures sat on what looked to Declan to be a trapeze, hanging high in the air from a line suspended between two poles.

"Is that *fire*?" asked Mason, pointing at layered triangles jutting from the bottom of the poles.

"*Two* women," said Declan, under his breath.

Shee looked at him. "Does this mean something to you?"

Declan swallowed. "My ex-girlfriend, Stephanie, might be missing, too."

"*Might* be?"

Declan pulled at his chin. "Earlier, I got a weird call from her. I went to check and found a table turned over at her office. Her things were there, but she wasn't."

"Did you call the police?" asked Shee.

"No. She's got a history of crying wolf for attention. I figured she was up to something."

"Staging her own kidnapping?" asked Mason. "Seems extreme."

"Not for her," said Declan. "Not even close."

Shee looked back down at the drawing. "Well, if this is her

and Charlotte, I'd say *she's* the one in trouble this time." She tossed the book back on the desk. "Let's go."

"Where?" asked Mason.

Shee called over her shoulder as she jogged into the hall, "The Big Top."

CHAPTER THIRTY-SIX

Kitty ducked into the bushes as the big black truck pulled to the curb down the street from Felix's house. The headlights went dark, and three people climbed out.

She recognized the woman. The brunette had been with the younger woman—the one who chased her from the bar where she'd been watching Felix.

She didn't know the men. Both were big.

The group headed for Felix's house as Kitty receded deeper into the shrubbery. They didn't knock, instead opting to head for the side lanai, where they opened a small window for the woman to struggle through—the same window she'd shimmied through a few days earlier.

What are they doing?

The woman unlocked the door. Once all three had disappeared inside, Kitty crept to the kitchen window facing the back yard and peered through. As the strangers moved through the home, she moved to the next window, only to find her view blocked by curtains. She put her ear against the wall. Hearing nothing, she moved to the next window to watch the biggest man walk around Felix's bedroom before leaving.

They skipped the locked room.

She'd been trying to get into that room when Felix woke up and chased her out of the house.

Kitty spotted a bucket near the back door and placed it

upside down beneath the curtained window. Standing on it, she pressed her ear to the glass. Something crashed inside.

"She's not here," said one of the men.

Kitty pressed her ear tighter to the glass as the group talked, her eyes growing wider as they discovered and discussed more information.

"The Big Top," said the woman.

Kitty gasped.

They're going to Big Top's tent.

Jumping off the bucket, Kitty sprinted behind the neighbor's house and popped out to the street two houses down. Glancing to the right she saw the woman and two men leaving the lanai.

They're coming.

Kitty bolted to the back of the big truck and climbed inside the flatbed, curling into a flattened ball tucked behind the cabin. As she was wearing her black evening costume, she blended with the bed.

She held her breath as the people reentered the truck. The engine roared.

Soon they'd be back at Big Top.

Kitty smiled.

She'd see Felix there.

CHAPTER THIRTY-SEVEN

"Carry them inside," said Felix, pointing to the faux big top tent.

Colossus stared at the two bound women lying on the floor of the van and scratched his enormous balding skull.

"I dunno. This don't seem right."

"Just take them inside."

"You're not going to hurt them, are you?"

Felix huffed a sigh. "No, of course not. It's for a photoshoot, remember?"

Colossus nodded, wiping his nose on the back of his forearm. He grabbed the blonde's legs and slid her to the edge of the van. Hefting her to his chest, he lifted her, draped over his arms as if she were an afghan, and then tossed her over one shoulder. He pulled the brunette out of the van and threw her over the other shoulder.

Felix stared.

The giant would be *terrifying* if he wasn't such an idiot. Felix had met him at a bar. He'd been frequenting the waterholes favored by the Big Top circus folk for over a year, chatting them up and banking insider knowledge about circus life to enrich his own lies.

He'd met so many circus people and had gathered so many stories—still, all his research hadn't been enough to convince the Big Top board he'd been an *employed* clown. Baroness had figured him out—locked in on him with those squinty black eyes and seen through him.

How'd that work out for her?

The memory of his humiliating board review made his hands curl into fists and his vision turn black. To keep from exploding, he focused on the unconscious blonde woman's slack expression as Colossus ferried her to the big top.

Not so smart now, are you?

Self-satisfaction squelched his rage.

Who did Stephanie Moriarty think she was? Did she think he wouldn't come after her?

Though, he still didn't know how she'd figured out *he* was the Big Top Killer.

He'd been so careful.

Felix took a deep breath.

It didn't matter. Soon she'd be dead along with the detective. In the end, their meddling had proven serendipitous. He'd kill the women in spectacular circus fashion, and the murders would be pinned on the Big Top Killer—rightfully so. But their deaths would throw the authorities off his motives.

Perfect.

Then, he'd knock off the rest of the small-minded board members who'd voted against letting him retire in Big Top. Why should it matter he never actually worked in a circus? He was more devoted to clown life than half the idiots living there now.

He couldn't have quit the force to travel with a circus. He would have lost his pension. And he couldn't work as a clown on the weekends—his fellow police officers would have laughed him out of town. But he'd practiced every weekend to perfect his art. He'd read all the circus books and seen all the movies. He'd flown hundreds of miles to watch performances and collected over five hundred autographs.

How many of the clowns in Big Top were *that* dedicated to their craft?

None. That's how many.

The new board would understand. And he could tell them having an ex-cop around might be a good idea—especially with someone murdering all their residents...

Felix grabbed his satchel and followed the giant into the tent to direct him toward one of the tightwire poles.

"Put them over there."

While Colossus finished his job, Felix worked his way to the control room and used the switchboard to lower a trapeze to the ground not far from where the women lay. Reaching into his bag, he produced a roll of duct tape and strolled back out to Colossus.

"Here." Felix tossed him the tape. "Sit them side-by-side on the trapeze and duct-tape them to it."

Colossus stared at the roll of tape in his hand before looking back at Felix.

"Huh?"

Felix sighed. "Duct-tape them so they don't fall off when I raise the trapeze, but make sure they're sitting when you do it, like they're on a swing."

Colossus' expression twisted into the same mask of confusion and concern he'd had since first seeing the women in the van.

"I need it done by the time I get back," snapped Felix. He waited a moment to ensure the giant had started working and then strode outside to don his giant floppy shoes he'd had to remove to drive. When he returned, he threw his hands into the air.

"And now, introducing the world's greatest clown—*Felix Funnypants!*"

Colossus clapped his approval as Felix waddled forward. "You look funny."

"That's the idea. Are they secure?" Felix asked, tugging on the tape bindings holding the women in seated positions to the trapeze.

"Yep."

Felix nodded. Everything seemed tight. He couldn't imagine a way the women could fall off.

Not until the wire snapped, anyway.

"Good job." Unable to reach his henchman's shoulders, he clapped him in the center of his back and then slipped into the control room to raise the trapeze.

Button pushed, he stepped out to watch the women rise into the air with his thumbs hanging on his suspenders.

"Perfect. Here." He handed Colossus his phone. "I need you to take pictures. Hold on while I climb up."

Colossus took the phone. Felix mounted the ladder attached to the nearest pole and climbed to the platform above. The women dangled in front of him, their chins pressed against their chests.

"Okay, take a bunch—don't stop clicking," he called down.

Colossus pointed the camera skyward.

Felix posed, straining to lean as close to the women as possible as he grinned down at the camera.

"Get on the trapeze!" Colossus urged him.

Felix frowned. He didn't love heights.

"There's no room," he called back.

A few more poses and he climbed down the ladder.

"Did you get them?" he asked, snatching his phone from the giant's paw to flip through the photos.

Colossus nodded. "I got a bunch."

Pleased with the results, Felix moved back to the control room and motored the trapeze holding the women to the center, dangling equidistant from each pole. Satisfied, he asked Colossus to join him as he returned to the van to get his gas can.

He'd leave the soft-hearted moron in the van while he finished the final phase of his plan.

Felix's phone buzzed and he glanced at it to see the camera in the circus room of his house had captured movement.

He watched the playback as the door exploded open and three people entered.

Thieves?

As his stomach churned with dread, he saw the woman of the group open the notebook lying open on his desk.

All his plans were inside.

Not thieves.

They were looking for him.

They'd come to the big top next.

I need backup.

Felix flipped through his contacts until he found the number of a danger act he'd met—a strange, angry couple, obsessed with whips, guns, and knives.

They'd made it clear they'd do anything for a buck.

CHAPTER THIRTY-EIGHT

Charlotte opened her eyes and yipped.

"What? What?" asked Stephanie, her head popping up. She looked down. "What the—"

Charlotte jerked at the sound of Stephanie's voice so close to her ear and then gasped as her world wobbled.

"Why is the ground all the way down there?" asked Stephanie.

"Don't *move*," said Charlotte as they swung back and forth. "We're duct-taped to a trapeze."

"*Why?*"

"I don't know, but it can't be good."

Stephanie shook her head. "I have to admit, I did *not* see this coming."

Charlotte studied the duct tape around her left hand, securing it to the wire supporting her side of the trapeze. More tape wrapped around her waist, holding her fast to the seat—a rod about the width of a broomstick.

"I'm torn about whether it's smart to break free up here," said Stephanie.

"I had the same thought. Do you see anyone?"

Stephanie scanned the ground. "No."

"I guess we'd better try while we can." Charlotte gnawed at the tape around her left hand as Stephanie worked on her right.

Their opposite hands were secured to the bar between their hips.

Charlotte scissored with her eyeteeth and jerked on the tape with her molars until the bindings tore.

"I think I'm making progress," she said.

"Me too," came the muffled response. "Hey."

Stephanie's tone made Charlotte pause. She turned to find Stephanie looking at her.

"What's wrong?"

Stephanie sighed. "Some tiny part of me wants to apologize."

"To me? *Now*?"

"Yeah." Stephanie sighed. "You're not *that* bad."

"Gosh, thanks. Stop, I might cry."

"I just wish you didn't exist."

Charlotte nodded. "Of course."

"So, just in case something goes wrong here, this is my official apology for anything I've done to you in the past and may do to you in the future."

Looking pleased with herself, Stephanie returned to gnawing her bindings.

Charlotte remained staring at her.

"I can't decide if that was an apology or a threat."

Stephanie shrugged. "Can't it be both?"

Charlotte heard a door open and looked down to spot Felix entering the big top. He slammed the door behind him, looking to be in a panic. Placing something large and red on the ground, he tugged a small set of bleachers toward the door, as if to barricade them. Once he had them in place, he fumbled a phone from somewhere inside his crazy pants.

"Is that a gas can?" asked Stephanie.

Charlotte zeroed in on the red box near Felix's feet.

Oh.

She looked at Stephanie.

"Chew faster."

CHAPTER THIRTY-NINE

Mason's truck roared down the street parallel to the field where the circus community's big top stood. Shee slapped the passenger side window as she spotted a van parked outside the striped structure.

"*There*—that has to be him."

Mason hit the gas. "Hold on."

He jerked the wheel to the right and plowed the truck into the split rail fence surrounding the outer perimeter of the field. Wood exploded, rails tumbling, only to have the truck press them into the soft Florida turf.

A large man walked around the van to stare at them as they bounced across the field.

"He looks bigger than he did in his pictures," said Declan.

A smaller man in a clown costume appeared, breaking from somewhere at the front of the van, bolting for the big top. He ran quickly for a man in very large and very strange pants, holding a large red plastic container pressed against his chest.

"There's Felix," said Shee, pointing. "He's carrying something." She looked at Mason. "Did that look like a gas can?"

Mason charged his truck ten feet from the van and hit the brakes hard to slide to a stop. Before any of them could open a door, a gunshot rang out. Something struck the truck.

"Get down," said Mason, pulling his own weapon from the

center console.

The giant ran to the opposite side of the van and ducked down.

"We have to get inside," said Shee. "Charlotte could be in there right now."

Declan opened his door. "I'll go. You distract him."

Mason turned his attention to Shee.

"Get out. Get behind the truck."

The three of them exited the truck on the passenger side. Mason glanced at Declan.

"Ready to run?"

Declan nodded.

Mason released two shots, both striking the front of the van as Declan bolted to the big top. The giant ducked out of view and returned fire without looking, his hand peeping over the nose of the van like a bullet-spitting snake. He popped off five more before they heard the empty clicking.

"He's out," said Mason.

"I'm going to help Declan," said Shee.

Before Mason could answer, a loud crack popped behind them. Shee watched as the gun flew from Mason's hand as if it had been yanked by a string. He barked in pain.

Shee followed the path of the gun to watch it land fifty feet away in the tall grass. Between them and the weapon stood a man and a woman, both blonde, both dressed in leather. The woman held a long black leather whip in her hand.

"Where did *they* come from?" asked Mason, holding his bleeding hand. "Get out of the strike zone."

Mason took a few steps toward the pair. "This is going to hurt," he muttered.

Shee realized his plan.

"Are you *crazy*?"

Before she could talk him out of it, the woman slung back her arm and released the whip a second time. Mason ducked to the left, snatching the leather out of the air with his right hand. Grimacing, he jerked the weapon from her grasp.

Clearly stunned, the woman looked to the man by her side. They charged forward.

Mason tossed the whip far away behind them.

"Why'd you do *that*?" asked Shee.

He looked at her. "Do *you* know how to use a whip?"

"Um, no—" Shee looked over her shoulder to see the giant lumbering toward them from the other direction. She slapped Mason's arm to get his attention. "You take the big one."

The couple was almost on them as Mason and Shee squared up. Shee glanced back at the giant again, hoping they had time to dispense with the couple she'd nicknamed the Leather Twins before he arrived.

They didn't.

She had every confidence in Mason's skills, but she didn't like the odds.

"*Rowwwwwrrrr!*"

Shee jumped as an ungodly howl filled the air. As the Leather Twins reached them, a flash of black caught her eye, launching from the bed of Mason's truck.

Shee watched as human-sized black cat flew through the air to land on the male half of the hostile pair. Fingers curled, the cat gripped the man around his neck with her legs and clawed at his face.

The man stumbled back, screaming. "My eyes!"

His partner stumbled back and fell to one knee, gaping.

Mason motioned to the stunned woman. "Yours." He swung a fist over her head as she ducked away. She spun in time to see his fist connect with the giant's chest. In all the cat commotion, she'd forgotten about the approaching big man. He must have been seconds from grabbing her.

The giant stumbled back a step before reaching out, searching for Mason's neck.

Mason knocked away his hands.

That was the last move Shee saw before the blonde on the ground gathered her wits enough to fumble something out of the crossbody bag slung around her shoulder.

Something black appeared in her hand.

A gun.

No time to run away.

Shee took option two.

She sprinted toward her adversary, praying her instincts were correct. The woman didn't look comfortable with her gun. She guessed it would take a minute—

The blonde pointed the gun at her and, wincing, pulled the trigger.

No!

Shee threw herself to the ground hoping to dodge the bullet.

Nothing happened.

She looked up to find the woman frantically fiddling with her weapon.

Had it jammed? Did she forget the safety?

It didn't matter—Shee probably wouldn't get lucky a second time.

Having *metaphorically* dodged a bullet, the breath Shee'd been holding released as she jumped back to her feet. The woman raised the gun again. Shee dove at her legs like a linebacker.

The gun fired as she slammed into the blonde's thighs, and the two of them hit the ground. Air burst from the woman's lungs. Shee rose to her knees, straddling her foe, and jerked the gun from her hand by the warm muzzle, preparing to smack her on the side of her head with it.

No such luck.

The woman blocked her swing and punched her in the face with her opposite hand.

Ow.

Shee's jaw throbbed, the iron taste of blood in her mouth. She hadn't seen the punch coming. The woman's unfamiliarity with guns had tricked her into thinking she couldn't fight either.

Wrong.

The blonde tried to wrestle the gun back. Shee used both hands to jerk it away from her. Certain she wouldn't have the time to point and shoot before the whip-witch grabbed the weapon again, she tossed it away and raised a fist.

Grabbing her shirt, the blonde jerked her down while raising herself up. Their skulls banged together.

Shee saw stars. She fought to keep focus as the woman hauled back her own fist. This time, Shee saw the attack coming, but her head felt too fuzzy to dodge.

Am I losing this fight?

She couldn't lose. If she fell unconscious, the woman would double-team Mason with the giant. After that, Declan would be fair game, and Felix would be free to finish whatever nefarious game he had planned.

Charlotte had to be in the big top.

I can't lose.

Eyes fluttering, she jerked back to feel the breeze of the woman's fist blow past her chin. The woman scuttled back like a cockroach and pushed to her feet. Shee stood as well, taking a moment to steady herself on her wobbly feet.

She glanced over her shoulder at Mason. Clearly, he'd decided not to *wrestle* the giant. Instead, he circled the man like a gadfly, peppering him with lightning-fast rabbit punches, wearing him down. The giant roared.

Shee knuckled up.

"I'm over this," she said.

The woman's lip curled. She lunged forward, fist first. Shee dodged right, cracking the woman on the jaw as she passed her.

The blonde fell to the ground with a loud *oof!* Shee dropped onto her back and put her in a sleeper hold. It didn't take long before she went limp.

Shee scrambled to her feet. The male half of the Leather Twins remained on the ground, curled in a fetal position, moaning and covering his eyes.

The cat woman had disappeared.

Mason continued to dodge the giant's blows. One mighty

missed swing pulled the monster's momentum forward, and Shee expected Mason to take the clean shot at the man's head.

He didn't.

He let the monster stumble forward and then, shifting, kicked his knee out from the side. The big man screamed and collapsed.

"Stop, stop, stop," he begged, rolling on the ground, holding his knee. "Don't hurt them."

Mason wiped his bleeding lip on the back of his hand.

"Hurt who?" he asked.

"The girls." The giant pointed. "Felix said you were here to hurt the photo girls."

Mason and Shee's gazes followed his gesture to the faux tent.

"She's in there," said Mason.

Before they could take a step, the door of the building opened, belching a billow of gray smoke.

Declan appeared with a limp girl in his arms.

It wasn't Charlotte.

CHAPTER FORTY

"Got it!" exclaimed Stephanie, holding up her now free hand.

Charlotte stared down at Felix. "We have bigger problems now."

"How—" Stephanie leaned down to watch Felix shake the last of the liquid in his red cannister onto the pole. "Oh."

Felix gawped at the trapeze, pointing as Stephanie's hand broke free.

"Hey, cut that out!"

Using her teeth, Charlotte tore away the last of the tape holding her left hand in place and began working on her waist in earnest.

"I'm going to kill you, you know," Stephanie yelled down at Felix.

In response, Felix produced a lighter and set the pole ablaze.

"Good job," muttered Charlotte. "Antagonize the guy with the fire."

Without further comment, Felix toddled out the back of the big top through a pair of double doors.

Charlotte did her best to ignore the flames and concentrate on the tape around her right hand. Pulling it free, she held it up for Stephanie to see.

"I think you can slip out now, too. Try it," she said.

Stephanie jerked her hand a few times. On the third attempt, she groaned as the tape ripped away, taking arm hair and skin with it. She rubbed her wrists and twisted toward the burning pole.

"Does getting free even matter? The ladder's ash and the fall would kill us."

Charlotte pulled the rest of the tape from around her waist and whooped as the trapeze wobbled. She clung to the side wire with both hands.

"We'll swing," she said, knowing the math wouldn't work. Even if they swung as far as possible, it would only take them either back to the burning pole or short of the other pole. Neither spot offered a way to the ground without broken bones, internal injuries, and more than likely, death.

Stephanie peered down. "How far you think?"

Charlotte didn't bother to look. "Fifty feet. There's a fifty percent chance a person will die from a fall of four stories, which is forty-eight feet."

Stephanie looked at her. "How do you know *that*?"

Charlotte shrugged. "I read it somewhere."

"What good luck that was. It turned out to be useful knowledge."

"Charlotte!"

At the sound of the voice, both women whipped their attention to the front door. Declan's head poked through, visible between the seats of the bleachers Felix had used to block the door.

"Charlotte!" he called again as he shimmed through and shoved the bleachers aside.

"Declan!" called Charlotte. She wanted to wave but didn't dare let go of the wire.

"He sees me up here, too, right?" asked Stephanie.

Charlotte ignored her and, with great trepidation, let go of the wire with one hand so she could point at the control building. "There's a panel in there. You can lower us!"

Declan nodded and flew into the booth. He appeared again a moment later, cupping his mouth to create an impromptu megaphone.

"The wiring's torn out."

Charlotte felt the blood drain from her face.

Declan glanced at the fire and then bolted to the opposite pole to mount the ladder.

"Start swinging," said Charlotte.

Stephanie harrumphed once, and then, in time with Charlotte, swung her legs until the trapeze moved. As expected, the furthest they could swing still fell short of Declan's platform.

Declan grabbed the other trapeze hooked to the pole on the opposite side.

"I'm going to swing out and get you," he called.

Charlotte nodded, finding herself, for the first time, doubting her boyfriend's chances of success. She looked at Stephanie.

"You've known him longer than I have—has he ever done *anything* like this before?"

Stephanie hooked her mouth to the side. "That'd be a *no.*"

Declan took the trapeze in hand and then seemed to reconsider. Instead, he stepped over it and sat on it.

"Okay, here I come," he called.

"This is adorable," said Stephanie, grunting as she pumped their trapeze. "We all get to die together."

Charlotte glared at her. "Shut *up.*"

Declan released from the platform and swung toward them, coming up short.

"Hold on. I have to get this going," he said, gliding back toward the platform.

Charlotte glanced over her shoulder. The flames had nearly reached the platform behind them. Once it reached the connected wire suspending their trapeze...

Declan swung forward again, this time flying to the limit

of his arc.

"We still don't reach," said Charlotte, her stomach doing flips. "How is that possible?"

She could see from the expression on Declan's face that he'd come to the same conclusion.

"Hold on," he said.

Charlotte watched him straighten in his seat. He took a deep breath.

Oh no.

Declan flipped backwards.

Charlotte gasped.

"No!"

Declan's knees remained hooked on the bar, his torso hanging down. Pumping with his body, he forced the trapeze to climb again.

"I'm coming. Get ready to grab my hands," he called. "Charlotte, you first."

"Well, I guess that settles that," said Stephanie.

Charlotte blinked at her, her mind wrestling with the idea of leaping off her own swinging trapeze.

Declan arced back and flew toward them. As their arcs met in the middle, he reached out.

"Now!"

Not an ounce of Charlotte wanted to release her wire, but she knew if she delayed, it would only make things more difficult and more dangerous for all of them.

She fell forward, arms outstretched, reaching for Declan.

Declan's fingers clamped around her wrists, and she jerked forward...

And for a moment, she was weightless.

Then she felt Declan's left hand sliding from her wrist.

Stephanie screamed.

Everything stopped.

Charlotte's straining shoulder snapped her from her shock. She opened her eyes to find Declan staring at her.

He looked grim and...*still?*

How am I holding him here?

Charlotte looked down to realize her butt remained stuck to the trapeze. Stephanie had fallen and hung, dangling in mid-air, one hand on their trapeze, one gripping Declan's wrist and his gripping hers in turn.

"That worked *perfectly*," growled Stephanie. "Now what?"

Charlotte felt tape around her waist tearing. *She'd missed a piece.* It held her to the seat when she tried to jump.

"The tape's giving," she said, straining to keep her fingers locked around Declan's wrist. Her weight had swung too far forward for her to remain on the trapeze with the tape holding her there.

Declan grit his teeth. "When it does, climb up me to the trapeze."

Charlotte gaped at him. "Are you crazy?"

"It's our only shot," he said. "See if you can pull me closer, so I can grab your trapeze. That'll keep me stable."

Charlotte nodded. "Okay, hold—"

Before she could pull him close, a whipping noise sliced through the air behind her.

The fire had reached the wires and burned through the connections.

The trapeze fell from beneath her.

Frantic, she threw out her other hand so both gripped Declan's right. A moment later, she was swinging with him back toward his platform, Stephanie dangling beside her from his left arm. Somehow his trapeze still had support, but she didn't know for how long.

"Hold on!" roared Declan.

Their weight kept the trapeze from arcing back far enough to reach the platform. Stephanie spat words Charlotte didn't recognize but felt sure were curses in other languages.

Their swinging slowed as Declan strained to hold them both. It was clear he wouldn't be able to support them for much longer.

"Climb up," he croaked.

"There's no way," said Stephanie. She looked at Charlotte. "Fifty-percent chance, you said?"

Charlotte nodded.

Stephanie locked on Declan's beet-red face.

"Let go of me."

"No. *Climb.*"

She shook her head. "Let go." She smiled. "You know nothing can kill me."

Declan looked pained.

"I think I really did love you…" she added, before looking at Charlotte. "You, not so much."

She let go of Declan's wrist, her fingers splayed.

He roared and gripped harder to hold her.

"Steph!"

Charlotte watched as Stephanie's hand slipped through Declan's fingers. He was helpless to stop it.

"Steph!"

Stephanie fell.

She hit the ground with a sickening thud.

She didn't move.

"Take my other hand," said Declan, thrusting his left at Charlotte.

Charlotte grabbed his other hand.

"I'm going to pull you up. Grab my shirt, my pants, anything you can get hold of and climb to the trapeze."

She nodded and did as she was told. Declan bit his lip and strained, lifting her enough for her to grab his torso with one arm and grip the seat of his shorts with her other hand. Somehow, she found the strength to pull herself up, Declan helping every inch of the way until she gripped the trapeze.

"I've got it!" she said.

"Keep going."

Declan boosted her bent knee. She made her way up until she stood on the bar, straddling his knees. Holding the side wires, she bent to help him to a seated position. He wrapped his arms around her leg and pressed his face against her thigh.

"I thought I lost you," he said, panting.

She bent down to wrap her arms around his neck, holding him to her.

"I'm so sorry," she said. The growing smoke made it hard to see, but Charlotte could make out Stephanie's still form on the ground below.

Declan shifted to the side so she could sit beside him. "Hurry. The rest of the wires are going to snap any second."

They pumped their legs to start the trapeze swinging.

A loud *crack!* made Charlotte jump. She twisted, knowing what she'd find. The burning pole had snapped. It toppled toward them.

Charlotte screamed.

Wires whipped past her head. Declan threw up his hands to shield them as they fell.

Trapeze dropping like a wild elevator, they hurdled toward the remaining pole.

"Hold on!" yelled Declan.

His body slammed against the ladder, absorbing most of the blow. Somehow, he kept the presence of mind to throw his arms around the pole and stop their decent. Charlotte threw her arms around *him*. They bounced as their trapeze tumbled to the ground below.

Declan groaned.

"Are you okay?" she asked.

He motioned down the ladder. "Go. Go. We have to get out of here."

Charlotte found footing on the ladder attached to the pole and helped Declan ease himself onto it.

"Grab a rung," she said.

"Got it. *Move.*"

Charlotte led the way, hustling down the ladder as the building filled with smoke. When they reached the ground, she found the burning pole had hit the ground fifteen feet from Stephanie's prone body. They ran to her, burning embers dancing around them like molten rain.

Declan scooped Stephanie up into his arms and, they ran for the exit, smoke belching out after them as they threw open the doors.

Charlotte coughed, her hand on Declan's back as he led the way. As the smoke cleared, she spotted her parents staring at Declan. Their faces lit as they spotted her behind him.

"Charlotte!"

Shee and Mason ran to them, Mason taking Stephanie from Declan, Shee throwing her arms around Charlotte to help her away from the burning building.

Mason started CPR on Stephanie's lifeless form.

"*Aaaieee!!*"

A scream tore from the direction of the burning big top.

"Is someone still inside?" asked Shee.

"No. Felix went out the back," said Charlotte.

Shee looked at Mason.

"You got this?"

He looked up and nodded. Declan was already on the phone with nine-one-one.

Shee took off running around the big top.

Charlotte ran after her.

They both skid to a stop as they rounded the back of the tent. On the ground lay Felix, half naked, covered in scratches. His crazy pants had been shredded and used to bind him.

His eyes were wild. Flames reached through the door standing two feet to his left. Charlotte could feel the heat baking the man as they moved in to drag him from the danger zone.

"She's insane!" he wailed.

CHAPTER FORTY-ONE

The funeral had been small—just Declan, Charlotte, Seamus, Frank and Darla, and Mariska and Bob—the same people now stationed around the biggest table in The Anne Bonny, raising a toast.

"To Stephanie," said Seamus.

They took their sips. Charlotte rested her head against his shoulder, careful not to jostle him.

"Are you okay?" she asked.

He nodded. "Only hurts when I breathe."

She chuckled. "Not the broken ribs. I mean losing Stephanie."

"Oh." He nodded. "I'm okay. It's weird. She's disappeared and reappeared so many times in my life it doesn't feel like she's really gone."

She nodded. "She went out like a hero in the end, though. We would have all died if she hadn't let go."

"Yeah, no one saw that coming," muttered Seamus. He looked at Charlotte. "What about you? Things good with your parents?"

Charlotte chuckled. "Talk about *weird*—hearing someone talk about my *parents*." She traced the lip of her glass with her finger, nodding. "Things are good. They were pretty cool."

"Why aren't they here?" asked Darla.

"They had to get back for a job," said Charlotte, snapping from her thoughts. "I'm going to go visit soon."

Frank snorted into his glass. "They sure did a number on Felix."

Charlotte met eyes with Declan, and they shared a smile. They'd agreed to tell the police Shee and Mason had captured Felix and also taken out his circus henchman. It was easier than dragging Kitty into the mess. She wasn't the sort of girl who liked attention.

Even if Felix insisted he'd been attacked by a giant black cat, who would believe him?

Declan turned to the door. "Speak of the devil."

Charlotte followed his gaze to see Scotty the Skyscraper and Kitty enter. Scotty hunched more than usual, still weak after being shot by Felix. Kitty smiled upon spotting Charlotte. After the mess at the big top, they'd had a long talk. It turned out Kitty could speak—she just hadn't trusted anyone to bring down Baroness' killer other than herself. After they squared their stories about what happened to Felix—and it wasn't easy to explain why Shee and Mason would scratch a man so many times while trying to subdue him—Charlotte invited the couple to The Anne Bonny. She was pleased to see they'd come.

She walked over to greet them. "Hi guys, can I get you a drink?"

"I'll take a White Russian," said Kitty. She wore shorts and a scoop neck tee shirt—no costume. *Thank goodness.* Charlotte didn't want to think what might come out of Seamus' mouth if the Cat Girl arrived wearing one of her body-hugging cat costumes.

Charlotte placed the Big Top couple's order and noticed Darla whispering something into Mariska's ear. Mariska's attention shot to the front door of the bar. Charlotte followed her gaze to see two women entering. She didn't recognize them.

"Gianna, Tabby, how are you?" exclaimed Darla, standing. She hustled over to drag the women toward the bar and *away* from the table where Frank sat with Bob. The way Darla kept watching her husband as she moved, Charlotte suspected she wanted to keep her new friends away from him.

Hm.

Charlotte moved closer to be sure she could overhear their conversation.

"I was surprised to get this invitation," said the woman Darla had addressed as Gianna.

Darla waved the woman's comment away. "Oh, my pleasure. You really showed me the ropes." She looked at the other woman. "No hard feelings, Tabby?"

Tabby frowned. "You think you're fancy because your friend owns a bar?"

"Fancy? Have you seen this place?" Darla laughed. "Tell you what, Tabby, to make it up to you I brought you this."

Darla reached into her pocket and produced a small white piece of paper, folded in half. She handed it to Tabby.

Tabby leaned back, as if the paper were made of poisoned thorns. "What is it?"

"Well, I heard through the grapevine you're *single*," said Darla.

"So?"

"So this is a *very* eligible bachelor. I talked to him about you, and he's *very* interested."

Tabby softened. "Really?"

"Really. He's very strong. *Virile.*"

"He isn't a bum?"

"*No.* Has his own house. In fact, he's a bit of a celebrity."

"Really?"

"Really."

Tabby took the paper.

"Oh, look, here he is now," said Darla, turning to the door as Tony the Tiger Tamer walked in.

Charlotte gagged on her cocktail.

Clearly, that woman was *not* Darla's friend. She'd told Darla and Mariska about Tony. Darla couldn't seem to get enough, especially the part about how obsessive he became about women who reminded him of his cats.

She'd even asked where he lived, his real last name—

Now it all made sense.

"Tony," said Darla. "I want you to meet *Tabby*."

Tony kissed the back of Tabby's hand.

"Hello there," he purred.

~~ **THE END** ~~

THANK YOU!

Thank you for reading! If you enjoyed this book, please swing back to Amazon and leave me a review — even short reviews help authors like me find new fans!

GET A FREE STORY

Find out about Amy's latest releases and get a free story by joining her newsletter! http://www.AmyVansant.com

ABOUT THE AUTHOR

Amy Vansant is a *Wall Street Journal* and *USA Today* best-selling author who writes with an unique blend of thrills, romance and humor.

FREE PREVIEW

PINEAPPLE CRUISE

A Pineapple Port Mystery: Book Fourteen – By
Amy Vansant

CHAPTER ONE

I should make a list. Keep myself organized.

1. Trap them in one place like cockroaches
2. Kill them for being the scum they are
3. Especially him

Was doing it on the boat a good idea?

Sure, in a perfect world, I'd kill each where he or she lives, but *ugh*. So much travel. So many variables. I can't spend months scoping out towns and neighborhoods and account for every possibility. It's easier to bring them all to one place. That way, I can control the variables and keep the witnesses to a minimum. No one will figure out what these *strangers* have in common or be able to trace their deaths back to me. Not in a million years. They'll be dead before they can compare notes.

I'll whack them like moles.

They deserve it.

Like all pests, they make other people's lives *miserable*.

People should be *happy*.

Why do people make other people's lives so unhappy? People they *love*. Or, at least people they *claim* to love.

Anyway, this is a one-time deal.

Probably.

I can't solve everyone's problems, but I can help a few. A

few this time, maybe more next time.

We'll see.

But first, this list needs some work...

Hm.

I've got it.

I need a *sub*-list. Obviously, these people can't be killed in the same way without raising suspicion. A killer can't stab five people to death and think people won't jump to the conclusion there's someone running around *stabbing* people. Five people can't *accidentally* fall off a cruise ship or choke on their buffet.

So, let me see...

1. Trap them in one place like cockroaches
2. Kill them for being the scum they are
    a. Push overboard
    b. Poison
    c. TBD x 5

I'll figure out the rest later.

Maybe I *could* take out the whole ship. Or *part* of the ship? Something to make the other deaths less strange...A small explosion, maybe?

Eh, I've got a few weeks to figure out the details.

Oh, *wait.*

Maybe I should add something...

1. Trap them in one place like cockroaches
2. Kill them for being the scum they are
    a. Push overboard
    b. Poison
    c. TBD x 5
3. Be *happy.*

The last item on the list is for *me.*

Perfect.

I'll be able to figure out the rest. Maybe I won't kill all

seven. I'll play it by ear.

Except for the *one*, of course.

Well, the *two*.

CHAPTER TWO

When The Fine Swine Bar & BBQ opened in Charity, Florida, most residents celebrated the slow-cooked pulled-pork sandwiches and mouth-watering baby back ribs.

A select group had *other* meat on their minds.

Meat *Bingo*.

The joy of winning uncooked ground beef and pork butts had wormed its way into the hearts of Charity's retirees like few other activities had. Others had tried. Cornhole paled in comparison. Cosmic bowling inspired naked disdain.

Meat Bingo?

Bingo.

Today's Meat Bingo caller, the daughter of the restaurant's owner, held aloft the *O-30* ball with all the enthusiasm only a twenty-one-year-old girl, who'd much rather be someplace else, could muster.

"Oh-Thirty..."

She glanced at a piece of paper her parents had printed out for her and snorted a laugh.

"Dirty Gertie? Oh-Thirty."

Ball still in one hand, she worked her phone with the other, thumb bouncing and stretching like a yoga instructor on fast-forward.

Darla and Mariska watched in awe. They'd left the

Pineapple Port retirement community to try for the day's big prize: a brisket.

"Is she *texting* with just her thumb?" asked Darla after marking her bingo card.

Mariska looked down at her own card, horrified she'd been distracted by the girl. It could have cost her the brisket.

Delighted to see she had O-30, she marked her card and then stole a moment to slap Darla's arm. "*Shh*. Pay attention, or you'll lose."

Darla's attention remained fixed on the girl. "You have to admit, that's pretty impressive. I tried to text Frank the other day with two hands, glasses on my nose and a cup of coffee in me, and *still* ended up sending gibberish."

"Gee-Seventeen, uh..."

The girl checked her sheet of bingo nicknames again and delivered her findings with the same mixture of disbelief and ridicule as she had the others.

"Dancing queen? Gee-seventeen, dancing queen."

Darla sang the Abba song as she marked her card.

"Long and lean, only seventeeeeeen..."

Mariska grimaced, hovering over her bingo card as if staring at it could make G-17 manifest.

"It's *young and sweet*, not *long and lean*," she muttered.

Darla shrugged. "*Long and lean* rhymes better. Why are you so cranky?"

"I'm not cranky. I want the *brisket*. Those things are fifty dollars at the store."

"You don't even have a grill."

"You don't need a grill to cook—"

"Eye-Thirty-Two, Buckle my shoe." The bingo-caller girl rolled her eyes so far back into her head it looked as though she'd lose them somewhere in her sinuses. The whole episode spawned a new flurry of texting.

"BINGO!" Mariska jumped from her chair so fast she had to grab the table to keep from falling over.

Someone in the corner of the bar dropped an F-bomb.

"I won, I won!" Mariska held up the card as the girl schlepped over to check her numbers.

"Yep. You got it," said the young woman. She turned her head and bellowed to the bar. *"Mom!"*

A woman behind the bar pouring a draft beer turned at the sound of her daughter's call. She delivered the ale, wiped her hands on her apron, and disappeared into the back.

Mariska rushed to the bar and waited, staring at the row of stringed beads separating the front from the storeroom as if The Beatles were about to poke their heads through them.

Bartender Mom reappeared with a large beef brisket in her arms. With some effort, she hefted it on top of the bar. Mariska snatched it, offered a quick *thank you,* and then scurried back to her spot beside Darla before anyone could try and wrestle her prize from her.

"I can't believe I won. This will last Bob and me a *week.*" She rocked the meat in her arms as if it were a precious newborn.

"You saved fifty dollars, but now you need to buy a three-hundred-dollar smoker to cook it right," said Darla.

"Don't be bitter."

"You're the one who gets mean during bingo. Anyhoo, I have a right to be bitter. You're going to want to leave now, and I still have half a beer."

Mariska huffed. "You can't expect me to sit here with a beautiful brisket rotting on my lap—"

"Excuse me?"

Darla and Mariska turned to find a fortyish, cherub-faced woman staring at them. She seemed to be addressing Mariska, though her gaze remained locked on the brisket.

"Yes?" asked Mariska, clutching her prize a little tighter. One word lit in her head.

Wolves.

The woman pulled a piece of printer paper from her purse. "I was wondering if I could trade you something for that," she said.

Mariska blinked at her. "For my brisket?"

"You can trade her a hundred bucks," suggested Darla.

"No, she can't," snapped Mariska. Her head tilted as she did the math. "Um..."

"I don't have a hundred dollars," said the woman. "But I do have these." She held up three sheets of paper, and Darla plucked one from her hand for closer inspection.

"Is this a cruise ship ticket?" she asked.

Mariska leaned down to squint at the printout.

"The *Gulf Voyager*?"

The woman nodded. "I won them somehow, but I don't like boats." She cringed. "This isn't one of those giant cruise ships either. It's small. Brand new from what I gather."

Darla elbowed Mariska and leaned in to whisper. "The small ones are the *fancy* ones."

"Where does it go?" asked Mariska, straining to read more from the ticket in Darla's hand.

"The Keys."

"Oh, I *love* the Keys," said Mariska.

"You've been?" asked the woman.

Mariska shook her head. "No, but they have *wonderful* commercials."

"How do we know these are legit?" asked Darla.

The woman motioned to the paper in Darla's hand. "You can look it up online. You can call them to confirm the ticket numbers. I think there's a phone number on there."

"These have to be worth more than fifty dollars," said Mariska.

The woman shrugged. "Not if you don't want to go."

"Couldn't you sell them online?" asked Darla. She grunted as Mariska poked her in the liver.

The woman frowned. "I don't trust the Internet. Anyway, I'm having family over this weekend, and my husband bought a smoker, and this meat seems like the *perfect* thing. I mean, if you want the tickets."

Darla twisted to look at Mariska. "Think you can release the death-grip you have on those ribs?"

"It's not *ribs*, it's a *brisket*." Mariska considered her options. "*Three* tickets? You, me, and...Charlotte?"

Darla's eyes widened. "A *girls' cruise!* That could be fun. No Frank. No Bob..." Her head cocked. "Actually, it sounds like *heaven*."

"There's probably an unlimited buffet," said the woman.

Mariska felt her mouth water at the idea of pastries stacked high into the air. "Maybe a chocolate fountain?"

"Give us a second." Darla pulled Mariska away from the woman. When they'd reached the opposite side of the bar, she dug her phone out of her purse. "I'll look it up."

Mariska pet her brisket as she waited.

"*Gulf Voyager* is a real boat," said Darla after a minute. "New. Only holds a hundred people. Hold on, I'll call."

Darla dialed and chatted with someone.

"Ask them if there're unlimited pastries," prodded Mariska.

Darla waved her off, chatted a moment longer, and then hung up.

"They're legit," she said, holding up the one ticket still in her hand.

Mariska looked down at her prize and sighed. "I don't know. I *really* wanted this brisket."

"This is the maiden voyage. They're running with half the passengers. It will be like having the whole boat to ourselves."

Mariska grimaced. "Really?"

Darla nodded. "And hey, if we change our minds, we can sell the tickets and buy a *whole cow*."

Mariska gave her meat one last squeeze.

"Sorry, baby," she whispered to the meat as they headed back to the waiting woman. "Looks like we weren't meant to be."

BOOKS BY AMY VANSANT

Pineapple Port Mysteries
Funny, clean & full of unforgettable characters

Shee McQueen Mystery-Thrillers
Action-packed, fun romantic mystery-thrillers

Kilty Urban Fantasy/Romantic Suspense
Action-packed romantic suspense/urban fantasy

Slightly Romantic Comedies
Classic romantic romps

The Magicatory
Middle-grade fantasy

Made in the USA
Columbia, SC
11 March 2023

13639694R00141